LOST DAUGHTERS

HARDSCRABBLE BOOKS—
FICTION OF NEW ENGLAND

Other Books by Laurie Alberts

LOST
DAUGHTERS

Laurie Alberts

UNIVERSITY PRESS OF NEW ENGLAND
Hanover and London

University Press of New England

publishes books under its own imprint and is the publisher for Brandeis University

Press, Dartmouth College, Middlebury College Press, University of New Hamp-

shire, Tufts University, and Wesleyan University Press

Published by University Press of New England, Hanover, NH 03755

© 1999 by Laurie Alberts

Printed in the United States of America

5   4   3   2   1

Portions of pages 33–41 and 73, slightly altered: Reprinted from *Goodnight Silky
Sullivan* by Laurie Alberts, by permission of the University of Missouri Press.
Copyright © 1995 by Laurie Alberts.

Library of Congress Cataloging-in-Publication Data
Alberts, Laurie.
Lost daughters / Laurie Alberts.
p   .cm.   — (Hardscrabble books)
ISBN 0–87451–898–9 (cloth : alk. paper)
I. Title. II. Series.
PS3551.L264L67 1999
813'.54—dc21   98–48770

ACKNOWLEDGMENTS

The author extends heartfelt appreciation to Jody Lannen Brady, whose beautiful piece, "Talk of Babies," which appeared in *The Adoption Reader*, served as the seed inspiration for one aspect of this novel. Thank you for saying "Go for it," Jody.

The author also wishes to thank the University of Missouri Press for permisson to reprint some excerpts from the title story of the author's collection *Goodnight Silky Sullivan*. Some of these excerpts appear in slightly different form.

L. A.

To Rebecca

LOST DAUGHTERS

PROLOGUE

Your absence is the center of my life.

The day you were born, I didn't name you. Naming you would have made you too real, and anyway, I didn't have the right. But later it came to me, Lila, Lila for the lilacs blooming outside my window. I've always loved that flower. As a child in New Hampshire, I sucked their sweet pollen. Closed, the blossoms look like tiny fists; open, they resemble crosses.

I still don't know your eye color. Then it was that murky slate of newborns. I only saw you for a few minutes, long enough to feel a cramp in my innards, shut my eyes and turn away.

No. I'm lying. I didn't look away. Not immediately. I studied you: the cat-like smoothness of your newborn cheeks, drawn by the ordeal of birth, before baby-fat obscured their true lines. You nuzzled me. I felt your monkey grip on my thumb. I touched the silky top of your head and watched your pulse beat in that fleshy soft spot, the hole in your skull cap, eggshell of bone, and tried to match my breath, my heartbeat, to your rapid tattoo.

You had two little purple marks, one on your left eyelid, the other at the base of your skull. Stork bites, the nurse said, they'll fade. Birthmarks. Have you spent your life marked, wondering what made you, six-pound, nine-ounce you, so unlovable your mother cast you off? Did you sit in therapy groups mourning your primal rejection? Or act it out, in a string of unloving affairs, or do you count yourself among the lucky, the ones who escaped into the eager arms of the unfruitful?

I see those advertisements in small town throwaway papers,

Penny Savers and *Thrifty Nickels*. Adoption: Lots of hugs, beautiful home, and opportunities to offer, Happily Married Couple seeking . . . Call 1-8OO . . .

Who tucked you in, read you stories? I want to and don't want to know. I'm jealous of their history with you; it's like reading a lover's old diaries, hungry for and sickened by the details.

LilaLiLaLilaLilaLila.

I want to cry your not-name like those Arab women at a grave who ululate, a grief that vibrates out of the back of the throat. Or slow it down to make a lullaby.

CHAPTER 1

Lila slid out from under the weight of Kevin's arm, halted to be sure he was still sleeping, stepped gingerly across creaking boards. She dressed quickly: a cotton summer dress for a warm day in early May, no slip, natural fiber innocence, sandals in hand. She skipped her usual stack of bangles, dark lipstick. Today the object was not to draw notice, to blend in. At the door she glanced back at Kev splayed across her bed, taking up much more than his share of space. His freckled shoulders and lean hips, sandy hair, smooth white butt called out to her but a tiny string of drool attaching him to the pillow relieved her from regret. She closed the door carefully.

In the kitchen her roommate Marcia sat hunched over a psychology text at the table, coffee mug and buttered bagel on the side. Marcia's blond hair clung to her head greasily and she'd worn the same olive-drab teeshirt for days. Marcia took exams seriously. Normally Lila did too, but she hadn't even begun to study for finals.

"Kev asleep?" Marcia whispered without looking up. She scratched behind her ear with the business end of her ballpoint.

"Uh-huh." Lila poured a mug of coffee, sipped.

Marcia set down her pen, caught Lila's eye. "Sure you don't want me to come?"

Leaning against the counter for balance, Lila pulled on her sandals, buckled them. "It's not that big a deal, Marcy. I'm not having open-heart surgery."

"You know, they're just beginning to study the long-term emotional effects."

Lila turned back to her mug. "That's pro-life bullshit, Marcia. Anyway, you're making me feel worse. Let me live in denial if I want to."

Marcia sighed. "So, did you tell him yet?"

Lila shook her head impatiently. Marcia and she had different ideas about the role of honesty in relationships. It was just too complicated to get into with Kevin. He'd want to marry her and keep it, even though it would disrupt his orderly vision of their future together after he finished law school. Kevin might have lifted himself out of the limited vista of his South Boston boyhood on the strength of good grades and determination, but he was still a Southie at heart. It wasn't just his accent that tied him to his Catholic school, Boston College past.

Besides, there was a small chance that the baby—fetus, Lila reminded herself, don't picture little waving fingers, just a blob of cells still, but dividing, dividing, ticking away inside her like a basketball clock—wasn't Kev's. She'd had a quick fling with her History of Design professor two months ago.

Marcia shouted "Shit!" but it was only spilled coffee. She mopped at pages. "I'll be home by four," she said, refilling her cup at the counter. Lila recognized that she was leaving out the words—". . . in case you need me."

She wanted to thank Marcia for trying to be a pal, but if she did, she'd have to acknowledge that there was a reason to need her, which there wasn't. All she really needed was her period, and she could attend to that by herself. "See ya," Lila said. She grabbed her purse and opened the front door onto a view of the sagging wooden row houses of Porter Square brightened by spring tulips and jonquils blooming in their minuscule yards. She slapped down the tilted sidewalk to the subway station, shoved her token into the slot, rode the impossibly long descent and waited briefly on the platform for a train. Seated, she glanced at her reflection in the window: the harsh geometry of her boyish haircut, bony collarbone bridging hollows that could hold water, arched nose. Dark, perhaps Latina skin. The face of no one she knew.

In the reflection, a tiny silver ring pierced the flange of her left nostril. So much for natural fiber innocence. She'd opted for the usual art student affectations: the nose ring, a small tattoo of a snake swallowing its tail that rode her right shoulder blade. Kevin loved to run a fingertip over the snake, fascinated by its odd intrusion. Why did straight-ass law school types go for artists anyway, she wondered. Marcia would probably say that everybody wanted to find in their mate the missing parts of themselves. So what absent part of herself did she find in Kevin?

Well, as Marcia would be eager to point out, there were always the missing biological 'rents. Kevin offered stability, commitment, family. But so did her adoptive mother and father. Ambition, then? Kevin had it in spades, while she was slipping off the dean's list faster than an ice cube on a griddle. But that was recent. She'd always been a good grade grubber. So, then what? Fuck these simple psychological formulas. A little knowledge was a dangerous thing. Though in this particular case, a little knowledge made it easier. If she actually knew for sure that it was Kevin's baby, it might be harder to go through with.

Lila emerged out of the ground behind the kiosk in Harvard Square, blinking in sudden light. She could have gotten out at the Brattle exit but she preferred walking above ground. Usually she enjoyed the eyes of Harvard boys on her as she crossed crooked brick. Today it was a dark, sad-eyed man with a drooping mustache seated across Mass. Ave. at an outdoor cafe: Pakistani? Bosnian refugee? He stared over a brioche as her legs flashed by. The dark ones always stared, wanting to claim her as one of their own. If he knew her mission he'd probably stone her.

Lila squeezed past the sidewalk magazine racks where kids pored through porno, caught a quick glimpse of the cavern between the two halves of the Harvard Coop, the florist shop's canned bouquets. Up Brattle Street to the quiet of the mansions, the professors' palaces, elaborate fences and big yards raked like combed hair, the wet dirt a smooth brown scalp between tender blades. Lilac hedges, painted gates. Old Cambridge's picture book perfection always stirred some secret anger, because it wasn't hers, and never would be.

Like Kevin, she was a pretender, a scrambler up the slopes of brick, always secretly hoping the ivy she gripped in her teeth wouldn't pull loose. It was surprising they hadn't both been drawn to their true opposites, someone with automatic admission.

Kevin with his Southie accent. Lila, good chameleon, like any military brat, knew enough to leave her Southern drawl behind, erase those later vowels flat as prairie lands. She was a girl of air force bases, parade grounds and commissaries, red dirt and boiled peanuts. Her elementary school classmates were rickety civilian kids with nits, untouchables who lived outside the sterile order of military housing in Georgia and Mississippi. Later, she shared classrooms with beefy Kansas blondes.

It was only when Dad served his final stint at Hanscom Field in Bedford, offering her the shock of good suburban Boston public schools in her junior year, that she came to learn what SAT scores really meant. Ivy and brick and all the right words. She had to suffer her schoolmates' smirking condescension toward military life, their horror at the Gulf War bombardments, a contempt she shared but only here felt reflected back at her. And the disappointment of Lesley College when her classmates went off to Wesleyan, Amherst, Cornell, and Brown. It was too much catch-up to play, and she was at a disadvantage because of geography: if they'd still lived in Georgia or Mississippi or Kansas, she probably could have slipped into Harvard.

Her parents lived in Colorado Springs now. Dad was semi-retired, teaching one class at the Air Force Academy, and Mom had retired too, from the life of military wife, throwing herself into the activities of the first church she'd be able to attend for more than two years running. A Methodist now because that's what her community offered (though in the past it was Baptist and Lutheran), and what she wanted more than anything was to belong to some civilian unit and follow their marching orders.

Dad had served in Nam; Mom fought the fertility wars. Lila tried to imagine what kind of woman married a military man in '67. The summer of love. Lila had heard on the radio recently that in a huge number of cases it was actually the man who was the cause of infertility, low sperm count being so common these days (the prevalence of plastics in the environment, molecular imitators of estrogen, had been blamed). But twenty years ago society still ganged up to protect male egos. She bet Dad never jacked off in any test tube. High irony: their infertility, her unwanted fertility. The echo of another woman's problem, the one who had carried her to term.

And what would Mom say about the "procedure"—as the clinic staff referred to it—toward which she was now headed? Lila knew too well. Mom would be shocked, angered, disappointed. It went against the tenets of her various religions. Lila rejected the dogma, but she couldn't blame Ruth. It must be hard for a woman who spent years mourning miscarriages, crying over unwelcome blood returning every month, to fathom another woman ridding herself of what she so wanted. If Lila painted a portrait of her mother, it would be in a cloud of ghosts, the souls of her lost babies. Somewhere in the canvas, she'd have to include herself, a candle—no, a nightlight—flickering at the heart of her mother's shrine to maternity. In the end, Lila knew, Ruth would forgive her.

Lila turned off Brattle onto a side street; the houses were more tightly spaced but still impressive. Saabs and Volvos in the drives. She checked the slip of paper with the address again: Cambridge Women's Associates, 219 Sunderland Court. It sounded like some feminist consulting cooperative. Everything had to be euphemized now, a sign of the times. It wasn't so long ago that a receptionist was murdered at an abortion clinic in

Brookline. The sign was small and unobtrusive, the entry on the side of the grey Victorian hidden from the street.

Lila opened the door. The waiting room displayed the usual institutional Cambridge decor, a mixture of worn Orientals and Scandia design with the recent air of fortress. She slid her insurance information to a middle-aged woman behind a counter topped by bulletproof glass. An elderly uniformed guard sat not very discreetly amidst the patients. Lila pegged him as a retired Irish cop and wondered if he judged them.

She glanced at her comrades in shame. A girl way younger than herself, thin, hunched, miserable looking, scraggly blond hair and knobby knees. Another woman, forties, wedding ring, business hair. Professional. Perhaps she had three kids at home already. The only clients this morning. Of course, they served up more than abortions here. Perhaps she, Lila, was the only one to be vacuumed today. The young girl could be getting a pregnancy test, the businesswoman in for her regular pap smear, like going to the dentist.

Lila looked down at her sandaled toes. They bore a light scrim of city dust. She pictured herself on her back, legs up, dusty feet in some doctor's face. And inwardly mumbled the mantra she'd been repeating for weeks: I can't have it, can't have it, can't. Not like her own birth mother did, ruin your body and your life for nine months, then give it away to strangers. Create another kid who'll grow up wondering why.

A woman in a white lab coat, short grey hair brushed back, came in and spoke softly to the teenager, led her behind swinging doors. These women doctors and assistants were heroes, Lila supposed. Bravely continuing what they believed in, despite the threats of Operation Rescue fanatics. She should have been grateful. Yet, when the woman returned and beckoned her with practiced sympathy, Lila's heart seized, she felt dizzy. Tears came to her eyes. What was she doing here, eliminating the only blood relative she might ever know?

CHAPTER 2

Lila, I'm staying this week at the Jemez Bodhi Mandala Center. Don't worry, I'm not a shaved head Zendoist. They have a little motel and they rent rooms to the public as a means of supporting their center. I take my meals with them (near silent meals, finding myself mimicking their earnest piety though not their pressed palm ritual bows as they get up for a second helping of tofu scrambled eggs or miso soup). They leave me alone and they have absolutely beautiful hot pools, natural springs gathered into rock-lined lagoons from which you can listen to the gentle peal of wind chimes and stare up at the impassivity of cedar-spotted mesas, or at night watch the steam rise off the sulfurous waters as the moon draws you into a certainty that you are the most alone of all living souls.

Before you curse my lounging spa-indulged butt, Lila, know that I'm here for this, for the silence in which I can invent myself for you.

At supper tonight, in the polished pine dining room, we sit in a great U-shape of linked tables, nearly silent. The visiting disciples include a stiff young businesswoman who owns a make-your-own wine and brewing shop in Santa Fe, two middle-aged matrons from Phoenix of the Sedona, crystal-worshipping variety, a Parisian dance therapy teacher, a pony-tailed man who works in an Albuquerque bicycle shop and has the classic shrivelled look of the long-time vegetarian.

And I, the lone motel guest/infidel? I am a freelance travel writer of no great fame, Lila, though my profession has taken me all over. I know the prices of rooms and the best deals on rugs in Bukhara and Samarkand. I've drunk sweet tea with Bedouins and been slathered with mud in a Sardinian spa. I know the surfaces of many places and the smiles of those receiving adequate tips. I know how easy it is for an American woman, traveling alone, to get laid. Excuse me, is that inappropriate? I'm new at this mother business. Does that word sound obscene, coming from me? Mother, I mean.

Okay, I'm a travel writer, but for this week, the week before your twenty-first birthday, the week before they open the files to your possibly interested eyes, I am determined to focus only on this inner landscape, the scratch of pen that will shape my version of a history for you.

I can't help looking though. From what I gather, some of the Bodhi students stay for months, some are only weekend visitors, here for a quick serenity fix. They are each given work assignments as part of their practice: planting the considerable vegetable gardens, caretaking the priestess' eight-year-old twin hellions, cleaning the Bodhi motel rooms, washing dishes. They rise at four A.M. for ritual chanting and bow their heads piously over their meals. Some meals are officially silent, others not, but it seems they're all unwilling to talk until given a cue by the ordained Buddhist priestess. During talking meals, she smilingly questions each of us about where we've come from and what we do there. She could be a charming cruise guide if not for her shaved blond head and floor-length muslin dresses.

While the disciples clear the tables and wash dishes, I stroll back to my room, to what I've come to think of as my time with you, Lila. Don't grit your teeth, please.

I sit at a desk in my Bodhi cell, which isn't a cell really, but a reasonably graceful room with a little altar at one end, some Japanese scrolls with swooping ideographs pinned to a grass cloth wall. A low futon frame. A windowless bathroom in which the toilet runs ceaselessly, leaving a green mineral stain on porcelain. Outside the New Mexico stillness—bright hot light on mesas, the regular spacing of cedar and pinon separated by thirst. What would it be like to share a practice with my hosts? To bow my head to an overarching simplicity, to chant myself into something resembling peace?

An old boyfriend used to say religion was like knocking teeth off your mental gears, an odd comment from a man who ended up drinking bourbon for breakfast.

No peace here.

Lila, it has occurred to me to try to seduce you into contacting me by promising you the name of your father. But that's so manipulative. You owe me nothing, not even your voice. So I'll tell you and leave your decision unclouded.

I'll begin with your beginning, that accident of pollination. Your father was . . . no, wait. I'll get to that. As much as I'm trying to make sense of this for you, I'm trying to make sense of this for me. Coherency comes from narrative, right? Or at least that's what a therapist used to tell me.

I could begin with a dark New Hampshire ranch house, before we were rich enough to buy the big colonial on Berkely Road. In a room, a basement TV room, with me rocking on my little wooden rocking horse, creak, creak, until my foot slipped off the peg and I slammed down hard and screamed at the pain between my legs. And my father's face from the armchair: enormous, laughing.

So what comes in the gap between that crying child and a teenager spreading her legs? And before that? I have to believe, or pretend to believe that you'll want to know—even if only to know why I surrendered you—as I want to know each knee scrape, the titles on the spines of the books you've read, your taste in clothes.

I'll try to stick to the facts because truth has always been such a slippery fish. It's not my fault: it comes from a legacy of mothers who lie. So here, daughter, is your inheritance.

When my mother's mother, Gramma Rose, was a teenage beauty fresh from Russia, two brothers vied for her hand. After it became clear that she favored the one who was to become my grandfather, the older brother walked into the room where my grandmother and grandfather sat on a couch and slit his throat from ear to ear before them. He died leaking blood onto the rug.

As though this weren't enough gothic horror for one family, my mother's cousin informed me a few years ago that my grandfather killed himself too. "Of course," he said, "your mother won't admit it."

I sucked in breath at my cousin's words. It explained so much. My mother, in the parlance of our family, is a ghoul. She's a rubbernecker at accidents, a reader of obituaries, a hospice volunteer. In her story, they said her father went away on a trip, then they slapped her for playing while everyone sat shiva.

Shiva. In case you don't know, that's the Jewish version of a wake, without the celebration. We were Jews. Lousy Jews, but Jews. And as my daughter, you are too whether you know it or not. By the law of return.

My mother waited and waited for her father to return. Later, Gramma Rose told her kids they caused their father's death by making too much noise.

"He died of pneumonia," my mother always told me. "Exhaustion and pneumonia, depression too," as though depression were a killing virus. His partner had cheated him, it was 1932. My mother was only four years old. Her mother was thirty-five, pregnant, with a baby in her lap and seven older living children. The first baby had died.

They were just words, all those years when my mother told me this story over and over: "The first baby died." I never stopped to consider what they meant—a sixteen-year-old wife and refugee with parents half a world away whose belly swells for nine months then yields up loss, a tiny red-faced squalling infant who one day refuses to breathe. A teenage girl mute with grief . . .

When I queried my father about my grandfather's suicide he

said, "I knew all along. One of the brother-in-laws told me, but I would've figured it out. It was for the insurance money, the only way he could save his family, so they hid it."

"Does Mom know?" I asked.

"She knows, but she doesn't want to know."

"You never mentioned it?"

"Oh, once in a while, I hinted at it to be mean."

I can believe that. That's the one thing I am sure of.

I never told my mother what I know about her father. It seems too cruel; although I was often cruel to her, it's the one line I won't cross.

According to my mother, her father was a cultured man, a lover of the classics who spent his Sundays under an apple tree rereading his treasured books. In the family photo, taken four months before he died, he is pale, thin, with dark circles under his eyes and the delicate hands of a Talmud scholar, not meant to be a hacker of bloody beef. A man who looks too weary to have fathered all those kids.

Her father was a god, my mother always said. The kindest man. But she hid in the toy box when he hit the other kids. How do I put these opposites together?

Instead I imagine Grammy Rose fat and pregnant, waddling down to the butcher shop to call her husband home. She would have sent one of the boys, most likely, but this is *my* version. "Daveed? Daveed?" she calls. Opening the door to the cramped office, gasping as she sees him hunched over his littered desk, green liquid trickling from his lips, bills and ledgers spilling onto the floor. I paint it as an early van Gogh, like *The Potato Eaters*. Bleak light, muddy brush strokes, distorted faces. Or recast it as a perverse golden Vermeer.

No, that's too romantic. She finds him slumped among the hanging sides of kosher beef, ruby carcasses marbled with fat and dense with salt, the smell of blood like menstruation, like iron filings in her heart. And when she sees him, the baby in her belly, the one she'll abort two days after the funeral, gives a lurch.

This part is from my mother: Gramma Rose spent the next thirty years in the kitchen, except during thunderstorms, when she climbed the attic stairs to shriek her rage.

The gap between what they tell you and what they cannot tell you is where the lies take hold.

My other grandmother became a lying memoirist at ninety-five, in the Hebrew Home for the Aged near Boston. Her real life was fantastic enough—her father was a Socialist zealot who organized his fellow cigar makers and spent time in jail. At seventeen, Grammy Heller was a shop forelady at the General Electric plant in Lynn, Massachusetts, supporting her many brothers and sisters.

Grammy Heller's memoir never mentions her Socialist father, or how she had to sacrifice her own education to raise her sisters and brothers. No. She was a debutante, she writes, describing with great detail the elegant gowns and polished flatware at her coming out party. Where did she hear of such things? In the Boston papers? A shocking liar.

She was a girl who never sledded down a snowy hill. A woman who married the Lithuanian chair caner with an accent, because her mother said he'd always provide. A nervous, frightened woman who hustled to cook six different suppers every night to suit the demands of her family. Later, when there was money, she still made mean little blintzes thinly filled with grape jelly, carried home chipped, sea-battered tumblers from the beach and sported a beanie copter hat because she'd found it. She instructed us grandkids to look down when we walked to find useful things. She wouldn't kiss us because of germs.

At the GE plant, the women sit hunched in long rows in their shirt-waist dresses, soldering little nests of wires. Grammy Heller stalks the aisles, her buttoned shoes clatter on planks past caged windows opaque with dust, a smeared view of train tracks and loading docks. Hot metal sizzles and spurts. Pale-eyed, grim, corsets pinching her young girl's body, she gives the orders while the big-breasted Portuguese and Italian women workers curse and spit behind her back. She is the forelady, she is seventeen, her life will hold no joy. But in the factory she hears a debutante's waltz and twirls on parquet floors.

A reverse telescope, this short line of women: I know nothing of their families before them, you and I know nothing of each other. A sine curve, thick in the middle with my tales, petering out on either end with mysteries.

Is this what you care about, Lila, or just medical histories, things with practical application? I'm sorry to inform you that madness runs its course through many of these lives. Plus diabetes, cancer, obesity, stroke, bad hearts from the Roses—maybe not genetic, just too much meat consumed by a butcher's family. And on both sides, a shitload of depression.

Lila, I just heard on the radio, NPR, my bible, that infants with depressed mothers aren't stimulated in the areas that govern capacity for joy. Their brains are measurably different, never developing certain neuron paths or whatever. Hardwired for sadness, you might say. That awful interface of nature and nurture. Were you lucky enough, Lila, to avoid that one?

Little lamps light the curved path to the hot pools, and sulphurous steam hovers above the black water. At first all I can hear is the rush of the river not twenty feet away, and the pebble scrape of my flip-flop sandals. As my eyes adjust my ears do too:

the shape of the mesa, a bulky pyramid behind the river, looming, and the slick splash of another body surfacing as I lower
myself into the burning bath. The inescapable "aahhh" and then
my shy silence, as I try to make out the identity of the phantom
soaker, while looking away.

He is floating now on his back, not far from the small arched
bridge that separates the hottest pool from this one, the
medium. I roll to my belly and walk my hands in the knee-deep
water, the volcanic pebbles sliding under my fingers, a stream of
slime gliding off my forearms. Without speaking, we slowly
change places, I by the bridge, he by the river side. He is as
aware of me as I am of him, yet neither of us acknowledges the
other. I imagine he is the Japanese-American boy with shaved
head who serves as serene baby-sitter to the priestesses' twins. I
overheard him telling someone he'd recently graduated from
Bennington. Figures.

Now in the darkness and voluptuous heat of the pools, I picture his slender, hairless chest slick with hot water gushing from
a mysterious underground source, and stifle what might be desire: he is your age, child, not much older. More suited to you
than me, and guiltily I remember my purpose. When he leaves,
hugging a towel in darkness, I clamber from the steaming water
and lay myself supine on a flat rock by the river, watching the
steam rise from my own pinked flesh as the evening chill tingles.
I am hot and cold both.

The moon is revealed behind Albert Pinkham Ryder clouds
haloed white at their edges, and I think, tritely, I suppose, it is
the same moon that illuminates *your* sky even if we are miles,
perhaps continents apart. Where are you? It must be close to
eleven, but here in New Mexico it could be hours earlier or later
than wherever you are.

I spin scenarios: you are a college girl chugging beer at some
awful frat party, a drunken dufus' hand slipping under your
sweater while the moon spins emptily behind closed curtains;
perhaps you are a dervish whirling in tie-dye to the Grateful

Dead; or putting a crack pipe to your lips in some Washington Heights basement; or bent over an open book this cool March evening, chewing a pencil nub; or maybe you're making change at Dunkin Donuts, sliding your palms down your pink smudged uniform and planning your escape.

And I? Lila, I am the one who never planned, the one who thought she escaped.

CHAPTER 3

The doctor gave Lila Percocet for the cramping, and by the time her required rest period was up, she was drifting pleasantly. She refused the receptionist's offer to call her a cab, nodded serenely at the rent-a-cop, and was out on the street again in morning warmth. Except for the thick pad riding her underpants like a misplaced sub sandwich, it seemed as though nothing had actually happened.

Halfway back to the Brattle subway station, Lila had the bright idea of stopping by Richard Warren's house. Although she'd never been inside, she had looked up his address in the faculty directory and walked past it two or three times at the height of her classroom fascination. He lived in a lavender three-story Victorian with a wrought iron gate and a carriage barn, purchased, he'd said, by his wife's inherited money.

Their quickie affair had been conducted at the enormous, fake tudor Sheraton Tara out by Route 128, where no one was likely to recognize him. She had expected the colonial charm of the Concord Inn, or some little bed and breakfast. Better than a roll on his office floor, she supposed. Apparently he, a history of design aesthete, drew some mildly kinky pleasure out of the tacky monstrosity with its king size beds and highway view, its ponderously decorated lounge.

Perhaps he'd found her just as mildly diverting and tacky, an Air Force brat whose father flew fighter jets in a war he'd escaped by deferment. She didn't tell him about Kevin. But Richard Warren was a pro: he kept tight control over the number and emotional content of their meetings by referring casu-

ally but often to my wife this, my daughter that . . . The second
time he took her to the Tara, she wondered if it wasn't his own
ploy, a fear that a one-time fuck would lead her to feel used; the
specter of a sexual harassment case hovered. From the start he
was careful; he'd only called her after fall semester finals, when
she was no longer his student, and her grade was in, an A, natu-
rally. He displayed a line of practiced patter: praising her matu-
rity, brilliance, beauty. A drink in a dark bar in Somerville. A
kiss in front of her apartment.

That first time at the Tara he'd been eager, ardent, a connois-
seur of angles and curves, while she savored the guilt of betray-
ing Kev, her own sordid sophistication. But the second, final
time, watching him wash her smell from him, a tall bony man
with an elegant profile and sunken chest, knees folded in a short
hotel bath tub, hurriedly running a soapy wash cloth over his
long arms, his eyes already turned from her, sorrow settled
somewhere in her throat, a taste of a loneliness different from
the one she'd always known.

Later, when Richard didn't call, she decided, in self-protection, maybe, she'd used Richard as much as he'd used her, to
worm more room for herself from Kevin, to make space where
he was always crowding in. She hated Kevin for the same things
she loved about him: his insistence that they would inevitably
be, already were, a family.

It wasn't as though she'd been in love with Richard Warren.
She'd been flattered, intrigued. And something else . . . vulnera-
ble to a man old enough to be her father, only he was the father
she would have preferred: educated, cultivated, at home on cob-
blestone streets. She was afraid that his defection meant more
than that his curiosity or need for conquest had been slaked—it
was a judgment on her failure to make the Cambridge grade.

She wasn't sure if she had reason for bitterness against
Richard Warren, but now, with the remains of her abortion
seeping between her legs, a child that might have been, could
have been his, she didn't want him to escape unscathed. Lila

turned into his street, past trash cans out for collection, modest professorial cars crowding the curb, stickered cars with resident parking permits, the large houses set back underneath the branches of enormous old maples and beeches. An interesting phenomenon: here the houses were expensive, the cars cheap, just the opposite of so many places she'd lived. She read off numbers. In her Percocet daze, it didn't occur to her that Richard's wife might be home. Or she didn't care. His car, the smoke grey Toyota Camry whose upholstery had cradled her behind so promisingly two months ago, was parked in the drive.

In the yard next door, a woman in a denim skirt kneeled, gloved hands digging in soil. The woman pulled on an enormous, unyielding root. Lila lifted the brass door knocker. What would she say if his wife came to the door? She listened to the clomp of footsteps, ready to turn tail, but it was Richard, in jeans and a pale blue cotton shirt, sleeves rolled, towering above her, his face frozen in an anxious smile. He glanced toward his neighbor and pulled Lila inside.

"What the hell are you doing here?"

"Nice to see you too, Richard." She smiled. "Since you've asked, I'm pregnant." How easily the lie slipped out, as perfectly shaped as the enameled Chinese vase balanced on a pedestal at the base of Richard's graceful, winding staircase. Liar. But she *had* been pregnant, until only an hour ago. And the staircase led up to some bedroom he'd never let her see although she could imagine: antique sleigh bed and soft king-size duvet, ancient maps of Cambridge and his wife's dour ancestors on the wall.

"Oh, good Christ." Richard put a palm to his forehead. "This just about takes the cake. I mean, I'm awfully sorry, sweetie, but did it ever occur to you that there might be a more discreet place for this conversation?"

"You mean like the Tara?"

Richard groaned. "Lila, I really am sorry to hear it. I don't mean to be callous. But it's been a hell of a morning. My daughter just got herself kicked out of Milton for smoking, a semester's tuition down the drain, our fault, of course, and now this."

Our. That exclusionary word. A hell of a morning for him? Fuck him.

He checked his watch swiftly. "Come on in, have a cup of tea, and we'll talk for a bit. I have to go out to Milton to pick up Alix in half an hour."

Lila followed him toward the kitchen, glanced about as he filled a kettle and set it on a gas burner. It was a large "country" kitchen, with the requisite unused copper pots on beams, an oversized restaurant stove. And on the refrigerator, family snapshots. A sailboat, teenage girl in bikini, a closeup of a windblown blond woman, grinning against an ocean background: the wife, Emily. She looked pretty, merry—not the withered priss Lila had hoped for. Probably her only crime was sharing Richard's age. The kettle shrieked. Richard took down two mugs, set out milk, honey.

"Black or herbal?"

"I don't care." Lila hadn't eaten anything yet today. She felt hollow, but not painfully so. The Percocet was still thrumming inside her.

Richard turned off the burner but let the kettle sit.

She watched him calculate—legal ramifications. Job. Wife. Sympathy was called for, understanding, a delicate tact. But suspicion won out.

"Lila, not to be crass, but what makes you think it's mine? Surely you've had other men in the past few months."

If she said yes, she'd let him halfway off the hook but prove his insignificance to her; if she said no, she'd confirm his guilt but make herself pathetic.

"Just one. And he had a vasectomy." Oh, those lies were coming easier all the time.

"How nice for him. So what do you plan to do?"

"I don't know." Lila turned her back to him, gazed out through twelve-over-twelve windowpanes at the gardening woman next door. "Maybe I'll keep it."

"Oh, don't be ridiculous. Lila, you know you can't expect me to have anything to do with the child, if it is in fact mine, which hasn't been established, and you'll ruin your own life. You haven't even graduated college yet. Listen, it's awful, but you have to do what's best for everyone concerned."

"You mean what's best for you?"

He pursed his lips in exasperation. "You're determined to exact your pound of flesh I see."

"Nice choice of words, considering."

"God, that did sound awful, didn't it? I'm sorry. But you aren't thinking straight, either, sweetie." Parental now, soothing. "You've got everything ahead of you, you can't ruin it for yourself. Not someone with your promise, your ability. And think of the child. What kind of life could you offer it now?"

She gave up the game, uncertain now why she'd started this whole thing. It was already over, the pad between her legs proof. She'd intended only to throw him off balance, but Richard was like one of those kid's weighted blow-up clowns. Knock him down and he sprang back up. He was still the one in control.

"Do you need money?" Richard asked gently. "How much does . . . this sort of thing cost?"

"Four hundred." That's what it would have cost if her college insurance hadn't paid.

Richard stood. "Well. I don't have that kind of cash lying around, I'll have to go to a machine. That will be an interesting withdrawal to explain."

Already planning his own lies. She'd made no dent, she saw. She couldn't make a scratch on the waxed black and white tiles of the kitchen, she'd leave no mark on his smooth dark soul.

"We better get going," he said, looking again at his watch.

"Wait," Lila said. "Can I use your bathroom?"

"Of course. Just down the hall on the left."

Lila pattered on gleaming oak boards, closed the bathroom door behind her. A stained glass window admitted light but no view. Beside it hung a Corot drawing, stunted trees against a flat landscape. A real Corot, under glass, in a bathroom? Lila looked at herself in the mirror over the sink. No discernible change. She opened the medicine cabinet slowly, so it wouldn't creak: nothing but a bar of ivory soap and a wrapped new toothbrush. A guest bathroom. She shut the medicine cabinet and watched herself as she withdrew an earring from her lobe: an opal set in antique silver, a gift from Kevin. She lay it on the glass shelf under the mirror. Let Richard explain that one.

Lila checked her stained but not sodden pad, flushed the toilet, ran water.

Outside, the neighbor woman was gone; her gardening gloves lay palms up on the dark soil, a pose of supplication. A length of muddy tree root stripped bare. Richard opened the Camry's passenger door for Lila, ushered her in quickly.

They drove silently west on Mass. Ave., away from the Square, to a bank machine. Lila watched while he extracted money from the ATM, counted it carefully, folded it into a wad. He looked stooped in daylight, weary and grey complexioned in the May sunlight, and Lila felt a tiny surge of remorse, but perhaps it was only the throb beginning in her abdomen as the Percocet wore off.

"So that's that," he said.

For you, she thought, but what was the point of playing it out further? Tight-lipped, Lila stuffed the money into her purse and refused Richard's offer of a ride home. He didn't kiss her when she unbuckled her seat belt and she didn't answer when he wished her "Good luck." By the time she made it up the wooden steps of the house in Porter Square, she was doubled over and crying, from cramps and shame, the purse with Richard's money clenched against her belly.

She took two Percocets and fell asleep. She woke at two-fifteen, afternoon sun slanting through her western window, ashamed of her trickery with Richard and Kevin both.

Kevin who loved her, suffocated her with his constant certainties, his interrogations. "What ah yah gonna do aftah graduation, Li?" If she graduated. The thought of failing after years of diligence was almost seductive. Giving up. He made her so mad with his assumptions.

"Lila," he said, "someday, when ah'm working for a cah-pahration, yah can spend all day doing yah aht, yah can twiddle yah thumbs if yah want to, but not now, not yet."

Fuck him. Just because she was adrift didn't mean she was lazy. She simply didn't feel a pull toward any of the options. And Boston was a bad place for options, overflowing with graduates with advanced degrees doing secretarial work, too many colleges, too many PhDs. Kevin, ensconced at Harvard Law School, could play the parental role, suggest she take computer courses after graduation, something immediately applicable and worthy of money. He did, after all, have hefty loans, and they were planning to move in together in June. Or he was planning. She didn't know if she even wanted to.

"You need a strong parent, don't you?" Marcia offered. "Considering your father, and the absence of your birth parents. You think love is someone telling you what to do, then you have to keep pushing against it so they can tell you over and over they won't abandon you."

"Li," Kevin asked in exasperation, "what's the problem?"

She didn't know what the problem was. She'd tried to be practical, augmenting her major in art with courses in graphics. But she couldn't see herself as an illustrator or designer, creating brochures on a computer, whipping up someone's business card. She wasn't foolish enough to think her studio art impulses would ever earn her a penny. And didn't want to go on to grad school to become a lecturer in art history, even if there were academic jobs, which there weren't anymore.

What was the problem? Even before the bad news from a home pregnancy kit, she'd felt something in herself slipping, some vagueness coming over her the past few months. Worse than an ordinary case of senior-itis. Things just wouldn't line up or stay in their borders. Cheating on Kevin was part of it. If

Kevin knew what she'd done, with Richard or at the clinic, he might never forgive her.

Lila thought about the erasure of her genetic relative, a coded message from her birth family. Information that Mom and Dad had never shared. And she'd never been able to push because it made Mom so unhappy. Just a hint in that direction and Mom wanted to know what she'd done wrong, why Lila didn't feel at home with them. Why they weren't enough for her.

There were organizations out there that could help, of course. Searchers. Like those Nazi hunters, Simon Wiesenthal, digging out old war criminals from South America. Lila imagined someone surprising her birth mother: You are being extradited for the crime of . . .

What was her crime? Was it worse than what Lila had done today? An unknown woman, girl perhaps, who'd sacrificed herself, swelled her own body past recognition to bring Lila's own sweet self to life. Then ditched her.

Once she'd finally told him about the adoption, six months into their relationship, Kevin took her to task for dredging it up all the time. "What's the point?" he'd ask. "Yah've got a mothah, right? Yah bound to be hurt if yah pursue it. Yah nevah gonna fahgive her for dumping yah, so what good can come of it? Yah think if yah meet her yah'll be able to romanticize her into the one that would have made yah happiyah all these yeahs?"

Lila countered with, "You don't fucking understand. You never will." Which pissed him off, but he didn't. What else did he think she was doing but romanticizing her now?

"What about yah birth fathah then?" he'd badgered. "Yah nevah think about him. Kind of sexist, huh?"

"Will you please shut up?" He couldn't see it—it was *her* giving Lila up that made her magic. It wasn't the father who decided these things. For all Lila knew, her birth father hadn't been aware that she existed. As Kevin wouldn't know about this child—fetus, Lila corrected herself. Fetus. The clock had stopped ticking. The game over—but when your mother decided to throw you away, that gave her a power over you that no woman who went through measles and mumps, who called to nag about visits, could ever have. It was the ultimate version of playing hard-to-get.

The cramps had weakened. It was just like a bad period now. But her mind was reeling in too many directions, directions she normally tried to avoid. Maybe she had an infection. She got the thermometer from the medicine cabinet—shit, had she really left that earring at Richard's?—and took her temperature. Ninety-nine. No big deal. She often ran half a degree above normal.

Her real mother—a phrase she'd never use with her parents—was tall, Lila decided. No, short, fat, dumpy, with sagging arms sticking out of a muscle shirt and a cigarette dangling from her mouth. Or she was a hard-nosed Manhattan CEO in a power suit who couldn't be bothered with a pregnancy then but now had two perfect little preppie kids in elementary school who were picked up every afternoon by their nanny. Then there was Lila's dark coloring to think of . . .

It was strange that the Daleys had adopted her. They could have picked themselves up some Vietnam boat kid or an orphan in Guam. But they wanted white. Only, Lila wasn't white like they were. They were both as freckled and fair as springer spaniels, and Lila was black Irish, according to the joke. She figured, since she was born in Albuquerque—that much she knew, nothing more—that there was a good chance she was Hispanic. She pictured her mother as a scared Catholic girl who'd made it with some Anglo kid. Or maybe her father was the dark one, her mother a pale ghost whose parents hadn't approved. Maybe her mother was dead.

Lila fell back to sleep again. When she woke it was three-thirty. Marcia would be coming home soon from her job waiting tables for the lunch crowd at the Cambridge Sheraton. She wasn't ready for Marcia's sisterly concern, her insistence that Lila had to face her feelings over this one. Or Kevin's call.

She had to get out of here. She couldn't face Kevin. The doctor said no sex for three weeks. How was she going to explain that one? Her rent was paid until the end of the month. It was only May second. Where could she go? Everyone she knew was in college, facing finals week. No time for a visit. Only her parents would welcome her home.

Not a great time for that either. They were expecting to fly out for graduation in three weeks. How could she explain turning up at their door? But it was just their refusal to ask questions—or if they asked, not to probe too deeply—their desire to look on the ever-present bright side, to march forward without looking back, that she craved now. Their determined non-psychological approach to life that had infuriated her so often now appeared as appealing as a bank of muffling fog, a cushion of fog she could enter and rest within, until she was ready to come back here and figure it all out. She washed her face and brushed her teeth and changed the pad. It was bloody, but it wasn't like she was hemhorraging or anything. What she wanted most of all was to be out of here, to not have to face either of them, or finals, or anything about her everyday unsettled life.

She wanted a mother whose lap she could bury her face in.

What would she tell them? She'd come up with something, some line. She had two thousand miles to figure it out, and four hundred dollars of Richard Warren's blood money to pay her way. That would be more than enough for round-trip gas in her rusty little Datsun.

Filled with the euphoria of decision, any decision, Lila left a note for Marcia, threw a few changes of clothes and her Walkman into a bag. She knew it wasn't a great idea, taking a road trip the day of an abortion, but what *was* a good idea?

She locked the door, carried her bag to the car, jammed a Sheryl Crow CD into the player.

Route 2 jammed at the rotaries. Mass. Pike. West. Fresh crisp twenties from a Cambridge bank machine. Kevin at the law library studying torts. Richard Warren battling his teenage daughter. And all about, the light-filled evidence of spring: baby leaves, forsythia nearly gone by, tulips, green grass. She felt almost hopeful for no good reason except that she was leaving the place she most wanted to fit into behind.

CHAPTER 4

"Today is the day we give babies away."

That, Lila, was my father's answer to the question, "What day is it?"

My mother liked to say she got me from the gypsies.

My birth parents. My only parents.

Travel writer that I am, I once decided that if my father were a country he'd be Russia. Not the confused Gimme-quick Russia post-Gorbachev, but that somber mix of sentimentality and violence that Stalin epitomized and capitalized on, Brezhnev's cynical version or even the old Russia of Gogol and Dostoevski.

Quick, I see him twice: an enraged red face in the windshield, gripping the wheel, gunning the engine, as he threatens to run us down—my brother has an earache and my father, in the throes of his own furious logic, has forbidden my mother to drive him to the doctor; we're trying to walk there.

Change the channel and you'll hear his mournful, bad-voiced rendition of September Song—"the days dwindle down to a precious few," as he insists we make our yearly pilgrimage to the Barefoot Trader gift shop in Hyannis, three tanned, grumpy kids hopping from stone to stone on a pathway between glowing torches so that we can pay homage to seagull ashtrays and anchor design pillows we'll never buy. "The last day of summer," Dad says, nearly teary, as though all good things have already passed and our own young lives promise nothing but disappointment.

Russia: elusive, seductive, punitive, insane.

I have a picture of him on my wall, taken when he was seven-

teen and in the Navy: standing crooked in front of a barracks
covered in asbestos shingles, his dark woolen middy blouse
tugged too tight across his chest and pants tucked into gaiters.
His face so open and generously featured: full lips, thick chest-
nut hair, his green eyes startlingly light in black and white.

My mother said she married him because he had the saddest
eyes she'd ever seen. A blind date who offered to take her to see
the "submarine races" and she was naive enough when they
parked alongside the Charles River to expect underwater boats.
He told her some guys brought their date posies but he brought
them shoesies, opening up a box of pumps he'd gotten discount
through the family business.

"Why did you have kids if you dislike them so much?" I once
asked him.

"I didn't know how you got them."

Don't expect any straight answers from *him*.

There's a woman in my birth mothers' support group, Lila,
who says, "Look on the bright side. You may never find your
kid but at least you won't get endometriosis like the infertile
ones." I'm used to bad jokes. It's the currency of my family.

My father hooked up with my mother, whose boss, when she
showed him her dental hygiene school graduation picture, said,
"That's a squashy looking puss." She was soft, round-faced, ac-
cused by the Chinese launderers in her hometown of Newport,
Rhode Island, during the war, of being Japanese, her cheekbones
were so wide, so Tatar. They warmed to her immediately when
she explained that she was Jewish. Birth order apparently determined much of her fate. She was seventh out of eight, denied the
status of youngest along with any power. She liked her next oldest sister best, she said, because she didn't compete for food. She
hated her youngest sister most because she was the favorite, the
baby who sat on their mother's lap, saying, "I love you Mama,"
all the while dipping her finger into the sugar bowl.

I can't even imagine her as a country; she doesn't have enough
definition. Perhaps a state, amorphous and undistinguished:

Delaware? Or is that too harsh and not even true? I'm trying to diminish her because she loomed so large in my life.

For years she said she lived for her children, then admitted that she felt repugnance when she held me as an infant. I was stealing my older sister's thunder, an interloper. I was dark like my father's sisters, those pushy loudmouths who never seemed plagued by uncertainty. I was one of *them*.

What drew them together, my raging father and neglected, lost mother? When she begged him to set a wedding date and make an honest woman out of her—she swore, Lila, when I became pregnant with you, that unlike me, she'd been a virgin until marriage, a whopper lie—my father dismissed her with the phrase, "Come Christmas." She set the date for Christmas.

And so it started. Of course, those are all *her* stories.

For my own tale, I will begin with fragments, because that's how memory works, isn't it? Especially our oldest recollections. Images discrete as photographs, they have the force of something primal and prelingual. Totems of our earlier selves. Other pieces of our history are lost; there has to be *some* reason these scenes linger. If I put enough of them together, perhaps I'll find a trail that leads to you.

Two years old, I stood outside our first house in New Hampshire, a blue rented ranch. I raised my hand, rested it casually against the clustered green fans of a cedar shrub. Then I shrieked: a hornet had stung the center of my palm. Outrage smarted as badly as the sting: I hadn't intended the bug any harm, hadn't even known it was there. Why was I being punished?

Nearly three, in leggings and wool coat, planted on brown, winter-killed grass, I gazed at a crunched '55 Chevrolet in the driveway. Two neighbor boys, six-year-old toughs, swaggered over to tell me that my mother was dead, see the blood on the car? This one appears like a picture shot from behind, my small anguished face forever hidden.

Mrs. Watson came to care for my howling newborn brother, my older sister, and me. With her skinny neck and narrow wool dress, Mrs. Watson looked like Olive Oyl in the Popeye cartoons, only older. She had a high quavery voice like Olive Oyl and she could see through walls. I knew she could because she yelled, "Allie, stop picking your nose!" when I was in the living room and she was in the kitchen.

She brought me to her house, a rickety frame structure with a peaked metal roof at the edge of our housing development. Her husband Ollie rocked on the porch beside his beagle Hero. Ollie was as skinny as a rake, with an Adam's apple that prodded his wrinkly neck, and he was deaf. While Mrs. Watson bustled about doing chores, I sat on a scratchy couch, digging my finger into a split seam. An oval painting of a windmill hung on the wall, a strip of paint forever peeling into the millpond. Beside it a cuckoo emerged periodically from behind wooden doors and chimed its cheerful message, carved pine cones weighting the chains. When I walked outside to the driveway, Hero attached himself to my leg and frantically pumped.

Ollie's toothless mouth swallowed words. "Go gather eggs with him," Mrs. Watson translated, flapping a dish cloth toward the door.

Ollie led me into the chicken coop. Feathers floated in sunlight speckled with dust motes. The stink made me dizzy. Chickens squawked and fluttered as Ollie reached into the laying boxes, his bony fingers stealing eggs from underneath sitting hens. Ollie grinned, his mouth a juicy cavern, and held out a pale, manure-flecked egg. I wondered if it saddened the hens to keep losing their babies day after day.

Mrs. Watson served roast chicken for supper, and wax beans

she extracted from a blue glass jar. The only beans we ate at home were green and frozen. I decided the yellow wax beans had something to do with ear wax and refused to eat them. When I took too big a swallow of milk and gulped, Ollie gulped too and laughed. I stared down in shame at the rim of my plate, threaded with tea-colored stains, determined I wouldn't eat at all. After supper Mrs. Watson and I carried the garbage out to the chickens. Cannibals, they fell upon the bones and flesh of their own kind. They didn't even wait for them to die: one hen was scabby from being pecked. In the morning when we threw out the breakfast scraps, the scabby hen lay dead on its side, feet stiff and curled.

I thought my mother was dead like the chicken, but she wasn't. The car accident was nothing serious, she told us. She stayed in the hospital because she got too sad. She brought home presents: a baby doll for me, and for my older sister a little girl doll with painted hair.

"I want the baby!" Susy screamed.

I shrugged and offered to trade.

"Allie is so mature," my mother said. "Not like Susy."

Guilt squirmed in my belly. I didn't deserve the praise since dolls meant nothing to me. I loved animals. Susy squeezed the bald baby doll to her chest; I dangled the little plastic girl by her stiff arm. For my brother, three weeks old, my mother brought a bottle prop, a plastic support that fit the baby's chest so no one had to hold him while he nursed.

My mother wasn't always sad. One day she came out of her room wearing a black swirly skirt and danced around the living room with Davy in her arms. Susy and I sat by the playpen watching. "My mother always liked my youngest sister best because she could sing," my mother said, "but I can too. Listen. "Sol-apreee, Sol-apreeeeeeeeeeee." Her skirt twirled and her voice got so loud Davy began to cry. My mother stopped, looked around the room. "Dance, Mommy, dance," Susy and I pleaded. But it was over. She lifted Davy by the straps of his blue rompers, carried him like a package wrapped in twine, down the hall to his crib.

"Your father," my mother said, putting her head in her hands. "What did I do to deserve this?" The TV was on but there was no picture, just a grey hum. Davy napped, Susy was in school. My mother sat beside me on the couch. I put my arm on her shoulder. "Don't cry," I said, "don't cry." I feared she'd go away again if she got too sad.

"And my father," she said, "nobody even told me, they just said he went away." I knew this story, how my Grampa died when she was littler than me.

"He called you his best girl," I prompted.

"That's right," my mother said, looking up. "He'd say, who's my best girl, and all of my sisters were jealous." She smiled, squeezed me, said, "You kids are the only reason I still live."

"Let me out," my mother demanded, "right now!" The car veered to the right, slamming to a stop at the curb. "I can't take it anymore," she shouted, "I've had enough."

"Then do it," my father said, "abandon your kids, go ahead."

Susy sucked in breath. Davy dropped his rattle and began to cry. My mother got out of the car, walked away in the wrong direction, away from home. "Where's she going?" Susy wailed, "Daddy, where's she going?"

"To hell," he said, starting the engine. He looked scared.

"LET ME OUT! LET ME OUT! LET ME OUT! I WANT TO GO WITH HER!" Scrambling over Susy, I clawed at the door handle. "Shit," my father said, opening the door for me, "you go to hell too!" Susy watched me open-mouthed, faced pressed against the rear window, as the car disappeared down the road.

"It's the factory, my mother said, "if only he had enough courage to break away from his family. He's afraid of his brother but he keeps going back. All the noise there. He doesn't want to hear you kids when he gets home."

I tried to picture him in a big room full of people: The Help. When he yelled, did The Help get scared like the boy who came to mow the lawn and ran over the hose?

"They were so mean to him," my mother said. "When he left his clothes on the floor his sisters tied them in knots. When his parents went out he'd throw up and his mother would push his face in it like a dog." (I wanted a dog but he said not until I was old enough to feed it.) "Like a dog," my mother said. "He was so much younger than the rest of them, they were ashamed. And they used him like a toy. Taught him math problems for a parlor trick when he was three. His mother would give him five dollars when she went out to keep him quiet, then stole it out from under his pillow while he slept, and yelled at him for losing it in the morning. That was *their* fun."

"You were fresh," my father said.

"No I wasn't." I stood pouting, arms across my chest.

"You were fresh and now I have to lock you in the attic."

"NO NO NO!!" I had only been in the attic once, with my mother. I knew there were scary hornets up there, following mysterious trails on the window panes, trying to crawl through glass.

"Yup, I've got to lock you in the attic." He swung me up to his shoulder. A giant, he leapt stairs two at a time, holding me with just one arm. I kicked and flailed. My mother—my mother—my mother!—stepped aside to let him pass. He pushed me in and shut the door. I choked in the scent of baking pine boards, stifling air, my fear of being stung. I pounded, screamed. When my father opened the door he was grinning. His little joke.

"Red Belly. Red Belly. We want to play Red Belly!"

"Go look in my coat pocket," my father said, trying to buy us off with squirrel nuts, the candies he brought from the news store.

We scrambled for candy, but then it was "Red Belly! Daddy please!"

He lay us across his lap, pulled up our jerseys, slapped our bare bellies and then our bare tushies until they turned bright red. "That's enough," he said. "I said that's enough. Get them out of here."

At Miss Cole's Nursery School, a white Victorian house on a grassy field rife with daisies, a helper mommy showed us how to shape clay into little birdies in nests.

"God made the little birdies," announced a classmate. She was a goody-goody, the only one not scolded by Miss Cole when someone came in late during the Pledge of Allegiance and the rest of us turned to look.

"I hate God," I announced. I was as surprised as the mother that these words urped up like a bubble of acid to spill over my lips.

"Oh no you don't dear," she said quickly. "Why would you say such a thing?"

I scrambled to make it alright. "Because he made my grandfather die."

"Oh, sweetie, everyone's grandfather dies someday, that's no reason to be mad at God. You don't really hate him."

I congratulated myself for quick thinking, but on the way home, in the back seat of a car pool station wagon, I knew it wasn't over. God had heard me. *He* knew what I said and *He* was going to get me for it. The only way out, I decided, was to trick him. "Please God, *don't* make my stomachache go away," I prayed. "Please God, *don't* give me a china horse for my birthday." God wasn't that smart, it turned out, since most of the time it worked.

"Goodnight Silky Sullivan," my father called from the doorway.

"Come in," I pleaded, although my mother had already tucked me in.

"You got enough room in there," he asked, because of the stuffed animals crowding me under the sheets. I nodded, I had it all worked out: if a murderer came in to kill me in the dark, he'd stab the animals instead of me. "Silky Sullivan," my father said softly, leaning over the bed. It was the name of a racehorse. With a straight stiff arm my father reached out to pat my silky head.

"Allie," my mother said, "go back and shut off the living room lights, you were the last one there."

"It'll be dark. I'll have to come up in the dark.

"I'll wait for you right here. Be brave. Remember what Eleanor Roosevelt said—it's better to light one candle than to curse the dark."

"You talking about Bucktooth again?" my father called from the kitchen.

"Please don't talk about Eleanor that way. Now Allie, go down and shut off those lights. Your father's right in the next room."

In the kitchen, my father coughed loudly, yelled, "Why the hell didn't you mark it cat food, I thought it was tuna fish!"

"Oh, Sam, couldn't you tell by the smell?"

He coughed and coughed and coughed until I knew he was

faking. My mother started to laugh. I ran down, hit the light switch, ran back up the stairs.

He was waiting for us outside the theatre. We just saw *Swiss Family Robinson*, he saw a dirty movie across the street. "Did you learn anything?" my mother asked him, and they laughed together in the front seat. The snow had stopped falling during the movie. I pretended we were the Swiss Family riding on a raft through the night. When we got to our road the plow had been by, but only in one direction, leaving our road blocked. "Watch this," my father said, backing the car. He hit the gas and we flew forward through the drift, snow spraying like waves in all directions. "Yay!" everyone yelled. "Yay!"

My mother rarely swam, though we begged her. When she finally came in, she performed a frenzied ten-minute backstroke, kicking up a geyser of spray to keep us at bay.

I sat in the shallow ocean, my feet stuffed into the rubbery bindings of water skis. When my father gunned the outboard, the tow rope jerked, my arms threatened to pull free of their sockets, but I wouldn't let go, eager to prove I could do it, eager for the moment I'd be lifted free, poised on a surface slipping away yet still coming towards me: a world made wholly new.

"Sam," my mother protested, "you're scaring the children. You're scaring me. This was supposed to be pleasant." We were on our way for ice cream, our regular Sunday drive.

"Daddy," Susie said, "you're over the line, there's a car coming, look!" The oncoming driver honked and veered.

"Everybody just shut up," my father warned. "It's *my* road."

I huddled down in the seat behind my father. It was the safest because he couldn't reach me when he started to hit. No matter what, Susy always wanted to sit up front between them.

"Hey, Rasmus," my father said, eyeing my mother and grinning. "Hey Rasmus, what's pi r squared?"

"Not this again," she said.

"What you talking about Amos? Ev'body knows pi are round!"

"Sam will you please stop it? I don't like this kind of joke."

"That's right, my father said, "you and your nigger-loving Kennedy friends don't like this kind of joke."

"Don't talk like that in front of the kids."

"As long as I put gas in the tank I'll say what I want. Nigger lover. Nigger lover. Nigger lover."

My mother stared out the window.

"Hey kids." My father turned in his seat. "How do you make a hormone? Don't pay her."

My mother groaned.

"How does a die cutter order two beers?" My father raised his hand, hiding the middle fingers under his thumb, sticking up the index and pinkie.

"What's a die cutter?" I asked.

"Daddy," Susy cried, "you aren't watching the road."

"In the factory," my mother explained, "they cut leather. Sam, it isn't a joke."

In the factory, the floorboards rumbled under my father's pressure. He walked too fast, leaning forward, pounding. He wouldn't wait. Light fell through high cobwebbed windows; my father and I passed wordlessly through a series of dust mote rays. Below the windows, the Merrimac River swirled black. I was giddy with the pungency of leather, the factory's rich dark smell. It was Saturday and The Help was gone; stitching machines stood empty, row after row after row. We were here for Inventory, I was being paid to help him count: cutting machines;

piles of leather—brown, black, beige; burlap sacks of soles, heels, inners, uppers, welts; rooms full of racks; racks full of work boots, combat high tops, shiny black wing tips with funny holes. Pieces of shoes with dangling threads, unfinished; boxes and boxes of shoes ready to go.

Without warning he stopped, handed me a yellow pad on a clipboard lined with columns, then climbed on a pile of sacks. Flipping tags he shouted Inners R7834, six dozen, N57629 four dozen, G5873 five. I scribbled, scribbled, afraid I wouldn't get it all. We did this for hours, my father moving above me, climbing, leaping, grunting, while I followed along on the floor. His breathing mingled with the cooing of pigeons that hid in the factory walls.

Later, my father's shotgun phone voice boomed behind his office door. I stalked the room where the girls I'd never seen made up the orders. I sifted through wastebaskets, rifled their desk drawers, stole paper clips, erasers, pens. In the bathroom, big breasted naked ladies on calendars bent over to advertise Superior Hides.

When the windows were completely black, the factory dark with shadows, my father called me, a loud bellow that echoed through unlit halls. "Get your coat," was all he said when I came.

"Tell me about Tim the Woodhook and Dirty Julia when you were a little girl in Newport," I begged my mother.

Tucking me in, she stopped to consider the story. "You know," she said, "they had an old crumbling shack on Bellevue Avenue and all the rich people wanted to buy them out, but they wouldn't sell. Tim hooked wood off the beach and Julia, Julia wasn't too clean."

"Like you," I said, "like you when your bloomers were hanging and everyone made fun."

"Six-time hand-me-downs," my mother said, "I never had anything new."

"And you went to church with the O'Briens next door and when the rabbi found out he got mad at your mother. And you ran wild on the beach and you fell in the Vanderbilt's fish pond and the caretaker pulled you out."

"That's right. You know all my stories. But I was underwater so long I think I got brain damage. Just wait, you'll all see when I die and they do the autopsy, then you'll understand."

"Tell me about the cliff walk."

"Oh, I always wanted to go everywhere with my older sisters. Once Martha said she was going on a diet, and I said, 'Can I come?' Well, we went for a picnic along the cliff walk, behind the big mansions, all of my sisters and the neighbors' kids . . .

"That's enough," my father shouted from their bedroom. "Put them to bed and get in here."

"He's jealous," my mother whispered, clicking off my light. Even I recognized the pride in her voice.

Sleeping in the front seat, I was woken by urgent, angry voices. My father pulled the car over to the highway verge. "Goddammit son of a bitch! You're bleeding on the upholstery!" He got out, opened the trunk, returned with an army blanket for my mother to sit on.

"What's the matter, Mommy?" I pleaded. "What happened?"

"Nothing," my mother hissed, "go back to sleep." With a spin of gravel, my father jerked the car back on the road. My mother sat rigid. In the back of the finned Cadillac, my sister and brother mercifully slept.

Lila, I was a child who never knew what was going on. I could sit in my room weeping, weeping, until I grew fascinated by the bubbles I shaped with my lips, mwaaaa, mwaaaa, mwaaaa, and no longer remembered why I was sad.

I didn't even know my parents had gone to Europe until my sister told me. The woman hired to stay with us was a stranger; she locked us out of the house each day for several hours while she took her "nap." Even though she was dumpy and seemed old, she had a boyfriend. Wally took us places without her, in his old green coupe he called "The Puddlejumper." We sat at the movies, Susy on one side of Wally, I on the other, popcorn passing across his lap.

Eventually my parents returned with gifts of French and Spanish dolls too lacy and expensive for us to play with; they had to be displayed on a shelf.

Can I tell you this, Lila: how I sat—how I will always sit—legs open, knees up, on the walkway that leads to the basement, while ants file across the pits and boulders of sand trapped in cement? It is hot. The cicadas' loud rasp merges with the electric wires running overhead. Behind the rose hedge, lush with pink flowers and abuzz with the bees that I fear, is the pine forest, cool and dark and silenced by needles. Beckoning.

Like the man who leads me in. The man whose back I will always see, his back and his arm pulling me forward, the hummingbird iridescence of his Hawaiian shirt, the swell of veins on his thick forearm. He leads me into the woods to the softness of needles.

I sit on the cement walkway, bees droning in the blossoms and cicadas rasping overhead. On the other side of the house, away from the woods, are the lilacs. There it is safe, sweet when you suck the pollen from a lilac blossom, which has four little stem-like petals. The sweet dust reminds me of the powder from those paper lik-a-stiks, except the lilac powder is faint and wild. But lilacs bloom in spring. Now it is summer and I sit beside the roses, running my finger in the crack, feeling the rough edges of shattered cement and the dark smear of dirt that tastes like metal on the tongue.

The forest draws me, cool and dark and balsam scented, beyond the threatening hedge of flowers. The cicadas' shriek runs through me like an electric shock from the wires overhead and the cement is sandpaper under my hands. I lay my face against its warmth. The bees drone in the bushes and behind them stands the forest, dark and cool and silenced by needles, where no one can hear when you scream.

After my parents came back from Europe, I lay on the papered table, legs spread, while the doctor touched glass slides against my private places. I feared she'd cut me with her scary glass. Why her? A middle-aged lady doctor instead of our regular family doctor, a young man who drove to our house with his crew-cut and bow tie and his boxer dog. ("You had a urinary tract infection," my mother insisted years later, when I asked her about the doctor and her slides. But it wasn't an ordinary specimen that woman took, not pee in a jar; my crossed legs hid weeping sores.) When we got home from the lady doctor, my mother sat me in a warm bath—our special time together, she called it—and had me scissor my legs, water whooshing between them, both of us watching me heal.

CHAPTER 5

Lila's escape euphoria was lost long before the honk and screech of rush-hour Hartford. A determined hunch over the wheel carried her to the Pennsylvania turnpike—a great dark rising and falling of woods and ravines and then well past midnight the diminishing swell and flattening of eastern Ohio, a drone of land stretching west in squares of flat, cultivated fields. A double hypnosis, the blackness between towns, the familiarity of this landscape she had spurned.

Highways. Maybe it wasn't getting to her parents house she wanted but just to be en route, as she'd been so many times moving from base to base. There was something comforting about crossing great stretches of landscape. Those cross-country drives were the only time Dad was all theirs, stripped of his men, his planes for a couple of days. She could close her eyes now, here, on this highway, with the vibration of tires rolling on blacktop, and picture their usual lineup: Dad in the driver's seat, his prickly short hair in her line of vision, Mom in the passenger seat, Lila in the back with her cat in its travel case. And somewhere, ahead or behind them, a moving van with their boxes and beds, their wrapped dishes and silverware.

"It's got to be better than that backwater," Mom would say, hopeful, doubtful. Even though she'd said exactly the same thing as they'd headed toward wherever they were now leaving.

"It's going to be fine," Dad assured them. It would be fine for him. It always was, as long as he could fly.

"I hope the schools . . ." Mom fretted.

What did Lila hope for? A best friend, next door neighbors

she could stand, an art teacher who came to school more than
once a month with a paint-by-numbers mentality. A bedroom
with a view beyond barracks, missile silos, parade grounds. As
long as you were on the road you could still hope. It was only
when you got there, driving past the guards to one more row of
identical frame or brick houses, cheap flooring, scratched trim
boards, evidence of those who had come before and would
come after, that you knew it was never better anywhere.

"Let's play a game," Dad said. "Let's pretend we're not military, we're civilian, just regular folks moving. Ruth, what do
you want me to be?"

Mom wouldn't take the bait.

"C'mon, Ruthie, choose something. Plumber? Podiatrist?
Pretzel manufacturer? Proctologist? Prison guard?"

"Not a prison guard," Mom sighed. "No more uniforms."

Dad turned in his seat. "What about you, Lila, pick me a profession. What kind of daddy do you really want?"

She wanted him. At that age, at least, she wanted him just as
he was, only more often. "Does it have to start with a P?" she
stalled.

"Nope. Let's just make up the life your Mom wants to be living."

"Don't John," Mom said. "Please stop it."

"I'm just trying to make the time pass," Dad said, all innocence.
"There aren't enough signs out here to play the alphabet game."

"Okay then," Mom said, "a minister."

"A minister?" Dad was incredulous. "Presbyterian, I suppose. But ministers get transferred too. Sent to new parishes.
They live in crummy rectories and don't own their own houses."

"Forget that," Mom said. "Alright, a pharmacist."

"Oooh, that hurts," said Dad.

"You asked. I want you to own a drug store on a corner in a
nice little town. I want you to wear a white jacket with your
name clipped on and give advice to old ladies."

"Yes ma'am," Dad intoned in a syrupy voice. "Now don't

take more than one of those suppositories a day. That's right ma'am."

Lila and Mom giggled. There was no way. Years later Lila would read Isaac Babel's story about a pogrom in Odessa, his description of a Cossack with eyes that seemed to gaze over a Ural pass, and she would recognize her father. Nobody who looked like him could own a drug store.

"Mrs. MacGillicuddy. Mrs. MacGillicuddy. You forgot your Geritol dear."

Ruth ignored him, wrapped up in her own game. "And every day I'd meet you for lunch downtown. We'd go next door to a coffee shop and eat egg salad sandwiches and gossip about your customers."

"Yuck," Lila said. "I hate egg salad."

"Hey." Dad turned in his seat, raised an eyebrow. "Who said anything about you?"

Lila's breath knocked out of her, like on the playground when Gary Conner kicked her in the chest. Dad didn't want her. In their pretend life, it would be just the two of them.

"You'd be in school, honey," Mom said, glaring at Dad. "A beautiful school just down the block . . ."

"I was only kidding, Li-pie, you aren't mad are you?"

Lila sat back in the seat, poked her finger through the mesh of Kitten Caboodle's travel box so she could touch her soft grey fur. Kitten yowled softly, ready to complain about her incarceration if anyone was listening.

"Hey," Dad offered. "See that sign? A 72-ounce steak free if you can eat it in an hour. You want me to try? C'mon Lie-lie, Cow Pie, gimme a smile. See the trouble I get in trying to fit into civilian life?"

That night, Lila sat cross-legged on a plastic chaise beside the motel pool, a pair of terry shorts over her swimsuit, a book propped open in her lap. Dad sat down beside her and lit a cigarette. He was wearing his swim trunks and his hard-muscled chest glowed pale in the twilight.

"Watcha reading?"

"*A Tree Grows in Brooklyn.*"

"Is that a good one?"

"Uh-huh."

"I had a buddy from Brooklyn once. John Petrazzo. Shot down over Cambodia." They both listened while the bug zapper in front of the motel office fried a mosquito.

"There ain't much light left out here to read," Dad said.

"I can see." Though she wouldn't be able to much longer. The big halogen light on a pole at the corner of the pool didn't seem to do much but gather moths.

"I never was a great reader myself."

Tell me something I don't already know, Lila thought.

"Kinda wonder how I even made it to Captain."

Lila sighed meaningfully and closed her book over a finger to hold her place.

"I signed up the day I graduated from high school. I was just a hick kid from Della, Oklahoma, no Air Force Academy white gloves for me. I looked around and saw nothing but ruint farms . . ." He'd slipped into that hick way he had of talking about Oklahoma. ". . . and railroad tracks leading out. Too slow. I wanted one thing: to sit in the cockpit of a fighter jet and break the sound barrier."

"They don't let you do that anymore."

"Nope. Can't have that noise pollution. I met your Momma when I was stationed at Jerome, South Carolina."

"What was she like then?"

"Pretty. She's still pretty, but back then, wow. Her daddy died in World War II when she was just a baby and her Momma raised the two girls alone. All nice manners and no money. She was dead set against her girls marrying military men, and both of 'em did it. A headshrinker would probably have some theory about them looking for the lost daddy in a uniform. Her momma kept some kind of a shrine to him on the mantel. But she wanted her girls to marry up, marry solid,

marry in town. Your momma used to climb out the window to
see me."

"No way." It was hard enough to picture Mom climbing out
any window, let alone sneaking out to meet a boyfriend.

"Sure did. She was engaged to a fella in town. Nice boring
guy who was going to take over his daddy's drug store." Dad
nudged her bare foot. "Yup, think of it, baby. You coulda been
raised by some guy in a white jacket, had free candy and magazines all your life, lived in a white house with a maid. Instead of
spending half your life crossing the country in a station wagon
full of suitcases."

"Do you think that's what Mom really wanted?"

He flicked ashes onto the cement pool apron, smiled. "She
married me, didn't she? Hey, Lie-pie, you wanna see if the old
man can still do a back flip?"

He dropped his shirt, snuffed his cigarette with his thumb,
and walked around to the deep end where a rickety diving board
was fastened. Lila closed her eyes, heard the bounce and give of
her father's weight on suspended wood, then opened them in
time to see him hurtle backward, a neat slice and splash. She
waited, waited, and then he popped up in front of her grinning,
reached out and grabbed her ankle.

"Come on, bookworm, time to get wet."

"Dad, I got my shorts on . . . Da-ad!"

But she was sliding in, releasing her book just in time, sucked
under as powerfully as her mother must have been.

When Lila couldn't drive any further, when the center stripes
and dashes turned to indecipherable morse code, and she could-
n't stomach another cup of styrofoam road coffee, she pulled off
at a rest area, giving wide berth to the rumbling semis, and
parked at the far end of the lot past the bathrooms, under the
halogen glare. She locked her doors, bunched a sweater under
her head and leaned against the rolled window. The car immedi-

ately grew stuffy, but when she rolled the window down an inch mosquitoes entered, buzzing annoyingly in her ears. She opted for the sauna effect and the relative safety of closed windows, and slept.

When she woke, cramped and sweaty, it still wasn't light out, though the headlights and street lamps filled the sky with a garish glow. She ran her tongue over unbrushed teeth coated with fuzz; her eyelids felt gluey, her head ached, and her bones did too. She'd only slept an hour.

The semis roared and rumbled, engines never shut down. Lila got up and went to the fluorescent bathroom to change her pad, brush her teeth. She filled her coffee-stained styrofoam cup at the faucet on the side of the "convenience" station, drank, aware of the trucker who stopped to watch her, the pause in his bowlegged gait. "Hey girlie. You alone?" he called. Stiffly she walked back to the car, keys clutched in her palm, his stare like a cocked gun, making her shorn neck prickle. And all the while rehearsing bluffing words: I'm packing a .45 police special, my boyfriend, a karate expert, is in the men's room.

Lila unlocked the Datsun, hurled herself in, pushed down the buttons, twisted the ignition key until the starter ground. Fuck. She blew a gust of air into her bangs and restarted the car. Then backed up fast, jamming a Cranberries tape into the player to reestablish her own atmospheric sovereignty. Laying rubber on the access ramp, counting off the miles until she could relax again into the mind-numbing black and white world of nighttime driving.

Then a sun rising behind her, the great green grasslands and chunky plowed earth capturing angled early light, a sky dim at its corners lifting to the pale emptiness of her girlhood. She tried to compose it into a layered wash of watercolor, or recompose it into saturated canvas smeared with oils. Instead she remembered fighter jets' contrails scarring the bleached prairie sky.

She and Lisa Morris had sat cross-legged on top of a picnic bench, on scuffed lawn behind identical officer's quarters, planning their futures while Lisa's brothers slammed a basketball on asphalt, aiming for a netless hoop. Will was the oldest, the one on whom Lila had a violent crush. Watching him sit shirtless and spread-legged in an arm chair, lifting an RC Cola to his mouth, his black shiny hair—the only Morris dark like she was—was enough to make her swoon.

Lisa and Lila, only one letter separating their names, a coincidence they found significant. Lisa and Lila, eleven years old, sure that all was right in a world where Reagan ruled, everyone was Republican, kids could safely run from house to house on Halloween without tagalong parents, and rank was an inalienable fact of life. Here flatness was an acceptable view. Lisa and Lila, sitting on each other's beds in identical family barracks, the only difference in their rooms the teen posters, the gewgaws: dolls, china horses, Lisa's stock of pilfered makeup—she had older sisters.

They would both marry at twenty-four, have twins, a boy and a girl, but Lila wouldn't want a military man while Lisa was set on nothing less than a general. Then she would be the one to hold those parties that all the wives had to attend. The one serving dishes of non-pareils and bridge mix.

They argued about college and careers. Lisa didn't think it was necessary for an Air Force wife. Lila didn't want to be stuck at home like her mother. Moreover, she was leaning toward something investigative: reporter or private eye. Lisa was the only one Lila confided to about her desire to search out her "real mother," whose discovery would ensure a glamorous, though as yet ill-defined, future. Together they invented her birth mother's whereabouts and occupation: she was a ballet dancer (they'd been taken to see the *Nutcracker* last year in Kansas City) who wasn't allowed to have a child and had to hide it away; she was a movie star always on location. Lisa openly envied the romantic possibilities of Lila's secret life while Lila envied (though never admitted it) the simple sureness of Lisa's—a sister who looked like her even if she was bossy and mean; a little brother nursing at his mother's breast and Lisa's knowledge that she'd done the same. No faraway stranger tied to you by blood and rejection.

She also envied Lisa's chaotic house: toys and snack foods left on every surface, with brothers and sisters pushing you out of the way for the best chair or TV channel; two different TV's blared constantly, one in the kitchen for Mrs. Morris and her soaps, another for the kids. Lila's house was as spotless as the enlisted men's barracks. Her mother didn't have enough to do with only one kid. At that age, Lila suspected that she'd proved such a disappointment they didn't want to risk adopting another. Though no one ever said. But her mother's unspoken dissatisfaction was always present, in her constant scrubbing, her sighs, the whirring of the sewing machine, her foot on the pedal pumping angrily, her ladylike cursing: sudden aggrieved bursts of "Sugar!" or "Darn!"

Lila spent as much time as possible at Lisa's, even though Lila had her own room and Lisa had to share with Sherry, her younger sister who was only eight and fat from constant candy gobbling. They walked the paved roads cutting through flat fields, holding their ears against the repeated jet roars. They giggled about the cute enlisted man who called them babe and made them promise not to break hearts when they grew up. Two little girls without breasts, bony-kneed, biking around a base past squadrons of marching uniformed men, sharing the bus to school where civilian kids had their own mysterious codes and cliques.

That too was a world stratified by rank but not one so easy to divine. On base, everyone knew everyone else's and kowtowed accordingly. At school it was different; they were bussed twelve miles to the county school where life was divided into farm kids and town kids; Air Force kids were on their own. Everyone knew they never lasted. Rank depended on looks, and looks in Fairlee County meant Barbie doll blond. Lila with her dark eyes and hollow cheeks and black braids might as well have been from Calcutta.

Looks and cars. Rock groups. Clothes. With the country kids it was 4-H livestock projects and horses. You had to have attitude; you had to appear sure of yourself and people would act like you had a reason to be. Kids gravitated to the smart aleck boys, the bossy girls. Lila watched and took notes, sure in her friendship with Lisa.

Lila closed her eyes, that sweet seduction—how easy to simply fall asleep, to loosen her grip on the steering wheel, to give in to the tires' gentle hum. She opened them again, startled by a memory of Lisa's house:

She'd gone upstairs to use the bathroom, opened the unlocked door. Stopped, frozen. Lisa's brother Will was sitting on the toilet seat, pants at his ankles, hand gripped around the straining pink swell of penis, moving up and down. An open magazine—flash of crotch, enormous pink nippled breasts splayed on the floor at his feet. He looked at her, his face a quick grimace of exposure, then he grinned.

"Shut the door," he commanded. The speckled linoleum, green with gold glitters, the shower curtain mildewed and clouded with scum, the white cornice of the porcelain sink, the dark shellac on the knotty pine trim imprinted themselves on her brain the way details do in an accident.

She didn't know if he meant from the inside or outside. She hesitated, face burning.

"Come in and shut the door," he said. Because he was so much older, a high school senior, because the crush she'd had on him gave him power, because she didn't know how to break the spell she was in, she stepped in silently and closed the door. It clicked, a neat meshing of tapered bolt into hole. She only had to turn the knob to release it, yet she stood there, trapped.

"You want to touch it, don't you? You want to. You knew I was in here all along." His voice low, nearly a hum. But his hand never stopped moving up and down, up and down, a bizarre motion that seemed to have nothing to do with the situation. And then his penis, looking red and agonized, spouted milky goo against his tee shirt. He collapsed against the back of the toilet seat for an instant, then rose quickly, swiping at himself with his shirt. He pulled up his pants, grabbed his magazine. His voice different now, threatening:

"You better not tell or I'll say you came in here to watch. How you wanted to." And he was out the door, shoving past her, closing her in, and Lila was sitting on the edge of the tub, knees shaking, until she could rise and wash her face.

Would she always be doing that? Washing her face in men's bathrooms, stalling for time, as she had just yesterday (yesterday? the time blurring into road time) at Richard Warren's.

Then there was one secret she couldn't share with Lisa. Afterward she shrank at the sight of Will, his leering wink. Fortunately, Will graduated two months later and went off to a base in Georgia.

"Prick," Lila said now, to the bug-spattered windshield. As these things went, it was a pretty trivial story, nothing compared to the molestations professed by so many of her friends. Still, he was a prick. Probably on his way to being a major.

Things went back to how they'd been, and then as it had to happen, it happened. Lisa's father got transferred to Washington State. It was the first and last time Lila wept at a separation. They promised they'd write constantly, and they exchanged gifts: Lila gave Lisa the aquamarine heart ring her mother's sister, faraway Aunt Dee, had sent for her last birthday, and Lisa gave Lila a baggie full of pilfered cosmetics: sugar rose lipstick, peach blush, a tube of cover up for the zits that hadn't yet appeared. Lila watched from the sidewalk as the van filled with the Morris' broken and sagging furniture, and then she ran and hid behind the squadron housing, a place officers' kids were not allowed to go, because she figured no one would come looking for her there. She spent half the afternoon huddled in weedy grass between a propane tank and a prefab bunker, the sour stench of the tank running low the ever-after scent of loss.

Lisa wrote twice from Seattle about her boyfriend Paul, and

kissing parties. She had a bra. In September, they would have started junior high together. Lila suspected Lisa would have slipped into the world of the civvie kids, she would grow breasts faster, learn to play spin the bottle, while Lila clung shyly to the sidelines, and then Lisa would have left her altogether, even if she hadn't moved. A new family inhabited Lisa's house: their father a major, two boys, thirteen and fifteen, who called her "squirt" and shot baskets endlessly on the driveway just as the Morris boys had, and spit and smoked when only she was looking. Lila turned her concentration to mimicking the habits and codes of the kids in junior high, civilian kids, until she could discern the mysterious difference between popular and geeky, and she too was invited to kissing parties and overnights.

A year later they were transferred to Nevada, then Hanscom Field in Bedford, Massachusetts, and everything she'd learned of the Kansas and Nevada kids didn't apply. But she was already skilled at scoping out the situation and adapting accordingly.

In Massachusetts they lived in a house they owned, for the first time. Dad had decided to buy so that he could sell at a profit when he retired at fifty-five; he wouldn't have to pay capital gains tax. For Sudbury, it wasn't much: a sixties "contemporary," lots of glass and dark-stained vertical siding, cheap panel room dividers, on a woodsy lot. But for once Dad was the one who commuted and Lila got the benefit of Lincoln-Sudbury High School.

The hot sport at Lincoln-Sudbury was soccer, not football, at least not for the crowd to which Lila wanted to belong. She did layout for the high school paper and struggled with her lack of academic preparation. She took rides into Harvard Square with friends who had cars and hung out at Boston clubs to see performers she'd never heard of in Kansas or Nevada. But it was on an outing at the Concord Bridge that she had an epiphany, though one she was careful to hide from her friends.

She drove over after school one bright October day with a

couple of friends from the paper: Jason, with his Druid teeshirt, his unruly hair and early admission to Brown; and Sarah, who worried about getting a mere 1475 combined on the SAT's and went to France on vacations to see her father and his new family.

"We used to come here on school trips. In fourth grade we spent the whole year on the history of our town," Jason said, lighting a cigarette as they crossed the road and walked toward the famous bridge on a dirt path bordered by stone walls. "We lived in Lexington then. Concord was our rival. It was like some big deal, where was the shot heard round the world fired, here or Lexington. Plus we played them in sports."

"In Kansas they took us to view a John Deere factory," Lila said, rolling her eyes. "In Alabama, it was the Bear Bryant monument. They've got a Bear Bryant highway, and Bear Bryant burgers."

"Who's Bear Bryant?" Sarah asked.

"Some stupid football coach," Lila said. "That's what they consider history down there."

"Not the Civil Rights movement, huh?" Jason said.

"Not if you're white, boy. At least here you don't have to see Paul Revere burgers everywhere."

"Hey Sarah," Jason said, "who rode with Paul Revere?"

"William Dawes."

"Excellent. Ten points. One if by land, two if by sea. Take a shit or take a pee. The fourth grade version. These towns are so full of themselves."

Lila carefully noted his tone of disdain, but it was easy for him to dismiss them since he belonged here. They studied the bronze Minuteman, stepping away from his plow, rifle in hand.

"This is the part I like," Jason said, reading off a nearby plaque. "'I haven't a man who's afraid to go.' Wow. You know these guys were the originators of guerilla warfare? They hid behind these walls, the British came marching in their neat formations, all bright in their little red coats, blam."

Lila knew that already. It was the one bit of colonial history she did know. Military tactics.

They walked the incline to the center of the arched bridge and Sarah dropped her cigarette into the river. Pigeons cooed under the bridge rafters. Sarah leaned over the rail, long sandy hair hanging. A pair of swans floated out from the reeds, necks curved into white question marks. They looked serene, floating effortlessly, but Lila pictured their webbed feet, hidden from view, paddling furiously. Like me, she thought. Around the bend of the river, a couple of canoes slid out of sight. Sarah took a joint out of her pocket and lit it, passed it to Lila. Two mallards swooped down and skidded to a landing. Behind them, two tiny V-shaped wakes.

"Pretty fucking picturesque," Lila said, releasing smoke slowly. "So old Thoreau used to canoe right here."

"Yup," Jason said. "D'you ever have to read that Thoreau essay about Mount Katahdin? He really loses it up there in Maine, wilderness was just too much for him. It blew his nice little Concord mind. Like that turtle in the King Leonardo cartoons. Take me back, Mr. Wizard!"

"Do you think he ever got laid?" Sarah asked.

"I doubt it." Jason always assumed all conversation was directed at him. Lila and he had been an item for a while, but now they were just friends. Jason's know-it-all energy had worn on her. "You know, when he died his basement was full of unsold copies of his books."

"FYI," said Lila.

"FYI."

A troop of elderly tourists approached the Minuteman statue. Lila, Sarah, and Jason moved away, down the slanting boards, sheltering their joint. Across the bridge a path led through scruffy wetlands toward a large brick house that served as some sort of museum. Shafts of late sun caught in the weeds, cattails along the path. Lila picked a milkweed pod, cracked it and released the fluffy seeds with their little parachutes. If each mother pod released a zillion offspring, she wondered, why wasn't the world made up of milkweed plants? The survival rate must be miniscule. The ephemeral fluff rose, shimmered in the oblique afternoon light.

The tourists were gone by the time they got back to the bridge. They detoured, climbing over a stone wall by the Minuteman, crossed a pasture, and peered in the windows of the Old Manse, the big grey clapboard Dutch colonial where Emerson and Hawthorne had lived. Jason pointed out the bullseye glass over the door, the window where someone had scratched a picture of a sailing ship with a diamond. They walked the neat quadrants of dried up garden behind the house. Vines crackled underfoot.

"Once in ninth grade Zack Stanton and I rode our bikes out here and ate mushrooms," Jason said.

"Did you have any heavy historic revelations?" Sarah wanted to know.

"We puked a lot. It was a hell of a ride home."

Don't, Lila thought, don't make this place not mean anything. But she knew better than to say it. She didn't understand her own visceral pull. She wasn't fond of history in school. She couldn't stand reading Emerson, that transparent eyeball crap, and Thoreau was just a pretender who paddled his canoe home to Mommy regularly for cookies and home-cooked meals while writing about self-reliance. No, it wasn't the literature or the history, it was the feel, the aura, the look. Okay, so she was shallow. She preferred the grace of colonial structures with their symmetrical windows, their perfectly pitched roofs, their ancient maples and beeches, to split-level ranch developments and mobile home parks sprouting out of flat farm land.

She weighed this place against a lifetime of barracks and guard houses and identical officers' housing, of jet hangars and phantoms and reverence for the B-52, and she knew she'd found the home she wanted to claim as her own. It was more than just surfaces. It was an aesthetic that summed up everything she craved: a continuum.

Of course it was mostly illusion, as Jason would be glad to point out. Probably half the people living in these suburban Boston towns came from elsewhere, not even New England. The computer industry ringing the city, the Route 128 blight of high tech corporate strongholds, each with its carefully landscaped winding drive and logo designed by experts, had long dominated the area, drawing to it ambitious communications geeks from across the continent.

Lila didn't care. Concord, Carlisle, Lexington, Lincoln, Sudbury—towns with white clapboard frame houses, black shutters, historic monuments from a war long before General Robert E. Lee. Parents who read *The New York Times* as well as *The Boston Globe*, who voted Democrat and had shelves of books. Who displayed photos of ancestors instead of fighter planes on their walls.

That day on the Concord Bridge she knew she wanted all of it. Still did.

Instead she had Kevin.

Lila squinted through the windshield at the gentle oceanic roll of Indiana fields, tried to imagine what Kevin must be thinking. What story had Marcia given him? What exactly had she put in her note? Tell him I'll call. She ought to phone him at the next gas stop. She glanced at the dashboard clock. It was only eight fifteen A.M. Later maybe. He had probably stayed up late studying. It was a rare night he wasn't over at her place and Kevin would surely make use of the time.

They had been together since the summer after her first year of college when they met on a housing rehabilitation project, members of a team stripping old plaster and lath off the walls of decrepit city apartment buildings, scraping old molding and window sashes, painting freshly sheetrocked surfaces. Lila had figured it was better than waitressing or working in a copy shop. The pay was the same and the do-good aspect of it vaguely appealed to her, along with the physicality, after nine months of sitting in the library or at her desk. Besides, she loved the old

buildings, their detailed grace revealed under layers of cock-
roach droppings, stained wallpaper, chipped linoleum. She wondered if she might want to go on to architecture school. Her
hand-writing wasn't neat enough, she joked to herself, but she
knew something inside her would rebel against the gridwork of
blueprints, the angular geometry of functional structures. It was
the curve and embellishment of hundred-year-old crown mold-
ings and window trim she loved, not the load bearing capacity
of joists and beams.

Kevin was into the sociological merits of the work, immune
to the old buildings' aesthetic charms. "Low-income towah
housing is a proven failyah," he reported, scraper in hand, bare
legs beneath his shorts speckled with chips of paint. "Look at
the projects in Cambridge neah Fresh Pond." Lila thought he
was excessively earnest that first day, even as she judged his
South Boston accent low class. But she couldn't help noticing his
own fine architecture: a rack of shoulders wide and straight as
cross beams, biceps flexed and stretched under taut tan skin,
light eyes in a face planed smooth and neatly angled.

The other team members were less appealing: the thirty-year-
old union carpenter, Eddie, who was already bald, had a significant beer gut, and despised them for being in college; a dizzy,
stoned Dead Head named Shane from Bard whose aunt was on
the city Redevelopment Authority; and whining Isabel from
B.U. with the tragic ever breaking fingernails.

At five o'clock that first Friday, when they'd finished sweeping up the day's mess, Kevin surprised her by asking her out for
a beer. She wanted a shower, a change of clothes, but instead let
him drive her to a dark and dusty Irish bar located in a neighborhood not far from his own. The Shamrock was decorated
with Celtics pennants, faded Erin Go Bragh banners from some
long ago Saint Patrick's day, and a line of bent-backed men at
the bar. When a nun in habit came shuffling in, collecting for the
poor innocents in Belfast, Lila shook her head in wonder.

"I don't believe it. This is like a stage set," she said.

"Hey," Kevin said, setting two beer mugs on their booth table, "this is the real thing." He went into a fake brogue: "Jesus, Mary, and Joseph. I'm a walking stereotype meself." Then in his own laughable voice: "So wheah yah from, Brookline? Concahd? Cahlisle?"

"Hanscom Field, by way of Kansas, Mississippi, Georgia, you name it."

"And I thought it was money I heard in yah voice."

"Just middle America. If I had money why would I be slaving my summer away?"

"Wanted to help the poor? Wanted to meet nice boys from Boston College?"

"Is that where you go?"

"Yup, scholarship, loans, and work study." He crossed his paint speckled, corded forearms on the table. "Grounds crew."

"I work in the dining hall during the school year," Lila admitted.

"Do yah weah one of those little hayuh nets? I'm a suckah for girls in hayuh nets." He reached up to brush paint flakes from her bangs.

Lila held steady under the sudden intimacy, unsure if she resented or liked it.

"Weah gonna have a hot, dirty summah," Kevin said. "But it could be fun."

Lila swirled her beer. His ease with himself disarmed her, despite the Southie accent. Kevin McCarty wasn't ashamed of where *he* came from. And, it turned out, he was in no rush to make a move. Even though it was backtracking for him and she insisted she didn't mind riding the T, he gave her a gentlemanly ride back to Cambridge where she shared a summer sublet with her dorm mate Marcia. And that was that.

A week later, Lila rolled a coat of primer on the new living room ceiling while Eddie and Kevin wrestled the old painted cabinets out of the high-ceilinged kitchen.

"Ugh, we have to do ceilings today?" Isabel flounced into

the room, half an hour late, her voice a bray, a New Jersey whine. No sign of Shane yet. Lila silently dipped her roller in the tray.

Isabel pouted. "Somebody could've told me. I didn't even bring a hat."

"Eddie told you Friday." The hat was the least of it. Isabel never dressed for the job to which she was so ill-suited. The first day she appeared wearing sling back pumps with little heels, white shorts gathered at the waist, a lacy blouse. Today she wore black stretch leggings under a silky tee. Isabel was too busy worrying over her scarlet fingernails, or displaying a bruise on her long smooth leg to get much work done, although she collected her weekly paycheck like the rest of them.

Lila gestured with her roller to a sack on the floor. "Check out that bag." Several cheap white visored caps advertising Sherwin Williams lay among the stirring sticks and drop cloths and rags. Isabel examined a painter's cap doubtfully.

"I'll do the ceiling, you start on the walls," Lila offered.

Isabel turned away from the living room, wandered to the kitchen. "What are you guys doing?"

"Weah having a tea pahty," Eddie hissed between clenched teeth. Wood screeched under his crowbar.

Lila smirked. Don't think about it, she warned herself. You're getting your salary no matter what she does or doesn't do. She tried to put herself back into her favorite work fantasy: she was renovating her own colonial home into antique perfection.

Isabel screamed.

Lila dropped her roller onto the dirty floor, and stepped into her paint tray. "Shit."

"Kill them!" Isabel wailed. She rocketed back to the living room, cowered against the wall. Baby mice scurried about the kitchen in confusion, their nest dislodged by the yanked cupboards. Isabel shrieked as though knifed.

"Jesus fucking Christ," Eddie swore. "Somebody shut her up!"

Two of the mice ran into the living room, straight into the spilled Latex and out again, trailing tiny white foot- and tail prints as they scurried in circles, frantically seeking a hiding hole. Just then Shane slouched in reeking of marijuana. He lowered his headphones. "Hey, cool," he observed of the mouse floor-painting. "Just like Jackson Pollock, dude."

Isabel whimpered. Kevin and Lila broke out laughing. Eddie slammed his crowbar to the floor and stomped toward the door. "I'm working in a fucking nuthouse heah."

Kevin gave Lila a conspiratorial wink. "That white really sets off yah tan."

Lila looked down at herself. Her arms and legs, darkened by a weekend at Marcia's parents' house in Manchester-by-the-Sea, were splattered with white latex. Kevin was already heading back to the kitchen, whistling "The Girl From Ipanema."

After that it was a continual series of private jokes. They had a running bet on how long it would take Isabel to quit, how many joints Shane could smoke on the landing between lazy hammer blows. How soon before Eddie blew a gasket. They took turns making ice tea runs to the corner store. The city smelled like garbage and exhaust fumes. The summer heat and humidity grew stifling in the stuffy third floor apartment; Lila grew intensely aware of each time she and Kevin bumped shoulders or had to slide past each other in the narrow kitchen. Lila carried home a mental picture of Kevin's tee shirt stuck to his bent back, his strong, corded throat flecked with sweat and grime.

Kevin took her to a night game at Fenway Park, because, he said, she was woefully ignorant about Boston cultcha. When he wore headphones to listen to a game while working, Lila found herself wanting to rip the little foam pillows from his ears, insist on his making the time go faster as she stripped and spackled and painted.

She couldn't care less about the Red Sox, but found herself in the bleachers, wondering if, when Kevin drove her back to Cam-

bridge, she should invite him in. She had dressed more provoca-
tively than usual, a halter top appropriate to the city heat if not
the rowdy Bosox bleacher fans, a denim mini, strappy sandals.
After all, he'd never seen her in anything but grubby work
clothes. But Kevin shouted and threw popcorn and swore with
the rest of the fans as if they were actually there to watch a
game.

"So, yah don't like baseball," Kevin said. "That's really
tragic." He led her back to the morass of honking, swearing dri-
vers in the choked lot. "Okay, next time yah'll take me to the
oprah."

"I don't like opera." What was this game of Oscar and Felix
he was forcing her into?

"The ballet? The Museum of Fine Ahts?"

"Bowling," said Lila. "Professional Wrassling. Mud Bog
Boogie at the Boston Gardens."

But it was *Farewell My Concubine* at the Brattle Street Cinema, with the gorgeous Gong Li. Kevin, it turned out, had spent
his junior year of high school on an exchange in Beijing. Even at
seventeen he was heading for a career in international law. Afterward, they ate noodles at Panda Wok and Kevin showed off
his chopstick expertise.

"Did you learn much Chinese?" Lila wanted to know.

"Nah, I suck at languages. Can't yah tell by my English?" He
grinned over a heap of spicy noodles. "But I do a hot T'ai Chi
numbah."

"No," Lila laughed. "Shane maybe. I just can't see you doing
slow motion stuff in pajamas."

"Try me," he said.

The rush of desire puzzled her. After all, he was a guy still living at home with parents who didn't know enough to stop having kids after numbers four, five, six, seven. What could she
want with him?

By the Fourth of July, Eddie was drinking six-packs on the
job, slapping up sheetrock with untapable gaps, grumbling

about crybaby college cunts and potheads. Isabel had quit in a huff—Kevin won the bet. Shane didn't show up until after lunch and then he was worthless. Only Lila and Kevin climbed willingly up three flights of stairs to rooms of gypsum dust and paint fumes each day. But she couldn't be sure if Kevin's enthusiasm had anything to do with her or if it was just his good nature.

"I wish he'd *do* something," Lila told Marcia. "I mean, it isn't love or anything, just lust. But still."

Marcia rested her sore waitress feet on a hassock, raised an eyebrow. The Crash Test Dummies guy with the impossibly deep voice growled from the stereo.

"He must have testicles the size of basketballs," Marcia mused.

For a second, Lila thought she meant Kevin. "I wish he'd just make a fucking move," Lila complained.

Marcia laughed. "Some nineties woman you are."

It wasn't dating etiquette that held her back; there was simply no way she'd chance a rebuff. Especially when they'd be stuck working together for the rest of the summer. Better to cruise along, buddying up. Maybe she wasn't his type. Maybe he went for blue-eyed blonds with peaches-and-cream complexions, not small dark minor exotics like herself. Maybe he was gay. She didn't believe it. She was sure she'd caught him watching her butt as she climbed the ladder, or sneaking a peek at her breasts when she reached up to paint door trim. So what was the problem?

"Invite him over for supper," Marcia suggested. "I'll cut out before dessert."

"I can't cook," Lila whined.

"He's Irish," said Marcia, who was Irish herself, though from a fancy North Shore town. "He won't know the difference. Heat up some Ragu. Overcook some vegetables."

Lila ended up ordering a pizza, because she didn't want it to look like she'd put much effort into the evening. Self-protection was the name of the game. Though she couldn't believe it mattered. It wasn't like he was someone she wanted to end up with or anything. Kevin appeared on time, with two pints of Ben & Jerry's under his arm. Lila hustled the ice cream into the kitchen, suddenly shy. Over beers, pizza, Marcia carried the conversation, asking Kevin questions as though she hadn't heard it from Lila already: his major, Boston College, his neighborhood, his siblings. Even though she was irritated with Marcia's overly diligent efforts, Lila panicked when, as promised, Marcia headed out to see a movie with a friend.

"I like her," Kevin announced, leaning back from his paper plate of pizza crusts and tomato sauce smears.

"Of course you do. Who don't you like?"

Kevin raised an eyebrow. "Yah don't want me to like her?"

"I didn't mean that. She's great. You're just easy to please. You even like Eddie." She didn't know where the peevish tone came from, why she was giving him a hard time.

"I just undahstand Eddie," Kevin said patiently, oblivious to subtext. "Two of my brothahs ah in construction. They'd have a hahd time with ah crew too."

"So how come you made it to college and they didn't? Nobody stopped them from getting loans."

Kevin turned his palms out. "Maybe they didn't really want to go. Anyway, they both got girls pregnant and did the right thing."

"The Right Thing. So you're anti-choice," Lila said. "That figures." She started collecting the paper plates and ravaged pizza box from the table.

"Whoa. I'm just saying what I believe, not telling anyone else what to do. How come yah want to fight with me tonight? Usually when someone invites yah ovah, it's 'cause they're feeling friendly."

Lila continued to clear the table. She felt like a jerk.

"Did I do something wrong heah?"

"No. I don't know. It's what you haven't done."

"Ohhhh." Kevin took that in. "Come heah." He reached out and grasped Lila above the wrist, pulled her toward him. Lila clutched the trash. "Put that stuff down fah a minute," Kevin suggested. When she didn't move, he gently removed the box and plates and set them back on the table. He pulled Lila onto his lap. "I really like yah Lila. A lot." When he put his lips on hers, Lila's heart lurched in her chest. This was what she'd wanted. Then why did she feel so scared?

It wasn't the sex with Kevin, which turned out to be good, but the way he lay in her bed the next morning, as comfortable as if he lived there, as friendly and sure that everything was just as it should be, not a doubt in his mind.

There was something inescapable about him. As much as she didn't want to care, he kept easing his way into her life. Taking her out for breakfast that first morning. Showing up with tickets to a Radge concert, driving her to Falmouth so they could spend a day on Martha's Vineyard. Talking about things they'd do when school started up again in the fall. Monday through Fridays he was as steady as ever on the job. She hadn't decided that she wanted him as her regular boyfriend; Kevin just acted like it had always been true and Lila found herself carried along by his certainty.

They never even had a fight until that first Christmas when Lila revealed she wasn't going home for the holidays. Kevin was apalled that Lila, as an only child, would deny her parents her presence. They were Christmas shopping downtown, crushed in the crowds around Filenes. Salvation Army Santas rang bells over big kettles. A mean wind blew off the harbor, whipping through the canyons of highrises and tenements.

"I just don't have your sense of family, Kevin, okay? Quit trying to force your values on me. Anyway, I'm adopted."

"Yah what?" Tears from the cold ran from the corners of his eyes, and a little drop hung from the tip of his nose.

Lila turned away. "Adopted."

"Well thanks for waiting six months to tell me something impahtant about yahself."

Of course he was hurt. Why hadn't she told him? Maybe she'd been afraid it would make her seem even more rootless than she already felt, comparing her sense of disconnection with his solid family connections, even if his attachments were not what she had in mind. She'd suffered through a chaotic Thanksgiving at the McCarty house—Kevin's great aunt got looped and sang quavery old favorites at the piano, an uncle asked Lila to open her mouth so he could admire her teeth, while a million nieces and nephews ran through the rooms shrieking. No one but Lila seemed to be put off their feed by the agony of a bloody crucifix hanging over the dining room table.

Maybe her silence about the adoption was just habit. Through the shoulders of oohing adults and over the wool-hatted heads of little kids, she studied the twirling mechanical figures of a Christmas display. Little dogs beat cymbals together, elves swung useless hammers in alternating rhythms. "I didn't think it was that important," she lied.

"Then why ah yah using it as an excuse not to go home? I don't buy it," Kevin insisted. "Just because yah mothah didn't give birth to yah means she doesn't count?"

Lila turned away. "You don't know anything about it."

He shook his head as though trying to clear it. "Yah don't love them. Did they treat yah bad?"

"I *do* love them. They treated me fine. You don't understand."

"I'm trying to. Explain it to me."

"I just don't fit with them, okay?"

"No, it's not okay. Two people went out a theyuh way to sacrifice fah yah, to wipe yah nose and buy yah clothes and keep yah from wasting away in some ahphanage and yah don't fit with them because what, they didn't go to college or something? Yah pilot dad has the wrong politics? Yah think I like everything about my folks? My Dad fought against school busing, okay? My mothah calls Blacks monkeys. She thinks Jews should be punished for killing Jesus. I don't have to like them to love them."

Why didn't she want to go home for Christmas? She'd told her mother on the phone she had a make-up paper to write, she'd caught the flu near the end of the semester and gotten behind. "You can do it here, honey," Ruth had said. "We won't bother you."

Kevin, who hadn't even left home, couldn't understand that going home hurt. *She* didn't understand why her parents' love made her feel so ill at ease with herself. So restless and eager to be away from them. As parents went, they'd done little wrong. They'd tried their best. But since she'd hit adolescence she'd known she wasn't theirs and never would be. Nature, at least in this case, must have triumphed over nurture. When she spent more than a few hours in their presence this fact shot home to her, carrying with it inevitable questions: Where did she fit? Who did she come from? Why had that other mother ditched her? It hurt to see her parents, because she no longer believed they *were* her parents.

Of course, plenty of people raised by birth parents felt the same way. Marcia had pointed that out. "It's just a stage of late adolescent development," she informed Lila. "A continuation of the two-year-old's struggle for individuation. You've got to say 'No' all the time, even when you mean 'Yes'."

If she gave in to loving them, she'd be in danger of becoming like them. . . .

No, that wasn't it. Lila knew it was more than that. She wasn't trying to forge a separation because they'd been too close. The adoption *did* matter.

Lila cruised up behind an RV towing a Volkswagen bus. A sticker on the back of the VW read: "I know I'm slow but I can't help it. I'm pushing a big trailer." She pulled into the left lane and pressed the gas pedal.

So why, then, was she running home to them now? Some variation, she supposed, on the old Frost line: home is where, when you have to go there, they have to take you in.

The hell with it. Lila zoomed past the RV's window, a quick

glimpse of a Willie Nelson look-alike, all grizzled beard and grey braids, Mr. Ancient Hippie hauling his microwave and VCR on the road again . . . Lila revved to eighty, then steadied herself back in the right lane. She wasn't in the mood to call Kevin. Maybe tonight.

CHAPTER 6

"Is it a silent meal?" asks one of the priestess' twin eight-year-olds, dashing into the Bodhi's dining room for supper.

"No," their mother responds.

"Alright!" He high-fives his brother. Identical little freckled linebackers, as thick as their mother is slender.

"Miso soup again? Yuck," the first twin bellows, leaning over the large pot. All about me I can sense the unhappiness of the newly enlightened. Their serenity is being tried. And more so after dinner when the priestess requests her sons to give us a joke. One of them stands up and sings a ditty that includes Ajax cleanser and puke. The other showily burps. Their mother laughs merrily while her disciples stare at their plates. I like her brand of Zen. The graceful young man assigned as their keeper shuttles the boys off to watch the Simpsons and play Nintendo while I return to my little room, cheered at kids' insistence on being kids wherever they're raised.

I want to ask so many questions about how you were raised, Lila. Until then—if there is a then—I can only offer my own tales.

At our house, Lila, the television glowed in the darkened room. The Bride of Frankenstein loomed, her two-toned electric-shock hair rising from her head in staticky waves. Trapped, alone, I could neither move closer to shut if off, nor leave the room to escape. Through the door, the lit kitchen rumbled with voices, but I was, as I would so often be, in thrall; I had neither the will nor permission to step out of this nightmare.

When programs got too scary, my sister wisely climbed into the cabinet beneath the TV shelf and closed the doors.

In the mornings while my mother hid behind her own doors, we poured milk into the miniature wax-lined box of Sugar Smacks and settled in front of the television. In the afternoons when I got home from nursery school, while my brother napped upstairs, Susy was away at grade school, and Mom still hid in her room, I watched *The One O'clock Movie:*

A man and a woman were in love. She wore big shoulder dresses, he a felt fedora. They inhabited a Manhattan world of sophistication: maids, silver tea sets. One day he went out to buy cigarettes and was hit by a car. He woke in a hospital with amnesia. Months passed as she searched for her beloved husband. She finally found him and took him home, but he had no memory of her, or of their love. She was nothing to him but an oddly solicitous stranger. Until the day he went into her room for something, a lighter perhaps, and spied a necklace he'd given her before the accident and it all came flooding back in a wave of violins—his own history, their love. On screen, creamy letters took shape: "The End."

Lila, I can't forget this minor sentimental movie, viewed thirty-five years ago and already old then. What does it trigger? Some childish belief that I'd someday find an enchanted object that would make my parents wake from their tortured amnesia into the realization that they loved me? Or that I was the amnesiac; any day I might snap to and recognize my true home?

You have every right to accuse me of amnesia, Lila, to imagine it's only now that I remember you.

You know—no, of course you don't, sorry—I came to occupy a Manhattan world, though not the one of the movie. I'm almost afraid to tell you how I live, afraid that you might be disappointed. I rent a fourth floor walk-up, an illegal sublet, for ony $311 a month, an unbelievable rent, on the Lower East Side. Just a narrow living room with a closed off fireplace and one brick wall, a bathroom in which some former tenant painted the tub in flaking primary colors. The ceiling plaster is crumbling, but when you're in an illegal sublet, you don't complain. The bedroom isn't really a bedroom, just a niche large enough for a bed and desk. But the cheapness gives me freedom.

Freedom. A questionable concept here.

My sublet sits on East Sixth Street, the Indian restaurant block, between First and Second Avenues. I'm used to the smell of curry wafting up through my window along with the clinking of silverware being washed in the restaurant below. The Hells Angels live two blocks down, and a police station is situated across the filthy courtyard that separates the backs of the buildings on Fifth and Sixth. Between the two of them they keep order. It's not a dangerous neighborhood, not like Alphabet City, the world east of Tompkins Square. Just grubby, overrun with Tandoori-seeking yuppies, bums from the nearby bowery, and up on Eighth Street the junkies selling their goods.

I could show you so much if you ever came to visit me, Lila. Although one of us would have to sleep on the floor . . .

It's not a grownup life, is it?

I've been thinking about leaving the city. Like so many others, I moved there and got convinced that if I lived somewhere else I'd miss out on excitement and opportunity, then, as the years passed, I grew afraid to leave my friends. Where else but New York are there so many single people my age? Where else but in New York would people in their thirties meet to play kickball, a children's game? One thing I loved about the city when I arrived was that I no longer heard my mother inside my head warning me to keep my voice down, to wear more muted colors . . . the legacy of a New Hampshire Jew, I guess.

Of course, I don't have to go back to New England. I could move anywhere. California, Italy, Burma. My job is portable, I wouldn't need working papers. I've already got my contacts established for assignments, such as they are. But I won't make a move until I give you a chance to find me—in case you want to.

At least, if you read these pages, you'll know what you're getting into.

Back to the story, then.

Across the street from our house in New Hampshire lived the Rileys; they had seven kids and went to a different school. Sometimes I rode with Mrs. Riley in the station wagon when she took them; everyone made a cross on their chest before they got out. Jane Riley and I made crowns of clover in the meadow behind their house. She said, "Mine's a crown of thorns like Jesus, why'd you kill him?"

"What?"

"You killed Jesus," said Jane. "You made him die."

"I didn't," I said, "I didn't."

"Yes you did."

"I didn't."

"Did too."

So I hit her. Then my mother came out and Mrs. Riley, who started yelling. "You're bookish," Mrs. Riley said, "*we feel.* Jane, if I ever catch you at their house again I'll kill you."

"Let 'em keep off," my father said, "anyone touches you, hit them in the head with a brick."

"Sam," my mother said, "don't say that!"

I wondered what Mrs. Riley meant, calling my mother bookish. My mother never read books, but she went to a psychiatrist in Boston. She took me with her for company and let me wander the city streets while she disappeared behind an office door. A block away, I discovered a store window and in it a pink plush puppy with a blue bow. I engaged in elaborate rankings with my own collection of stuffed animals. My favorites slept closer to me, the less favored pushed to the outside. The white curly poodle that my mother brought back from some trip didn't get to sleep in bed at all, because I feared its haughty demeanor would make my other animals feel bad. Then my mother washed it in hot water, and its multicolored stuffing bled swirls of reds and blue onto the pristine white fur. Once it was debased, I cuddled the poodle close.

As I stared into the shop window, waiting for my mother to finish with her doctor, a woman appeared at my side. "Ain't he cute," she offered. "Boy, I wish I had a little stuffed dog like that."

I looked at her: shirtwaist cotton dress, simple, narrow face, greying hair, and experienced a horrible surge of pity: stuffed animals were for children. How awful to be a grown up and want one so badly. In the car driving home, my mother spoke sadly of the medical student who'd rejected her long ago, recited once again the poem she'd written for him: two hearts that beat as one. Now, she said, she loved her doctor. Transference, she called it. I wanted to tell her of the lady and the stuffed dog, my own Chekhovian tale, but I had no words for the grownup ache I felt.

My sister, who sucked her thumb until twelve, went to a psychiatrist too. She reported that all they did was play checkers. I wanted to go somewhere special and play games with a grownup but I was considered too well-adjusted.

Well-adjusted? At day camp my mother was called to take me home because I was acting strange. I didn't want to go in the water. A counselor had held me under, I insisted. He forced my head. At sleep-away camp I borrowed my bunk mates' Barbie and Ken during rest hour. While the other eight-year-olds drowsed, I made the dolls perform mysterious, unspeakable acts.

And one day I refused to go to school. I hated my teacher, Miss Tessier, who punished us for giggling at a picture in our music books: a discreet water color of kids skinny dipping. The day I rebelled, my mother dragged me around with her, first to the hairdresser, where, amidst clouds of choking hairspray and the stink of perms, she informed Mr. Isadore that she had an incorrigible child. She told the checkout lady at the grocery store, the post mistress, the gas station attendant. I suffered their frowns and slowly shaken heads. The next day I returned to school carrying a saccharine aplogy to Miss Tessier that my mother didn't need to make me write.

If she could read this, my mother would say that I'm forgetting all the good things. I hear her protest: "I read you kids books. I took you to the library, even if I didn't get books for myself—I can't seem to allow myself pleasure—but I brought you there. Remember the day you got your first card when you were four? You practiced writing your name on a big sheet of cardboard all the way there, you had to be able to sign your name to get a library card, and then the librarian pulled out this tiny little index card with lines, but you did it!"

Or, she'll insist, "What about the horse? I drove you everywhere, gave you every kind of art lesson, riding lesson, took you to tack shops, watched you in horse shows. I moved our whole family to Massachusetts, put up with your father's complaints about "Taxachusetts," just because I knew you were a child who deserved a better education . . ."

It's true, she did. Why do I want to blame her for that, to say that her focus on me once she pegged me as "gifted," her ignoring the others, was parasitic, that she wanted my life?

Lila, I know it's shameful to be my age and so ungracious, so unforgiving. To be angry still. It ought to help me understand how you might hate me now.

"I hate you, I hate you, I hate you," I screamed at my mother in a child's fit of pique. "No you don't," my mother replied calmly. "You hate yourself."

Later, she said, "You have an artistic temperament. You are incapable of love."

She didn't know it, but I was filled with love. I spent long hours tromping through the woods with frozen toes believing that I could find a baby bunny whose mother had abandoned it.

I'd take it home and save it. I kept newts—those fluorescent orange salamanders—in a window box and begged for the kitten crying in the rain under my father's car. I named the cat Pixie and she slept under the covers with me, head sticking out beside my stuffed animals.

I also loved my best friend Wendy. We skated on a neighbor's pond together, and afterward, when it got dark, we walked home singing, still wearing our skates, our blades sparking on asphalt, winter firefly light.

I even loved a boy. Though the rabbi's son, geeky behind his glasses, pulled me aside to show me the special way he tied his sneaker laces to indicate he had a crush on *someone special*, I reserved my first-grade affections for Butch, a thick lumbering kid assigned to my lunch table. He must have been fourteen and still in sixth grade. He wore a brush cut, a whiffle of hair standing above his low forehead and wide dull face. At home I tried to shape my pixie cut to match his, wetting my straight black bangs and combing them back. I don't know if I wanted to mimic his toughness or succumb to it.

Another older boy, Johnny Williams, lived in a large new house in our neighborhood. In high school already, Johnny attempted to draw us little kids into his peculiar games, games in which he fashioned all the rules. He stood at the edge of a newly dug foundation hole and gestured: If you want to join my club, you have to take off your clothes and pee in front of me. You have to lie down in that dirt and spread your legs. I ran home, panting with panic. My mother shrugged it off—boys.

Instead she warned us away from Peewee, a lanky unfortunate who wore a black wool overcoat, winter and summer, a knit watch cap, and ceaselessly trudged the streets of our neighborhood. His chin collapsed towards his upper lip because his teeth were gone. That was not all he was missing. My mother said he'd been lobotomized, a complicated procedure I didn't understand. The kids laughed at Peewee but I was haunted by his aimless, endless wandering, the fact that he carried, on his stem of a neck, an empty, hollow shell.

My sister and brother didn't need an operation to have their memories removed. Davy recalls nothing of our childhood beyond random, inexplicable slaps, and Susy, when pressed, asserts that whatever occurred in her childhood has no bearing on her current life. She doesn't remember our father beating her, then climbing in bed to cuddle and hold her while she cried. But *I* do. Susy lives in the cupboard still.

Even ugly memories are precious to me, Lila. I've hoarded them all, like the Halloween candy I used to make last until Christmas, though my sister sorted through mine, taking all the good stuff. Do you think I am using you as an excuse? A reason to tell this fractured tale? Perhaps, but I'm also building a case, trying to convince you that I couldn't help my long-ago defection. What I truly seek isn't an excuse, daughter, but a pardon.

CHAPTER 7

Bleary and beat, Lila turned left, right, left in the maze of drives and cul-de-sacs that comprised Mountain View, a recent development a few miles out of Colorado Springs where her parents now lived. The architectural inspiration of these stucco and cedar-sided houses appeared to be the mine shaft: great jutting upthrusts towered over centered double garage doors. Landscaping included a few new shrubs around the edges of emerald lawns, sprinklers shooting droplets into the evaporative air.

The development looked deserted at eleven A.M. Tricycles and swing sets stood empty in yards, the kids all in school, Lila supposed. Probably the land of double income families, the retired usually went elsewhere, to condos with golf courses. What had attracted her parents, besides the Air Force Academy's closeness, was access to a small private airport where her father could keep his World War II Staggerwing biplane. The development offered a Pike's Peak view as frosting. The one time she'd visited here, a year ago, her parents had taken her on a tourist loop: up the mountain, to the Garden of the Gods, and the zoo; she'd pitied the timber wolves their yellow-eyed insanity, long legs shaped to run for miles, weaving, weaving.

Lila parked in the empty driveway, checking the number. When she got out of the car, she felt dizzy and weak, more than just road weary. Crampy in her guts, wobbly in the knees, and little tracers danced at the edge of her vision. She knocked, waited. Behind the door, voices babbled gaily: the radio her mother left on to scare intruders. With some relief Lila found the key tucked into the zipper pocket of her purse and let herself in.

The door opened onto a vista of fresh vacuum tracks in the pale carpet. Lila sniffed at the odd department store odor, something used to coat new fabrics before they were washed. The room was both familiar and strange, arranged with furniture she'd known from so many other houses on or near bases, heavy oak and maple pieces able to withstand all those moves, but the beige couch was new. On the mantel stood the same framed photos of Dad in uniform, Lila in high school cap and gown, Mom in the peaked nurse's cap she'd only worn for a year. In the fireplace, behind a hearth of shiny slate, lay fake logs ready to emit blue jets of gas.

Lila wandered the rooms like a half-hearted customer at a realtor's open house, curious and detached. In the den, she surveyed Dad's pictures of fighter jets, squadrons, commanders, a snapshot tucked into one larger frame: herself, dark and small, standing between her large fair folks, with her pixie bangs and barrettes and Mary Janes. Too young to know that she didn't belong.

Upstairs, she walked into Mom and Dad's room. Their king-size bed stood awash in a creamy new quilt. She opened the closet's bifold doors, touched Ruth's flannel nightie, Dad's ties, the matching terry bathrobes she'd sent for their anniversary. In the dresser mirror Lila caught a glimpse of her reflection: hair greasy and mussed, eyes circled, dirty clothes. She looked like shit, she observed from a great distance, as though it wasn't her own image but that of a stranger on the street. She ran a finger over the dresser's polished shine, picked up no dust. If Ruth wasn't that kind of woman before she married, she'd had to become one, joined to a man who was trained to military tucks and white glove tests.

The dresser ornaments were the same as in every house they'd inhabited: a line of foreign perfume bottles pooled with darkened liquid that had evaporated over the years; a red cotton pincushion shaped like a tomato, attached to a baby tomato by a string; a cheap leather jewelry box stamped with fake gold

leaf—a Christmas gift Lila had bought her mother years ago.
Two photos: a wedding picture, crossed swords, bouffant hair; a
blown-up snaphot of Ruth carrying Lila in a receiving blanket.
By the time that picture was taken, Ruth had been trying for a
kid for years. She was already a woman in her thirties heavy
with disappointments, looming large in her love.

Lila went down the hall to the guest bathroom. She ran
shower water, then changed her mind and dropped the metal
button to fill the tub. She needed a good soak. The bathroom
was tiled in pale pink and grey. Little dishes of untouched shell-
shaped soaps, unopened bottles of creams and shampoos and
lotions filled the shelves. When the tub was half full she remembered the doctor's injunction against baths. Sighing, Lila
drained the tub and started again. Under the shower nozzle she
could barely maintain vertical. It was too much to think about
going back out to the car to fetch her bag of fresh clothes.

She dried herself, threw the towel into the hamper, stole a tee
shirt out of her father's drawer and hobbled to the guest room.
She felt fluey now, achey in her shoulders and back and legs. Her
abdomen throbbed. On the guest room bed, atop a flowery quilt
and double puffed pillows, lay Lila's old Lucy doll, one eye forever closed, dynel hair braided tightly, pink puckered lips awaiting a bottle. It was the only raggedy touch in this otherwise ho-
tel-perfect room. She wondered if Ruth had hidden the doll the
last time, when she knew Lila was coming. What did it mean
that her mother had dragged this old doll from a box stuffed
with Lila's cast-offs and set it on display? Lila didn't have the energy to consider that one.

She climbed under the quilt, the cool sheets setting her skin
ashiver. The ridiculously soft mattress sank under her weight.
Her head whirled. The textured paint on the walls stood out in
too much relief, a topo map of peaked egg whites. Lila had the
odd sensation that she was spinning inside a mixing bowl of
meringue.

At the Sheraton Tara, Richard Warren refused her entrance to the room. She knocked futilely, then went down to the lounge. Kevin sat at the bar with his back to her, beside a trucker who turned on his stool to look her over. "Girlie, you all alone? You want a drink Girlie?" Kevin sipped his beer, ignored her. The liqueur bottles behind the bar glinted chartreuse, creme de menthe, candy colors aswirl. "I'm not alone," Lila insisted to the trucker, who opened his mouth to reveal a toothless cavern. Lila gripped the counter, fearing she'd slide into that wet red hole. The lounge turned into a whirling vacuum; a mechanical roar filled her ears. She was being sucked downward while she soundlessly screamed "No."

Lila lurched forward but Ruth held her fast. "I was dreaming," Lila croaked.

"You're burning up. Let me take your temperature, honey."

Lila sank back onto the damp pillow. Under the quilt her legs were sticky. It was more than sweat. She lifted the covers and saw blood smearing her thighs, the sheets. Oh, shit. She sat up fast, too fast, headed for the bathroom but dizzily sank to the floor. Ruth lifted her up. "I'm taking you to the doctor," she said.

"It's my period," Lila whimpered. "I just need a pad." But she allowed herself to be supported by her mother's large freckled arms. She didn't have the energy to be embarrassed when Ruth swabbed her crotch and legs with a wet facecloth. Clean again, securely padded, Lila leaned back in the car seat, thermometer sticking out of her lips, pondering the properties of mercury. A mysterious metallic fluid to measure the heat of blood. Something that when smashed could separate into perfect little replicas of itself, then rejoin to become whole again, only larger. Quicksilver. Wasn't that the name of some song?

"A hundred and four," Ruth pronounced, squinting at the glass tube as she drove. "We'll just go right to the emergency ward." Her arm jiggled as she shook the mercury down.

The hospital blurred into nightmare faces of the sick and hurting. A man who'd cut off a toe mowing his lawn. A child screaming with earache. Lila hunched in a plastic chair, shivering while her mother stood at the reception desk, filing insurance, spreading Lila's wallet on the counter. Finally Lila was set on a papered table, examined by a foreign intern to whom she had to admit the probable source of her fever. He had the dark, mustachioed face and sad demeanor of that man at the cafe in Cambridge, a singsong subcontinental accent. "This kind of infection can be causing infertility," he chided. "You must be taking it seriously." She was hooked to an IV, pumped with antibiotics.

In an hour her temperature had dropped and her head was clearing. That was the thing about antibiotics shot in a vein; they worked so damn fast. Lila would have preferred the reprieve of a night in the hospital, but her insurance wouldn't cover it. They checked her out with a supply of pills and drove home silently. Busted, she thought. If not for this stupid infection, they wouldn't have known. It wasn't intentional. "But you went to their house right after the abortion," Marcia, with her psych texts, would say. "That wasn't a coincidence. There are no coincidences according to . . ."

"Oh just shut up," Lila said.

"What?" Ruth asked in surprise.

"Nothing, sorry, just thinking out loud."

Ruth spun the radio dial, tuned in an easy listening station.

Back at the house, Lila sat on an armchair while her mother stripped the bloody sheet and mattress pad, remade the bed. Then Lila climbed in and allowed Ruth to prop her against the pillows, ferry in a TV set with remote. If only she just had measles or mumps it would be so great. She could pretend she was in second grade, home sick from school.

Ruth lingered at the door, the dirty sheets bundled to her chest. "I was worried you might've had that thing that killed the muppet guy," Ruth said. "Septic something or other."

"'Fraid not." Lila pushed the power button on the remote, trying to stave off the inevitable. She jockeyed channels looking for MTV. She needed her tapes from the car.

Ruth came over, sat down on the edge of the bed, blocking Lila's television view.

"Why did you lie to me honey?"

"Oh, Mom. I didn't want to go into it. I know how you feel about abortions and I figured it was my business."

"You were always so secretive, Lila."

Lila groaned and flicked off the remote. "Mom, can I just sleep for a while now? We can do the big guilt scene later, okay?"

Ruth got up from the bed, setting Lila awash on the soft mattress as though it were a waterbed, sloshing, sloshing. The hurt showing in the stiffness of her back, her turned face.

"Mom, I'm sorry," Lila called, but Ruth was already thumping heavily downstairs. Pans rattled in the kitchen. Lila rolled over, stiff from her waning fever, stiff from driving. The textured walls were no longer looming meringue. There was nothing familiar in this room except for the old Lucy doll. No sounds or odors, no crack in the walls she knew, no pattern in ceiling tiles. Which house, of all the houses they'd lived in, could she even remember?

The earliest she could recall was a shotgun shack in Georgia. A parched red dirt yard. Paint peeling off the windowsills. White trash accomodations, but at the air show the jets whooshed overhead in a princely display, tilting, tilting, wings close enough to touch, the swoop of steel and anodized aluminum dazzling. She stood in the bleachers, face upturned, safe between Ruth's knees. She thought the show was something her daddy had arranged just for her. She was certain back then that she too would fly large silver planes someday. Her father had already taken her up, turned her upside down; she never feared leaving the ground.

Just exactly when had she come to believe that she'd grown up in someone else's life, the wrong people had taken her home?

Even before she'd learned to think it herself, the world was bent on informing her of that fact. First grade, and she'd run

home crying because Gary Conner said Ruth wasn't her real
mother; his mother had said so.

"I *am* your real mother," Ruth insisted. "Your daddy and I
chose you out of all the babies in the world. Gary Conner's
mother didn't have a choice, she just got him, poor thing."

Lila stopped sniffling, breathless at the enormity of Ruth's
revelation. "Chose me how?"

"Lila, Mommy couldn't have babies even though she wanted
to have them more than anything in the world. And the girl that
gave birth to you couldn't keep you, so Mommy and Daddy
were lucky enough to find you and keep you for ourselves."

"But why couldn't she keep me?"

"She didn't have a husband, and it's very hard to raise kids
without a daddy too."

At six Lila didn't know about single mothers—you weren't
apt to see them on military bases—and accepted that part of
Ruth's explanation.

"So," Ruth continued, "she needed to give you to people who
could be your Mommy and Daddy."

"Well why couldn't *she* get me a daddy?"

"I don't know, honey. Let's not worry about that, okay? The
important thing is we have you and you have us. Right?"

Ruth wanted so badly for Lila to agree that she had to. At
school she told Gary Conner that his mother hadn't wanted him
but got stuck with him, so there. Then he slugged her.

A few years later, the one time they'd visited Dad's relatives,
they'd also been happy to make it clear that she wasn't kin. Dad
had just been transferred and they were driving from Mississippi
to Kansas. Head on the car seat, Lila woke to urgent whispers
and continued to lie there, listening.

"She doesn't even know her family," Mom argued. "We're
going right by . . ."

"I don't see what the big deal is. They aren't really her family."

"Of course they are. She's your daughter."

"Well *I* don't want to see 'em."

Mom flounced in her seat. "Why won't you ever let me have some semblance of a normal life?"

"Sorry babe. I didn't mean to give you a hard time. If you want to stop, we'll stop. I don't even know who's left these days. You know I never much looked back."

Lila sat up in her seat, peered out the windows at flat red dirt, sparse grasslands dotted with Herefords and small pumping oil wells, mechanical dinosaurs raising, lowering their heads. She rolled down her window, stuck her hand from the air-conditioning into a wind that lifted but didn't cool her at sixty miles an hour.

At the Della exit, Dad turned off the interstate, drove past the usual cluster of gas station/convenience stores. It wasn't big enough for a McDonald's or Kentucky Fried.

"Where we going?" Lila asked. "How come we're not on the highway?"

"We're going to do some visiting," Mom said. "John, don't you think we should call ahead?"

"Visit who?" Lila demanded.

"Your Aunt Betsy," Dad said.

"I didn't know I had an Aunt Betsy. Does she have kids my age?"

"Maybe grandkids your age," Dad said.

"Dad was the youngest," Mom explained, "and you know it took us a while before we got you. Betsy's kids were already all grown."

Lila frowned. It sounded boring.

They travelled through the small, false-fronted town of Della. It looked dead. Plywood covered some of the storefront windows. The movie house was closed, a couple of random letters tilting on the marquee. Only a few cars nosed the headless parking meter posts on Main Street. Then they were cruising country roads again, past fields of sorghum, big wheeled irrigation lines spouting over the alfalfa, mobile homes on bare lots and white farmhouses hidden behind windbreaks. The dirt tinged red like in Georgia, but bare of the Georgia pine forests.

Dad turned onto a county road marked only by a number and a row of battered, leaning mailboxes. He drove another two miles of ungraded gravel, pulled into the yard of a slumping unpainted frame house. A large yellow dog on a chain looked up, too dispirited to bark.

"What a dump. Is this where you grew up?" Lila asked.

"Lila," Mom warned.

Dad seemed unfazed. "Same thing," he said. "Next farm house down the road."

Dad parked and got out. Lila and Ruth sat quietly. The fan whirred on to cool the car engine. They watched Dad stroll up to the door. He stood for a moment with his hands in his back pockets. He looked strange without his uniform; he could be anyone's father. He knocked. Waited. A frizzily permed, chubby woman with an incongruous, narrow, long-nosed face, wearing a shirt that stuck to her belly and butt, came to the door, peered out, glanced toward the car, suspicious. Then she put a hand to her chest as though suffering heart attack. She grabbed Dad, hugged him.

He turned, beckoned Mom and Lila out of the car.

"What about Kitten Caboodle?" Lila asked. "She'll get hot with the air conditioner off."

Ruth grimaced into the rear view mirror, running lipstick over her open mouth. "Why don't you take her out and set her box in the shade, honey. I don't know how long we'll be here."

On the porch, Aunt Betsy pulled her close in a suffocating hug. There was nothing in her that looked like Dad. And her house was stunningly dirty. Paper sacks of garbage sagged and spilled onto the floor. Sticky amber ribbons stuck with flies hung from the ceiling. Lila didn't want to drink the Kool-Aid her aunt offered her out of a spotty glass. She excused herself and went outside to explore.

The dog lifted his head, sniffed in Lila's direction, then lay his greying snout back between his paws. He'd made himself a circle of hard packed dirt around the tree to which he was tied. Behind the house chickens scratched in a wire pen. A hog stood patiently while a litter of piglets scuffled at her teats. Despite her gross bulk, her mud stained hairless flanks, there was something touchingly delicate about her closed eyes, tilted, and palely lashed.

The back yard, which gave way to a line of cottonwoods and behind them fenced fields, was littered with trash: tires, tractor parts, a lidless washing machine. Lila couldn't believe that Dad, with his military neatness, his insistence on beds made with tight folded corners and no candy wrappers in the car, could have grown up like this with these people. No wonder he never wanted to come back.

A tire swing hung from a Chinese elm. Lila tested the frayed rope, then climbed into the tire and sat listlessly waiting for the visit to end. Instead she heard the sound of a heavy truck pull into the driveway and her name being called.

Uncle Chuck delivered propane on a rural route and was allowed to drive the truck home at night. It sat in front of the house like a fat white bug. Uncle Chuck looked like a fat white bug too. He had round goggly glasses, a bald head. His left arm was burned red from hanging out the truck window. He took his shirt off as soon as he came in the house, repulsing Lila with the sight of his white, sagging belly. He sat down at the dinner table shirtless, making her stomach lurch.

"Who's this un?" he asked, poking a finger her way.

"Our daughter. Lila," Ruth said.

"She don't look like either a you two. Looks like you got her from the gypsies. Har har." His mouth full of mashed potatoes.

"If only I'da known you was coming, Johnny," Aunt Betsy fussed, "I'da set out a fancier spread."

"No bother," Dad said. "This'll do fine, Bets."

"Maybe it was the milkman," Uncle Chuck persisted. He winked at Lila. She busied herself hiding chunks of tough grey meat under a pool of greasy pink gravy.

"Lila's adopted," Ruth said.

"Huh," said Uncle Chuck. "Now that's something I can't feature. If the Lord saw fit to deny you children, he had his reasons. Adoptin's just going against nature. Kinda like raising a cuckoo in your nest."

"Chuck," Aunt Betsy said. "Hush."

"Well we don't see it that way," Ruth said stiffly.

Lila waited for Dad to say something, but he kept his head down, chewing steadily.

Lila pushed away from her chair. "I got to go check on Kitten Caboodle," she mumbled.

"Lila," Mom called but Lila ran for it, through the backyard and into the line of cottonwoods and brushy alders which leaned over a sluggish creek. She took off her sneakers, sat on a bent cottonwood limb with her feet in the tepid mud brown water. She wondered if there were snakes here, maybe moccasins. She didn't care. Let them bite her. Then her dad's stupid dumb relatives would be sorry. Mom and Dad would be sorry too. It was Mom's fault because she'd made them come here. Dad didn't want to. His family were stupid jerks but he didn't want to see them. And nobody'd even bothered to look for her. Nobody even cared. She'd hide, and after they'd driven away, she'd follow the creek until it came to some river, follow it to a town. She could hitch a ride somewhere far from this dumpy state. But where?

"Lila?" her mother called from a distance. Then closer. "Lila? Honey?"

"Wha-at?" She pitched her voice angrily, although she was relieved that her mother had followed.

"You're in here." Mom pushed her way through the alders, sat down beside Lila on the cottonwood branch. "Surprising how pretty it can be where there's water. Everything looks so parched out here."

"Kansas' probably just as bad," Lila said.

"I think it's humid there." Mom inspected the tip of one of her sandals that she'd muddied.

"Great. Ugly and humid."

"Lila, don't let what Uncle Chuck said bother you, honey, he's just an ignorant man."

"He's disgusting. I'm glad I'm not related to them." She wasn't. Hadn't she heard Dad say it, in the car? "Chuck looks like a stupid old hog. I wouldn't want to be related to him."

"I've got to agree with you there," Mom said. "Anyway, it's only by marriage. Aunt Betsy is the one that's Daddy's sister."

"Well she looks like a chicken. Blawwwk. Blawwk." Lila flapped her wings. "A fat chicken. She probably has a brain the size of a chicken too."

"Oh, honey." Mom reached out and rested her arm on Lila's shoulder. Lila stiffened—it was Mom's fault, even if Dad was the one who'd said they weren't her family, like she wasn't his family either—and then she slumped into her mother's side, letting Ruth stroke her hair while she cried. Ruth felt so soft, her skin yielding under Lila's hot cheek. She wished they could just stay there under the cottonwoods, rustling now in the faintest of breezes. Ruth hummed a baby lullaby. After a while Lila quit crying, hiccuped, wiped her runny nose with the back of her arm.

"How come Daddy didn't tell Chuck to shut up?" she asked.

"Honey, he hasn't seen his sister in years. He didn't want to make her unhappy. I mean, look at her. Look at how she lives. You can understand that, can't you?"

"What about making me unhappy?"

Ruth sighed. She sat up. "Did you check on Kitten Caboodle, honey? She probably needs some water."

"I'm not going back to that house. Not until it's time to go. We aren't going to sleep in that dump, are we?"

"We'll find a motel."

Lila wiped her nose. "I bet they don't even have HBO in this stupid state. Can we at least get one with a pool?"

"We'll try. Let's go find Daddy, honey. He's probably worried about us."

Not likely, Lila thought, but she knew her mother couldn't leave him for long.

Lying now in a too-soft bed, in her parents' unfamiliar house, Lila thought it strange that there'd been a time when she wanted so badly to belong to them. Really, for half her life. And in all those years, only once had Ruth seemed wholly hers. Lila closed her eyes. Here, in Mountain View, jammed up against the Rockies, two thousand miles inland, Lila caught a whiff of ozone, the aroma of ocean salt.

They had taken a vacation alone while Dad was stationed briefly overseas. They drove from Ohio, where they were living, to visit Mom's sister, who'd married a Navy man and lived in Virginia Beach. The town was crowded with sailors, tee shirt stores, tattoo parlors. Her aunt's house was a blur of indistinguishable teenage cousins slamming in and out of doors, cousins who were paid to babysit but dragged her on their dates and made her promise not to tell or they'd pinch her blue. What stayed with Lila was the detour they made on the way home, driving down the coast because Lila had read *Misty of Chincoteague* that winter and was dying to see the wild ponies.

They crossed a bridge over a canal between salt marshes. Chincoteague itself was disappointing: a tacky motel strip, the only ponies penned beside a hotel where you could pay a quarter to feed them a handful of hay. But the next day they rented old-fashioned one-speed bicycles and pedaled across another bridge to Assateague with their towels in their baskets, their swimsuits under their shorts. They biked the nature trail, peering across salt marshes at a herd of horses as distant and unknowable as the herons and cranes. But at the beach, a small scruffy herd of wild ponies stood in the parking lot, wandering among the cars. The stallion was almost horse size, his mares delicate ponies with narrow legs, long scraggly manes. Paints and bays, foals at their sides. The horses seemed both as wild and yet as at home among the litter barrels and cracked asphalt as the seagulls swooping over parked cars.

On the slant of sand, Ruth spread their towels, oiled herself. She wore a beach hat over her reddish hair, a demure skirted suit. The beach stretched on, sandy and warm and dreamlike. Lila ran down to the water. It curled and hissed around her toes. She ran the edge between sand and sea, imagined herself a wild pony escaped from a Spanish galleon, swimming to a strange wild shore. Her own bony brown legs left hoofprints in the sand.

When she came back to the blanket her mother was sitting up, hand shading her eyes. "Let's go in," Ruth suggested. The surf rose to their knees, then the cold hit their vitals, Lila's first. She hunched her shoulders up high, rose on tiptoe. Ruth's flowery suit skirt floated on the water about her hips. Then Ruth laughed and sank to her chin. She reached out to Lila, gently pulled her in. Hands joined, both of them screaming and laughing, hopping to keep their heads above water as the waves rolled in, rolled in, rolled in.

They splashed and dove through breakers and floated on their backs. Then a wave knocked Lila down, sending her face to the bottom. The wave drew back but didn't release her. Lila, on the bottom, watched amazed while shells and pebbles tumbled before her salt burned eyes. In an instant Ruth was sweeping her up, strong hands under her armpits, yanking, then hugging her close while Lila coughed and cried at the sting of water up her nose.

In the sun again, they lay on their blankets, baking in the ozone smell of salt on skin. And up on the crest of sand the stallion herded his silent mares, a sentry gazing out to sea.

That night they ate fish and chips and Lila's mother ordered a Piña Colada and let Lila dip the cherry and orange garnishes into the sweet rummy foam. In their motel room, they lay on the double bed and watched a rerun of *Come Back Little Sheba*. Both of them cried. Mom spread Noxzema on their sunburns and the air conditioner blew cool over their mentholated skin.

In the morning Ruth painted their fingernails and toenails

red. She gave herself a blond rinse and let Lila comb her wet, sunsparked hair. They pedalled the nature trail again and lay on the beach. That night they ate dinner in a grander hotel, then sat in the lounge listening to the three piece band—bass, sax, piano—play everything from swing to Beatles. Ruth danced with a man in a string tie who sent a drink to their table. But when he tried to join them, Ruth laughed and said it was time they got some sleep. Back in the motel, they stayed up late again watching Johnny Carson, a trick played on her mother's dancing partner. Lila knew that she was the partner here.

It was the first, maybe the only time, she'd known Ruth without Dad. Sure, he'd been gone before, and Ruth had always been attentive to her care, but there was something different here, a freedom in her mother she didn't recognize. Ruth loved Dad, Lila knew, but there was something about their life together that made her seem as rounded up, as controlled as the mares with their stallion. Maybe it came from living in places that weren't really places, just backdrops for the familiar geometry of bases.

The morning they left, they bought souvenirs in the tacky Chincoteague gift shops. A box for Lila, lined with red felt, lacquered shells glued on top, and a two-piece suit for Ruth that she swore she'd never wear at the officer's pool. They got Dad a paperweight with a crab enshrined in lucite. They filled a paper sack with penny candy for the trip home—sugary dots on paper, licorice whips, horehound sticks, and fireballs. Lila cried when it was time to knock the sand off their flip-flops and leave the motel.

"Why are you crying?" Ruth asked as she closed the car trunk over their suitcases.

"I like you better here."

"Oh, honey. I like me better here too. But Daddy's lonely, don't you think?"

On the highway they sang along with a hillbilly station and

ordered milkshakes for lunch. But it was over the minute they drove into the base. Ruth was lost in a whirlwind of laundry, as though intent on washing away every sniff of sun and seaweed and sand. For a week Lila slept with her shell box next to her pillow. Hidden inside was the purple paper umbrella from her mother's piña colada, and a little shell toy, made in Japan, that opened and released streamers if you submersed it in water. She didn't try the toy, saving it for a day she needed to remember the beach, the sand sliding away from her, and her mother lifting her high in the charged air.

CHAPTER 8

Lila, things slow down here. Sometimes I think my life both began and ended between the ages of twelve and fourteen with the Medford Street barn and its queen, Jill. Those treacherous middle years, when girls love horses and other girls before they go on to boys—those who are able to make the transition.

Let me catch you up. My mother, having lifted herself halfway out of her depression with the escape from New Hampshire, was consumed with perfecting our house with fake period decor. My father was afraid of being house-poor in "Taxachusetts" so we lived in a neat little Cape with matching dormers, a reproduction set on a quarter-acre lot. We had a bronze eagle over the garage and knotty-pine cabinets and matching imitation colonial end tables.

We weren't allowed to mess up my mother's kitchen. The greatest crime in our house was for someone to place a greasy palm on the flocked wallpaper. We walked through the halls with our hands raised as though we'd just been surgically scrubbed. My bedroom was wallpapered in ugly colonial colors I still loathe: mustard and rust and olive, in a tiny, monotonous print. I wasn't allowed to hang a picture in my room for fear of marring the wallpaper. At night I lay in my four poster twin bed—with the ruffled spread that had to be folded down just so—as though it were a straight jacket.

Each afternoon at five, never before (a fact that she was proud of) my mother filled a water glass with straight Chivas Regal and carried it around for the rest of the evening. Control was everything to her, although my mother was always in danger of slipping. Wielding a belt from my father's closet, a clothes hanger, anything handy, my mother occasionally chased us around the house, landing blows, shrieking that she couldn't stand it anymore, we were killing her. It was our fault, she insisted, when the mood had passed and she had regained her composure. My sister, brother, and I had driven her too far with our noisy voices, our demands, our bickering. After these outbursts, my sister whimpered face down on her bed, my brother watched TV—he had his own now—and I hid in my room, guiltily fearful that I would indeed kill my mother—she'd die mid-blow of a heart attack and it would be my fault.

Mostly I stayed outside and out of the way, finding solace in the grounds of the convent next door. I was crazy for wildness, for forests and fields without houses where I could stretch my legs and be free of the constricting corners of our neat little house, my mother's incessant decoration.

Then when I was twelve, by some miracle, I was allowed to have my own horse. I had saved close to $400 from birthday checks and odd jobs. Surprisingly, my father agreed to pay the board on a trial basis.   I chose a mean-spirited black gelding named Midnight who aimed a hoof at me the first time I saw him. We found a place to keep my horse—a squat cinderblock barn with a crew of junior high girls who did barn chores in exchange for riding privileges on the owner's nags. I think my mother was disappointed by the Medford Street barn. She'd probably pictured a stable replete with whitewashed paddocks and velvet-hatted girls but there wasn't enough land left in our town for that sort of place and my father wouldn't have paid the higher board if there were.

The Medford Street Barn's one claim to class was Jill Rojowski. Jill was nineteen, always wore high boots and slim breeches, and could vault onto a horse's bare back effortlessly. Her coppery hair exactly matched the color of Akbar, the gelding she cared for and begrudged its owner, a fat drunk named

Dickie who showed up about two weekends a month to flop about on a western saddle.

It never occurred to me then that there was something odd about Jill, a freshman at B.U., hanging about with a group of twelve- and thirteen-year-old girls. It seemed simple enough: we were all joined by our shared horse passion. But we weren't equals; we were Jill's disciples, her audience.

At Parkins Junior High I had a beloved friend named Debra Gurwitz, a large, heavy girl with frizzy hair, prematurely bad skin and a brilliant mind, who'd developed the body of a woman far too early. We were both in the AP—the Advanced Program by which "gifted" kids in our town were selected for a superior education and turned into social misfits.

The girls at the barn were the kind I'd never have known at school even if they attended my junior high, which they didn't. They were girls who laughed about skipping classes and groaned about math homework and didn't worry about ruining their college records. They knew things, such as the fact that Shirley, who owned the barn, came from a nice family but had gotten "into trouble". The two regulars, amidst a shifting cast, were Nancy Cummings, a mild-tempered freckled seventh grader and her best friend Lucy Carmenucci, a rawboned, awkward girl who made herself the butt of bitter, self-deprecating jokes, especially when she was "on the rag" as she called it, a mysterious, horrifying physical state I hadn't yet encountered. (I was still grateful to be wearing undershirts, deeply ashamed of the new wet cirlces that showed under my armpits when I raised my hands in class.)

While at school we little prodigies were discussing the Great Books and directing Shakespeare plays and deliberating over Supreme Court decisions, at the barn we held manure fights and taught the horses to rear on command. We learned that we could set the whole barn full of horses yawning by standing in front of their stalls and opening our mouths in enormous, exaggerated yawns. We spent hours grooming them, giving them baths, trimming chin whiskers, rubbing vaseline onto their noses to keep them velvety soft. We played fierce, dangerous games of hide and seek on horseback between the nearby greenhouses and tried barrel racing in the pasture or walked our horses single file on paved roads through housing developments until we found a stretch of woods or open land where we galloped madly, hooting and screaming in a phalanx of thundering nags and wild girls. When Jill led the way we were adventurers, fearless hordes; without Jill we were bitchy pubescent girls prone to fighting over which way to go or blaming each other for slapping branches.

One day Jill invited me home for lunch across a stretch of swampy woods to her ranch house—decorated in puce and orange, my mother's most detested colors. Out in the driveway, Jill's sister, an odd duck who wore a crew cut, swished a soapy sponge over her maroon Corvette. While I tried to swallow lumps of bland buttered bread and bologna, too shy to ask for mustard, Jill's mother, an Italian woman with a great beehive hairdo and tragic dark circles under her eyes, nagged Jill about our manure-laden boots, our crumbs on the counter. Jill ignored her, poured herself a glass of Instant Breakfast. She had to drink it, she said, to keep from losing weight. Sometimes she forgot to eat.

Although I was scrawny, I couldn't imagine forgetting to eat. I required a full bag of Oreos before supper each day when I came home from the barn famished. I thought it glamorous that Jill had to work to keep her weight up. She was very slender but big-breasted, and had been a cheer-leader in high school, according to barn girl scuttle-butt. Although her face was just a touch too narrow to be beautiful, she was "sensual," my mother said.

Jill studied me. "Do you know how lucky you are to have your own horse? Your parents must really have the bucks." She sounded angry, and I swallowed uneasily, but then her voice became smooth, caressing. "You're a very good rider, Allie. I can see you've had lessons.

I swelled with the compliment.

"The other girls just want to fool around, but you've got the makings of a real equestrian," Jill said.

That was exactly what I wanted to be!

Mrs. Rojowski rattled the refrigerator door. "Jill, don't forget to put that bread away. And I want those plates in the washer."

"Alright, Ma, Jesus."

"Don't think you can talk like that . . ."

Jill rolled her eyes. "Come on," she said, beckoning me into her room. "I want to change."

She showed me her closet full of poorboy sweaters and miniskirts, the white Mexican wedding dress she used as a nightgown. I didn't know where to look when Jill lifted her turtleneck—a flash of lacy bra and tawny flesh—and exchanged it for one equally spotless.

Jill constructed a jump course for us and coached me over fences. Midnight ran out or refused in every possible way. I fell off eleven times in a single day, but I went home bruised and happy. Eventually, I improved. I was afraid the other girls would be jealous that Jill had chosen me as her favorite but the following week she pulled Nancy onto Akbar's rump and rode off to her house, leaving Lucy and me to eat our lunches from brown bags in the hayloft, where we ended up throwing hay at each other and arguing over whether or not the Monkees were a real group. At the sound of Akbar's hooves, we hurried down the ladder as though delivered.

Summer came, an exquisite stretch of barn days. Jill and I competed at the local horse shows. We rode to a quarry and swam the horses. One day a group of teenage boys mooned us and yelled out a strange bad word I didn't know—"masturbation." Jill hooted and we galloped away, our dramatic exit marred by the release of loud, embarrassing horse farts.

I talked so much about Jill that summer my mother invited her over for supper. She raved about the house: the pewter sconces on the dining room wall, the flocked wallpaper that I detested. Alone with me, she whispered fiercely: "Someday I'll have a house just like this and everything that's in it." With my parents she praised the dinner excessively and acted amused by me, a little kid she was humoring. After she left I was eager for my parents' assessment. "Well, she's got a lot of style," my mother said. "Just like your aunt Belle. She could make a three dollar dress look like something from Saks."

"You should see how much she's done with Akbar," I enthused. "She's making him into a show hunter. He's got great conformation."

My father smirked. "I don't know much about horses, but your friend's got some pretty good conformation herself." He cupped his palms to indicate the size of Jill's breasts.

My mother clattered dishes. "What I don't understand is why she'd want to hang around with a little girl."

Stung, I fled to my room, insulted for Jill, and for myself, diminished by the entire evening.

In September, Debra Gurwitz was assigned to a deskmate, a boy with a ridiculous name, Maurice LaFontaine, whose mother was my former fifth grade French teacher. When I tried to commiserate after class, Debra shrugged. "I don't mind," she said. "He's nice."

I was flabbergasted. How could she like a boy? It was one thing to have a crush on the Beatles, but boys were noisy and obnoxious. Over the following weeks I studied Maurice. He had curly auburn hair, green eyes with long lashes. He was good at soccer and the smartest boy in our AP class if you left out Donnie Teitz, who had a blue vein running up his forehead and carried a briefcase. Maurice was mischievious; he climbed out the window during detention but the teachers liked him. When he came to school with a haircut, I mourned his shorn curls. By November I'd fallen madly, if secretly, in love.

Love didn't interfere with my barn life. Lila, I wonder how I had time for anything else when my days were so full of the barn: the two-mile bike ride from school, cleaning Midnight's stall, dragging water buckets from the greenhouse, riding. Yet I visited classmates, read in the trees of the convent, wasted hours training the family cocker spaniel to balance a biscuit on his nose, babysat to earn horse show money, in winter skied and skated and sledded. Maurice played hockey on the nuns' pond near my house. I bought a hockey stick and a puck and pretended it was hockey, not Maurice, that I liked.

In bad weather I holed up in my basement workshop. I painted, drew, made clay sculptures and earrings from beads and silver. I wrote stories about girls and horses and poems celebrating my love for Maurice. I watched massive amounts of television with my brother. "The Rifleman" and "Combat" were my favorites; I suffered intense crushes on Chuck "sodbuster" Connors and Vic "the lieutenant" Morrow.

The most peculiar aspect of all this rampant energy was that I kept my barn and school worlds separate. I had two lives. I never invited a classmate down to the barn although girls often begged to ride my horse. And except for that one time with Jill, I never invited the barn girls home. I tried to keep my family just as distant. My sister was no problem—she hated my horse because it was mine and she screamed because I came home stinking of horse manure every evening. "Make her take a shower first," she begged when I sat down with my cookies and glass of milk before supper.

One day my father decided he wanted to ride my horse. From the start he'd used Midnight as a weapon of domination. His favorite punishment was forbidding me to go to the barn the next day. Not only couldn't I ride then, but I had to make frantic phone calls to find someone to care for my horse. His trump card, brandished often, was the threat to stop paying the board. If I looked at him cockeyed he'd say, "That's it, the horse goes."

I didn't want anyone to ride Midnight. I couldn't bear the thought of anyone kicking him in the ribs or yanking his mouth.

And he was *mine*, the one area of my life in which I was in total control.

"It's my horse," I argued ungraciously. "I saved the money myself."

"Big shot," my father said. "I pay the board, I'll ride."

He showed up on a Sunday. He had trouble mounting, but once he was on, Midnight trotted off, my father bouncing awkwardly in the saddle. At the end of the field Midnight stopped abruptly, cropped grass. "C'mon horsie," my father said, flapping the reins. "Let's go." I had a moment of triumph, seeing him so powerless, but it was ruined. I was ashamed for my father in front of the barn girls.

"The check stops tomorrow," my father announced that evening from his throne in the den, the room we weren't allowed to enter unless beckoned.

"Just say you're sorry," my mother coached from the kitchen. "He'll back down."

"I didn't do anything," I protested hotly.

"You can't win," my mother hissed.

Feet up on the hassock, newspaper spread, my father grinned. "Apologize or I'll stop the check."

"I'm sorry," I lied through clenched teeth.

Jill could be equally imperious. One day she roared up to the barn in the passenger seat of a tiny sports car. Jill introduced the driver, a paunchy guy in a tweed jacket who smoked Gauloise (according to Lucy, who was a cigarette expert), as Arthur, her sociology professor who was helping her with a term paper. Lucy and I rolled our eyes. Men were always falling in love with Jill but none of them lasted. When she dated a Red Sox baseman, she listened to games on a transistor; when she dated a Scotsman, she wore a kilt; the realtor inspired demure Jonathan Logan dresses and an Etienne handbag. But she never fell in love with any of them; she only loved Akbar.

Now she and this Arthur were going riding, and Jill wanted me to loan her Midnight. The thought of Arthur sawing at Midnight's mouth made me ill. From my perch on the grain bin I bumped my heels and refused. "Take one of Shirley's horses. Dolly or Rex."

"Only Middy is good enough," Jill cajoled.

When I didn't relent she turned on me. "After all I've done for you? Really, Allie, I'm disappointed."

"C'mon," Lucy said when Arthur clambered onto Midnight's back, "let's go to my house."

We skulked around Lucy's house eating ice cream with potato chips while outside her father worked on a patio, the crack in his butt showing over his pants. In her room, the dresser covered with little tubes and lotions, Lucy bemoaned the fact that she was ugly (she wasn't, just plain) and that she had a terrible body. I didn't know what to say. She was thin but wide-hipped, not something you could change. Bodies weren't something I spent much time thinking about; I liked mine okay. When enough time had elapsed Lucy and I returned to find Jill happily brushing Akbar's tail and Midnight in his stall. Jill laughed as hard as we did when she told us that Midnight had dumped Arthur in a pile of compost. "What about your paper?" Lucy asked.

Jill shrugged. "I don't think Arthur was working out."

What could I do but forgive her?

Jill and I were cleaning up at the local shows and wanted to go farther afield. A friend of Jill's agreed to trailer our horses to a larger show for twenty dollars. I asked if she'd take fifteen—that's all I had from babysitting. Jill smiled slyly. "Allie," she said, "your heritage is showing." She was no more a friend than the sun was; I succumbed to her force like a plant following light.

Debra was my real friend. In English class Mr. Hail (Heil we called him, lifting our arms in mock Nazi salutes) gave us the odd task of reading the Communist Manifesto and putting Karl Marx on trial. Debra was voted defense attorney, I, her assistant. Maurice was chosen as Marx. The three of us were granted hours of unsupervised goofing off time in the hall in which to prepare our defense. We triumphed gloriously and Debra slept over to celebrate. That night we lay in the dark, rehashing our brilliant defense strategy.

"Boy, Linsky sure looked mad when the jury read the decision," I gloated across the gap between our twin beds. Jon Linsky, president of our AP class, was the head prosecutor, assisted by the delicate Donnie Tietz.

"It must have been embarrassing to lose in front of everyone," Debra replied.

"Well, *he* says they won, just because they got that one count of distributing prohibited publications. One count. Big deal."

It was quiet for a moment, and then Debra added, "Still, I felt a little sorry for him having his mother there and all."

I smiled in the darkness. Debra was a much nicer person than I was. I was glad to have a friend that nice. It made me feel safe.

"Why do you think Maurice's mother didn't come?" I ventured. I was burning to say his name aloud.

"She probably had to teach."

"Yeah." None of the rest of our mothers had jobs, although Debra's mother was president of the local Democratic Women's Club. I opted for a more direct approach to the matter of Maurice. "Do you think he appreciated our getting him off?"

"I don't think it mattered that much to him. He just got voted to play Karl Marx because he's cute. He told me he thought it was a good way of getting out of class."

I felt a bit jealous that Debra, his deskmate, had access to confidences that he hadn't shared when the three of us were out in the hall, giggling about how much Mr. Heil looked like the *Pig People* in a Twilight Zone episode.

"Debra?"

"Yeah?"

I took a big breath. "I've got a confession to make. I think I'm in love with Maurice."

"I know." Debra sighed deeply. "Me too."

"You? I just thought you liked him like a friend. And you knew about me all the time?"

"Uh-huh."

"Wow." I lay back on my pillow assimilating the enormity of the revelation. We were in love with the same boy and Debra had known all along. I sat back up again. I could just make out the curve of Debra's acne-covered cheek. I wondered if Maurice might overlook the fact that she wasn't very pretty and like her more than me on the basis of her goodness. The thought shamed me.

"Debra? Do you think that's okay, you know, us being friends and both liking the same boy? What if it hurts our friendship?"

Debra considered. "I think it's okay. We're only in seventh grade. It's not like we're ready for marriage or anything."

"Yeah, that's true. I guess we should just enjoy the fact that we've both got good taste."

Debra giggled.

I lay back down. The room filled with the aura of our shared confession. I could sense all the usual items of my bedroom—my shelves of china horses, my stuffed animals that no longer slept in bed with me but languished in a box in the corner, the school-books on my desk—transformed by this extraordinary moment. I felt close to Debra in a way I'd never felt close to anyone. I revered Jill, but Debra was the only person in the world I could talk to. I was overcome with feeling—for Maurice, for Debra— that made my chest swell.

"Debra?"

"Yeah?"

"I love you."

"I love you too, Allie."

"Can I come over there for a minute?"

"Sure."

I threw off my covers and climbed in beside her. Debra's shoulder and hip felt warm next to mine. She took my hand. My hand tingled, as though I could feel the love flowing between us the way electricity flowed from poles in Donnie Tietz' science fair project. The room filled with a strange glow. Holding Debra's hand, I pictured Maurice sitting up on the stage playing the beleaguered Karl Marx this afternoon. He'd looked so cute in a dark green polo shirt that matched his eyes. After a while the glow in the room dissipated. The narrow twin bed felt too cramped for both of us. I climbed back into my own bed and said goodnight.

Jill wasn't doing well at school. We had to whisper while she sat in the hayloft with her textbooks. Then suddenly it didn't matter. She didn't need college to be an equestrian. She needed money so she could buy Akbar from the disgusting Dickie. She went to work at a Cambridge night spot as a go go dancer. She showed us her little costumes, danced about the barn in a Frug or a Freddy, bragged about the men who wanted to buy her drinks.

Lucy and Nancy followed their own trajectory. They'd started high school and no longer had time for the barn. Lucy played field hockey and Nancy went out for cheerleading. They talked about hair styles and boys and finally stopped showing up. Jill had gotten more serious about riding, but she worked Akbar while I was at school, before heading into Cambridge. She had her sights set on the world of fox hunting and timed trials. I was happy enough sweeping ribbons at the local 4-H events. I wasn't the equestrian that Jill and I had imagined. I missed the trips to the woods, the camaraderie of the barn girls. I wanted things back they way they'd been.

It grew lonely at the barn. I rode by myself. Then cantering on a trail in the woods one day Midnight tripped and nearly went down. For the first time I felt fear—I who'd been in the hospital twice with concussions from riding accidents, who'd flown through the air when Midnight refused jumps and when he stepped in a hole while galloping. What if I got hurt? I'd lie in the woods and no one would even know I was missing until I didn't show up for supper.

I started skipping barn days, trading chores, and went home with Debra on the bus. After a healthy snack of fig bars (no Oreos at the Gurwitz house) we rambled her neighborhood. Debra pointed out the knoll where Cara Kaplan, our AP class "bad girl," swore she'd made out with a private school boy. Just two years ago Cara was a sweet plump girl who came to my birthday sleepover wearing kitty cat pajamas. Now she was class slut. She, like Debra, was prematurely developed, but she flaunted her cleavage, unbuttoning her blouses low. Although she was rather chunky, she wore the shortest skirts in class, tight sweaters, wide hip-hugger belts, and fishnet stockings.

Despite what I considered evidence to the contrary, Debra insisted that Cara was smart and only tried to hide it. I lacked Debra's generosity. As far as I could see, Cara acted ridiculous, leaning over boys' desks so that her boobs squished up in their faces and everyone could see up her skirt. She bragged that she had already been felt up and that she considered getting a boy to touch you the object of life. I couldn't see why. My passion for Maurice LaFontaine was chaste and cerebral. I wanted his love but had no idea of what I'd do with it if I got it. I was perfectly comfortable leaving making-out for the distant future.

Of course, I knew that making-out was something teenagers did. My older sister subscribed to *Seventeen* magazine. Once in a while she let me into her room and I'd pore over the articles and advertisements. There was one ad for a sandwich, with the headline: "Boy Trap." Glossy pages hyped blush and liner and shadow, acne creams, lingerie. Articles offered guidelines for getting boys to like you ("Learn the rules of football and go with him to a game; Talk about his interests, not yours"), what to wear to proms, and just how far to go when "petting." I was amused as much as interested, pleased to think there was a feminine world awaiting me with its rules and details, a world as complicated as that of horses and horse shows, but I was in no rush to grow up. It was enough for me to eat fig bars and ramble the neighborhood with Debra.

In fact, I felt guilty at how easy and pleasant the time with Debra was compared to the tedium of pedaling the two miles to Medford Street on my bike, shoveling manure, riding alone, then pedaling home again stinking of horse shit at dusk.

Not long after I had a date to accompany Jill to a large Class A horse show. I'd helped her fill out the entry form, selecting the classes she would participate in, and I was eager to be spectator at a big show where the competitors came from all over and the jumps would be high and tricky. I was looking forward to an outing with Jill. I rarely saw her now that she danced in the club.

I rode my bike to the barn early so that I could have Midnight's stall cleaned, his water bucket and hayrack filled before the trailer arrived for Akbar. At eight-thirty, when Jill hadn't appeared, I grew alarmed. At a quarter to nine I couldn't stand it any longer; I traversed the swampy woods to the Rojowski's house.

Jill's sister was already busy in the driveway, giving her 'Vette its weekly wash and wax. I knocked on the kitchen door. Mrs. Rojowski sat at the table, her head on her arms, as though napping. When she heard my knock she raised her head and I was startled to see that she'd been crying. I wanted to turn around, but she got up and let me in.

"She's in there," Mrs. Rojowski said into a kleenex, tilting her beehive toward Jill's room.

I knocked softly on the closed door.

"Who is it? What do you want?"

"It's me, Allie."

"Allie? Oh, Jesus."

"Can I come in?" I pushed the door partly open. Jill lay on her bed, legs stretched out, propped up against a couple of pillows. She had a magazine on her lap. She wasn't wearing her beautiful white Mexican wedding dress but a turquoise nylon nightgown. Her hair hung in greasy clumps and her face looked sallow.

"Are you okay?" I whispered. "I waited for you and you didn't show up. Aren't you going to the show?" I glanced about the room. There were no medicines, no boxes of Kleenex, but a wastebasket by the bed held bloody sanitary pads. I looked away quickly. It didn't make sense that Jill would stay in bed for her period.

Jill leaned back against her pillows and shut her eyes. "Does it look like I'm going to a show?"

"Are you sick?"

"No," she muttered.

"Then what's the matter?"

Jill didn't say anything. I stood half in her doorway, uneasy and uncertain. None of this made sense—Jill in bed on a show day, but she wasn't sick. Her mother crying in the kitchen.

"I thought we had plans." I could hear the whine in my voice, its rising plaintive tone.

"They got cancelled."

"Well, do you want to ride later? We could go to the quarry..."

"For god's sake, Allie, get off it. I can't ride. I can't ride for a week." Jill turned onto her side, facing away.

I hesitated. "Maybe if you can't ride, we could just go to the show to watch together. Would that be okay?"

Jill rolled over and sat up. The magazine fell from the bed. The rage in her face stunned me. "What do you want from me, Allie? When the fuck are you going to get your own life and quit sucking my blood?"

All the breath had been whisked from my chest, like when Midnight threw me and I got my wind knocked out.

"Get out!" Jill screamed, although I was already gone, rushing past Mrs. Rojowski, down the steps, and away from the house. I splashed through the swamp, not bothering to pick my way carefully across the dry hummocks, filling my sneakers with muddy ooze. At the barn I grabbed my bicycle, wheeled it around, jumped on and pedaled, pedaled as hard as I could away from there. "I hate her! I hate her!" I sobbed as my knees rose and fell, rose and fell over the ruts of the pasture.

It wasn't fair! She'd invited me! I'd never go back to her house, ever. I'd never talk to her. I'd find a new barn for Midnight. I'd . . . I didn't know what I'd do. I pedaled away from the barn, toward the center of town. I had money that I'd brought to buy lunch at the horse show. I headed for Woolworth's. Defying anyone to turn up a nose at the smell of horse manure on my clothes, I bought myself two boxes of Crackerjacks, a bottle of Coke, and a Chunky candy bar.

I spent the rest of the day pedaling around town, into distant neighborhoods, around the high school where boys shot baskets, past the synagogue that my parents only attended on High Holidays, through a cemetery where an old man bent over a spray of artificial flowers, a junkyard filled with wrecked cars, a golf course where men in ridiculously bright plaid pants swung shiny clubs. All human activity looked absurd and artificial from the perspective of my grief. "Get your own life," I sneered at them as I pedaled past. "Get your own life."

It was after four o'clock by the time I came home exhausted and hungry. The manure odor must have faded because my sister didn't scream at me to take a shower. No one even bothered to ask where I'd been. I watched *Community Auditions* on television and sat down to dinner as though it were any other night. My grief had faded to a dull throb.

But that night, when I was lying in bed trying to sleep, Jill's words came back: quit sucking my blood, sucking my blood. I remembered the wastebasket full of bloody Kotex pads and then I knew: Jill had had an abortion. Only bad girls had abortions. They were illegal, and Jill was Catholic. No wonder her mother was crying. But who could it have been? Not that professor. Maybe one of the guys at the place where she danced, one of the guys she talked about who bought her drinks. A picture of Jill grossly entwined with a faceless drinker in a bar merged with a horrible image of bloody fetuses. I had to count rapidly backwards from a hundred to block the pictures out. But I couldn't escape the echo of her shrill scream, "Get out! Get out! Get out."

When Jill showed up at the barn a few days later, she wore her usual breeches and high riding boots; her hair shone. She offered me molasses to make Midnight a sweet feed. She assumed her ugly words no longer mattered because they no longer mattered to her. Jill was queen of the barn and made all the rules, but her rules were too complicated for me.

That weekend, I arranged for the barn owner, Shirley, to feed Midnight and joined my mother on a trip to New Hampshire. My family belonged to a ski club that owned a lodge in the White Mountains; each fall the club held a work weekend to put the lodge in order before the first snow. Generally I begged off in order to ride, but this time I decided to go along and asked if Debra could join us.

In between sweeping dorm rooms and scouring bathrooms, Debra and I huddled close to discuss important matters such as the likelihood of Maurice attending the first dance our class was going to hold, and if he did, whether or not he would dance with us. Our AP class was just starting to get into the social swing that the rest of the eighth grade had enjoyed for more than a year. Except for Cara Kaplan, AP's were considered notorious pillow-kissers by the socially advanced kids in the other tracks.

Debra confided to me about the liquid nitrogen treatments she had to take for her skin, how they froze and peeled her pimply cheeks. And how happy she was going to be next month when they took off her braces. I knew that even if she had straight teeth and smooth cheeks she wouldn't be pretty, with her heavy woman's breasts, thick hips, wide face and frizzy bangs. Only her gentle brown eyes were beautiful.

I confessed that when I pedaled home from the barn in the afternoons, I often passed a boy from our school. Not a boy I liked or anything, just a boy who I feared would smell the odor of horse manure clinging to my clothes. I'd gotten into the habit of closing my eyes when I passed him, figuring that if I didn't see him I could pretend he wasn't there. Debra, who was sometimes mocked by non-AP kids, understood my shame.

When the work was done on Sunday morning, the club members took a hike in the mountains. Although the leaves hadn't fully turned at home yet, here they were at their brilliant peak. The air was crisp, the sky an unreal blue, and there was a clarity to the day that I had never noticed at home, as though every pine needle and birch tree was somehow more defined, more real.

Debra and I hiked ahead of the adults, stopping when we got too far along the trail to sit on rocks and gossip. The valley spread below us, a tapestry of maples and poplar mixed with pine and spruce. When the wind blew through the trees and rippled their tops, it looked like someone was flapping a bright woven blanket. I felt guilty to be having such a good time while Midnight languished in his stall. For the first time I wondered if I ought to sell him.

On the long ride home, Debra and I sat in the front seat with my mother. We listened to the detective show *Johnny Dollar* on the radio, ate grilled cheese sandwiches at a diner, and giggled over school secrets. At one point, Debra rested her hand companionably on my knee. My mother quickly removed it.

We dropped Debra at her house. "See you tomorrow, Allie," she promised, lingering at the window after slamming the door. "Thanks for everything, Mrs. Heller."

My mother nodded curtly. She didn't speak a word to me until we pulled into our driveway. As I was wrestling my overnight bag out of the back seat she grabbed my elbow. "Allie," she said, "please wait for me in the den."

Mystified, I lurked in the kitchen doorway while my mother filled a water glass with Chivas. She drew me into into the den, shut the door, and sat down in my father's green leather armchair. I took a seat in one of the uncomfortable and incongruous Danish Modern slingbacks with the pointy arms that jabbed unwary passers in the thigh. Behind my mother's head hung a naive painting of a colonial house, lacking all perspective. I wondered how my precision-loving mother could enjoy a painting in which all the angles were off.

"At first I didn't believe it," my mother began abruptly. "Jerry and Janice brought it up to me and I thought they were being ridiculous, prurient even. Janice is the sort who likes to stir things up. But then I began to notice."

"Notice what?" I was sleepy from the hike and the drive and wanted to go to bed. Whatever it was, I wished she'd get it over with.

"And then the others started saying things too."

"Saying what things?" I yawned.

"About Debra and you . . . The way you two kept running off and hiding from everyone else on the hike."

"We were the only ones our age. What's the big deal if we didn't want to walk with the grownups?"

"They kept saying how large and . . . well . . . mannish Debra is. And how she kept touching you." My mother shuddered.

"What are you talking about? Debra's my best friend. We like each other."

My mother searched my eyes. "Allie, do you know what the word *lesbian* means?"

I knew, without really knowing. I'd heard jokes about Miss Murphy, our gym teacher, who didn't shave her legs. You could see thick black hair flattened under her support stockings. But what did it have to do with me and Debra?

"Oh, I don't blame you, honey. I never doubted that you'd grow out of that infatuation with Jill someday. But some girls just aren't normal, and they can lead you wrong."

I stared at my mother dumbly. I was beginning to get her drift.

She reached out to grip my knee. Her fingers dug into my

flesh and her dark eyes searched mine. "You have to tell me, Allie. Did she do anything to you? What did you two *do*?"

"Nothing," I started to protest indignantly, then a hot flush rose to my cheeks and I turned my face away. I was lying. We *had* done something. There was that one time, when Debra slept over and I got into bed with her. We had lain side by side and held hands while the room glowed. My stomach sank. I hadn't realized it then, but we'd done something horrible, something perverse. The glow that had filled the room was unnatural, sick and awful. I was a lesbian, a pervert.

Voice deadened and flat, I shaped the lie for my mother: "We never did anything."

I lay awake in bed all night, ill with shame and fear. I was abnormal. My friendship with Debra was disgusting, corrupt. All the adults had been talking about us. Everyone knew. Only I hadn't known. But now that I did, I had to do something to stop it. I had to get back on track.

The next day, at school, when Debra smiled at me across the classroom, I refused to meet her eyes. Even seeing her brought back the terrible horror of our abnormality, the knowledge that everyone at the ski club had seen it, had known. In a move that still haunts me, Lila, I cut off my friend without an explanation. But what could I say? That everyone thought we were lesbians? That the sight of her questioning notes, her beseeching glances made me sick with shame? To explain would be as bad as to give no explanation. Eventually, when our eyes met by accident in class, she turned away as quickly as I did.

After the dangerous Debra incident, I realized it was time for drastic measures. Up until then I'd been lax. Now I saw that a crush on Maurice wasn't enough to establish me as normal. I had to learn about boy stuff, fast.

I quickly shifted my allegiance from Debra to Cara Kaplan. Cara seemed pleased to have an ally. Until sixth grade when I slipped in between them, she'd been Debra's closest friend. Although Cara exacted homage, frequently comparing her superior curves to my undistinguished little breasts, I became her willing pupil. With Cara, I shopped for minis and hiphugger pants, listened to tales of boys who had touched her in private places, learned the rudiments (in theory) of the French kiss. I told Cara about my lust for Maurice in order to establish my credentials as a normal girl. She judged him cute but backward and coached me on ways to get him to make a move.

At our first dance in the junior high gym, the same dance that Debra and I had giggled over only weeks before at the ski club, a boy name Klaus asked me for my first slow dance. Klaus was a big gawky blond boy with white eyelashes and pink lidded eyes whose father was a Nobel prize winning physicist. (Klaus would one day get into Harvard on his father's name and end up running a Chinese restaurant.)

Although I wasn't at all interested in Klaus and kept looking over his shoulder to locate Maurice, the minute he put his arms around me, I was wracked by a shocking arousal. A warm buzzing stirred me so intensely that I was afraid everyone could see, even hear it, a buzzing that might have been as loud as cicadas on a summer day. I don't think I even knew what it was, only knew that it was similar to a feeling I'd had once while riding Midnight when he wouldn't behave and I got tense. That buzzing had been localized between my legs, but this surged through my entire body. It was like being invaded by an alien force. When the song ended, I stumbled away from Klaus in shame.

There, in a corner, under a construction paper cutout of a chest full of jewels (the theme of the dance was "Treasure Island"), Cara was slow-dancing with Maurice. But she wasn't just dancing. Her mouth was locked on his; her hips were grinding away, and she appeared to be pushing him deeper and deeper into the corner. She turned and looked over her shoulder, saw me watching, and grinned. My eyes filled with tears. She'd done it on purpose! How could she go after Maurice when she knew I liked him? She didn't care about him.

I retreated to the girls' bathroom. Three tough girls with

teased hair sat on the sinks and leaned against the metal cage that covered the window. They were dropping aspirin into dixie cups of Coke—rumored to be a sure high. Cigarette smoke spiralled out of one of the stalls.

"Hey, what are you, a Guinea?" one of the girls inquired, looking me up and down. "Guinea Guinea, Wop Wop. Guinea Guinea, Wop Wop." Her friends giggled.

I splashed cold water on my burning face.

"Obviously," one of the other girls mimicked a stuck up Harvard voice. "She's one of those dink AP queers."

"Fuck you!" I said—the first time I'd ever used the word—pushing my way out just as Miss Murphy, the gym teacher, headed in. I hoped they got caught for smoking. It would serve them right.

I waited out the rest of the dance on a bleacher. In the swirling lumpy mass of bodies below me, I caught a glimpse of Debra dancing a jerky Pony with Donnie Tietz. She didn't look like she was having a very good time.

Driving us home, Cara's mother wanted to know if we had enjoyed ourselves. Cara flopped in the backseat, a satisfied cat who'd eaten the canary. I didn't deign to answer Mrs. Kaplan. I wasn't even angry anymore. It no longer mattered that Cara had been grinding away at Maurice in the corner. Either she'd wanted to get back at me for being close to Debra, or she just *had* to do it. Like Everest, he was there. What was Cara to me? What was anyone? I felt embued with a remarkable new strength. None of it mattered. I'd attained a state superior to ordinary humans. I could control all my feelings. I didn't have feelings anymore.

It was all so easy. At school, Debra, Maurice, and Cara no longer existed. I was impressed with my own ability to ice them out. If I was assigned to work with any of them on a group project, I simply did the work without speaking to them. Classmates whispered about how weird I'd become, but then got used to it. Other classroom intrigues took precedence.

The next time my father threatened to cut Midnight's board check, whipping out the old sadistic refrain "the horse goes," I looked him straight in the eye and said I thought it was a good idea. I'd been thinking of selling Midnight anyway. If earlier I'd toyed with the idea out of a desire to have more time for school friends, now I knew the most important thing was to strip myself of anything that would give someone power over me. As long as I didn't want anything, I knew I'd be free.

I put an ad in the local newspaper and sold Midnight for exactly what I'd paid for him two years before. When the trailer came to haul him away I patted his neck, and in the darkness of the horse trailer, touched my nose against his warm horsey flesh. I wasn't sure anymore why I was selling him. But something had been set in motion and now that it was rolling I couldn't make it stop. I stood in front of the cinderblock barn as the trailer rounded the corner and drove away. I had no more reason to be there. My life at the Medford Street barn was done.

Lila, my mother, your grandmother, likes to say that Nature abhors a vacuum. Perhaps she is right, because the vacuum left by the loss of both my school and barn lives quickly filled.

One day I looked down and decided that my calves and thighs, muscular from riding, were too big. Although I wasn't at all overweight, a diet seemed like a great idea. When I mentioned it to my mother, who was always on one kind of diet or other, she eagerly joined in. Finally, there was something we could do together. She cooked me my first diet breakfast—a poached egg on a slice of toast, four ounces of juice, tea—and set me in the dining room to mark the special occasion. Sun poured in through the windows, sparkling on the silverware, touching the room with a hallowed light. I glanced down at my carefully measured allotment, and felt imbued with power. Safe.

The problem was, safety was precarious. Soon everything turned into a measure of good and bad, and I was good or bad accordingly. I wanted to control myself as carefully as my mother controlled our house. An accidental sip of coffee that had sugar in it when I'd asked for coffee without sugar was as terrible as a mark on my mother's flocked wallpaper.

That fall I entered high school. Debra sat behind me in Ancient History but we avoided each other's eyes. Once in a while I'd see Lucy or Nancy in the halls, but the school was huge, there were thousands of students, and we were in different years and tracks. The enormity of the school frightened me. I was consumed with self-consciousness, certain that people thought I was ugly or fat. I went to one dance and spent two hours clinging to the wall, terrified, shamed, afraid of the jocks and the fashionable Honors Class girls who were smart without being dorks like AP's.

Some of my AP classmates became hippies. I went to one of those parties too, but it was just as awful. I was sickened by the smell of marijuana, the sight of people making-out on couches and on the lawn. I wasn't hip. I wasn't cool. I did my homework, locking myself in my room, and plotted the number of calories consumed against the exercises I performed for hours in our upstairs hallway.

Everything was in a perilous balance. At any moment, something in me could go flying out of control. I would consume everything if not kept on a leash, under the fierce control of willpower. I kept the perfect balance. No dressing on salads. No butter. I stopped eating any form of bread. I lunched on cucumbers sliced in half with a paper thin slice of cheese between them: my sandwich. My weight dropped and dropped. The one menstrual period I'd had in eighth grade was never repeated. My breasts didn't grow beyond meager bumps, but I was sure I was horribly, disgustingly fat.

The search for perfection grew all-consuming. There were college records to worry about. Grades. Homework after school. I lost interest in my basement workshop. I never walked the grounds of the convent or skated the nuns' pond near our house. It took all my energy just to do my homework and keep my eating in check.

I often dreamed about eating. It was always the same: I'd be stuffing Oreos into my mouth—the same cookies I'd scarfed so casually each day after the barn—and wake to incredible relief that it was only a dream. Once I had a nightmare that I was riding at the Medford Street barn and Midnight was running away with me, out of control. I awoke guilty, as though I'd consumed food in the night. Sometimes I saw girls riding horses on the street and I felt an undefinable pang, but it all seemed so distant, so far away.

I saw Jill Rojowski one more time. I was a high school junior walking home from school and a little MG hatchback pulled up beside me. Jill was driving. My first thought was that she'd see how fat I'd grown. I was a sinewy five-foot-seven and weighed 103 pounds, but I knew I was obese.

Jill rolled down her window. I asked how she was. Everything was terrific, she said. She'd married the owner of that club she'd danced in three years ago, a wonderful Jewish man named Sy who had a teenage daughter just my age. He'd bought Akbar for her, and another horse, a big thoroughbred jumper called Chrysalis. She'd taught Sy to ride and they'd joined the Pepperell Hunt Club. They kept their horses in Carlisle at the stable where I used to take lessons. Wasn't that a coincidence? Did I want a lift home?

I looked in at her, peering at a woman who couldn't be more than twenty-four but who suddenly seemed terribly old. She was elegantly dressed, still striking, but I noticed that when she smiled little lines fanned out from her eyes and she was missing a molar in her upper jaw. It bothered me—how had she lost that tooth? Now she had a man to pay for her horses, a Hunt Club. Did she tell Sy his heritage was showing when he didn't want to pay for something? I bet he always wanted to pay. I could picture Jill at another barn, with its own collection of preteen horse groupies, all of them in love with her. Jill would always be queen of the barn.

I insisted that I didn't need a ride since I was almost home. (I

always walked—200 calories an hour—to school and back.)
Jill drove off with a roar.

When I got home I did my homework and began my sit-ups,
but somehow I couldn't stick to them this time. No one was
home. I paced the house, into the kitchen, then out again, opening the refrigerator door, slamming it shut. I felt anxious, as
though facing a mortal danger. Some surge of feelings that I
couldn't identify, couldn't halt, rose in my gut. I rushed to the
metal cannister and took out the bag of Oreos and ate the whole
bag in fistfulls, horrified, yet at the same time relieved to succumb.

When the cookies were gone, I was still famished. A frighten-
ing emptiness overwhelmed me. I was hungry, hungry, hungry. I
needed to be fed. I gobbled leftover casserole from last night's
dinner, and then a frozen Sara Lee cake, not waiting for it to de-
frost. I gnawed on a frozen bagel. I ate dry cereal straight from
the box. My stomach ached as though it would split open. I was
horrified by what I'd done, but at least the echoing emptiness
was pacified, replaced by a dizzy vagueness, simple physical
pain, and self-disgust. I went into the bathroom and put my finger down my throat. Then I vomited and vomited, wiping my
lips on the matching hand towels (we weren't supposed to use
them, they were just for show) until I was as perfect again as I'd
ever be, and everything was under control.

CHAPTER 9

Lila was starving. She got up, wrapped herself in the bathrobe her mother had left on top of the guest room dresser, along with her washed, dried, and folded clothes. She met Ruth on the staircase.

"I was just bringing up a tray for you," Ruth said. "You need to rest, don't get up too soon."

Gratefully, Lila went back to the bedroom. Sitting up against pillows, she devoured her mother's crock pot stew—something she'd never eat away from home. The carrots and potatoes glistened with grease. The slow cooked beef shredded tenderly between her teeth. She hadn't consumed much more than road junk in three days. Ruth sat in the armchair watching.

"You must've been running on empty," Ruth said. "Want more?"

"This is fine." Lila wiped her greasy mouth with a napkin, slurped down half a glass of milk and attacked a brownie. When she was done, Ruth took the tray. She returned with two cups of tea and settled in an armchair.

Lila looked at her and tried to picture that woman on the beach at Assateague fourteen years ago. What had she done with that two-piece suit? Certainly, Lila never saw her wear it.

"Are you happy here, Mom?" Lila asked, stirring sugar into her cup.

"Yes I am. The climate is great and it's so wonderful to be able to plant some perennials and know I'll be here when they come up every year. And to know when I join a church group I won't have to leave in ten months. Your father's happy as a clam, of course. He has all his Air Force buddies over at the Academy. He's going to teach another seminar there in the fall. It's really just great. Of course he spends most of his time at the airport working on his darn plane. I thought when he took retirement we might do some more things together, but you know Dad."

"Right, I know Dad. But do *you* have any friends? I mean of your own?" Lila persisted.

"Sure I do, honey. I've got the gals at church and my mall-walking group and I volunteer at the library once a week. You don't have to worry about me."

"I wasn't worrying, Mom, I was just wondering."

"You'd do well to worry about yourself more, sweetie. Maybe you want to tell me what you're doing here. Don't you have finals coming up? It's a funny time to visit when we're coming out in two weeks for graduation."

"Well, that's just it. I'm not going to graduate. I mean I will, but not until the summer. It's some kind of technicality. It's no big deal, Mom, I just need a few more credits, and then I can graduate in the summer." Lying again, always closing off. A reflexive move.

"Well that's too bad. I suppose we can change our tickets. It's only twenty-five dollars extra, I think. That isn't why you drove out here, though, is it? Did you and Kevin have a fight?"

"No, Mom." Lila wished she could just put on some earphones, listen to something hard and loud, and block out what had to come next.

"Did he know about . . . the pregnancy?"

"No, Mom. And I'd appreciate it if you don't mention it if he calls. He's still mega-Catholic, you know."

"Well, you don't have to be Catholic to agree with him."

"You think I should've kept the baby and gotten married? You want me to live out your dream, Mom, but it isn't *mine*."

"I know we're different people. Believe me, I know. But I can't condone abortion, Lila. Aside from the moral issue, which

I won't go into, it just strikes me as selfish. I wouldn't have you, thousands of childless women wouldn't have kids if everyone just got rid of babies that were inconvenient. Babies are precious, Lila, precious."

At the sight of tears wobbling on Ruth's lower lids, Lila set her teacup down hard on the night table. "So this must be where you thank that unselfish girl, my birth mother, for donating her womb to you." Shit. It wasn't what she meant to say. Why did she have to harden herself against Ruth's grief?

"I *am* thankful. You don't have to be sarcastic about it."

"I know, Mom. It's just it's all so fucking . . ."

"Lila!"

"Excuse me. So *damn* theoretical. So abstract. You only want to talk about what this nameless generous knocked-up person did like she was some kind of pregnant angel, you never want to talk about her like she was a person, a person I'm actually related to."

There it was, the slapped-face expression. But Ruth was an expert. She'd regroup, shift away from the subject, something Lila had been edging toward for days without knowing, without saying it to herself. And wasn't she just as much a subject changer, jumping from the abortion to Ruth's refusal to discuss her origins?

"How could you have ended the life of a baby that was related to you, to you and Kevin, if you're so worried about having blood relatives?"

"It was a fetus, Mom. Not a baby. It was just a blob of cells. And I know what I did. I know that was my own little biological connection I severed, Okay? I'm the one that's fucking bleeding over it."

Ruth rose. "I'm not going to talk to you if you use that language with me."

"I'm sorry, I'm sorry, I'm sorry. But it really irks me. How can you glorify my birth mother as an example when you never even let me ask about her?"

"How can you say that Lila? That isn't fair. I never stopped you . . ."

"C'mon, Mom. Get real." Lila turned toward the wall, head in the pillow, her disgust as much with herself as with Ruth. She was acting just like the sulky teenager she'd been when she left four years ago. What was the point of going into it? Ruth wouldn't acknowledge how threatened she was. Mercifully, the phone rang down the hall. Ruth went to get it and came back with the cordless. "Kevin," she said. "Speak of the devil . . ."

"Oh God," Lila muttered. Great timing. She took the receiver.

"Hi Kev."

"Hi. Yah Mom said yah've been sick."

"Yeah, I guess I had the flu or something."

Ruth raised her eyebrows. Lila turned her back, hunched over the phone to signal she'd appreciate some privacy. Ruth shut the door behind her.

"Lila, what's going ahn? Don't yah think yah owe me some kind of explanation, taking off like that?"

"It's no big deal Kevin, I just needed some time away." She listened to his short, exasperated exhalation.

"I wish yah'd let me in on it. I didn't call fah two days because I thought it would take yah that long to get theyuh and I didn't want to scare yah folks."

Lila fingered the quilt's knotted tufts. He was always so considerate. Not like her. It was hard being around someone who was so much nicer than she was. She always suffered in the comparison.

"What about yah finals?" Kevin demanded.

"I don't know, Kevin. I'll do a make-up or something. It isn't your problem, is it?"

His silence ticked. Then, finally, "Listen, Lila, I'm into my own finals heah in a few days, in case yah've fahgotten. This isn't helping my concentration any."

"You'll do fine, Kevin. You always do."

"That's not the point. Jeez, Lila, I'm worried fah yah. I love yah."

"I know."

"Yah know. But do yah cayuh?"

"Please, Kevin, just give me a little time, okay?"

"Fine."

He didn't bang the receiver, but he didn't offer a goodbye or wait for one either. Lila groaned and pulled the pillows over her head. When the knock came she figured it was Ruth eager to do a post mortem on the phone call, but it was her father, home from messing with his plane.

"Can I come in?" he asked.

"Sure." Lila sat up, composed herself.

He looked tan, his scalp stubbled grey, and he was wearing glasses. He used to only wear them for reading. So much for the fighter pilot's perfect 20/20. Engine grease smudged his blue short-sleeved shirt. He sat down on the end of the bed.

"Well, you really know how to make an entrance."

"Daddy, I'm sorry. Are you mad?"

"I'm not mad you're here. If you mean about the other business, I don't see things like your mother. There's no point bringing kids into the world you don't want, there's enough of those already. I seen them all around the globe. I just don't like the lousy way you've been taking care of yourself."

Lila shrugged.

Her father shifted his weight. Lila waited for him to make another pronouncement, but none came. He reached out and touched her hair, then drew his hand back, stood.

"So," he said, "you get yourself some rest now. If you feel better tomorrow, I'll take you flying. If you want to."

"Sure Daddy, that'd be great."

"And do me a favor."

"What's that?"

"Cut your mother some slack."

Lila pursed her lips, but didn't answer. She flicked the remote.

Roseanne sat around a table with her twisted family, stuffing pizza in her mouth. Dad went downstairs for his own supper.

In the morning Lila's temperature was normal, her cramps light and infrequent as though it truly was nothing more than a period. While Ruth went off with her mall walkers, Lila followed her father's Buick past isolated new developments, then left the pavement and cut onto graveled country roads. They wound through hills green with new grass that would brown shortly: quilt squares spotted with dull Black angus and Herefords, stitched with barbed wire. Lila drove her own car, bug spattered and still full of styrofoam coffee cups and candy wrappers, because Dad wouldn't be ready to come home after flying. He'd have to tinker and talk shop with his fly buddies for the rest of the day.

A windsock announced the airport: a couple of hangars and a tiny office trailer. She waited while he gabbed about parts—magneto this or that—with a paunchy, coveralled guy at the control radio named Little Dick, and then she helped her father roll the plane out of the hangar and onto the gravel that led to a strip of paved runway. She'd flown with him in various planes over the years, but this was his baby, a taxicab-yellow biplane that had ushered some important General about in World War II. Like all small craft, it looked too flimsy to carry them skyward, as though it had been strung together with old cables, spit, and glue, though it was sturdier than the toylike Cessnas. Lila climbed into the cabin cockpit, belted in and adjusted the headphones that her father handed her—the engine noise would deafen without them—and watched his hands move over the welter of gauges and dials. The headphones filled with static and then her father requested clearance. A squawky voice granted it.

They taxied past a row of Cessnas, a Grumman, one Lear jet. The windsock flopped. Dad's fingers shifted madly, his attention complete. They turned and rumbled down the runway, building speed, and then Lila shut her eyes for the familiar but always odd sensation of liftoff, the moment when they were no longer gravity-bound. Dad turned to her and grinned.

He was, she imagined, the happiest man on earth. He'd always gotten everything he wanted. How difficult it would be to live with someone whose needs were fulfilled, whose passion was focussed on something unlike anything you could supply. She pitied Ruth this.

The world grew miniature below them: highways, steers, houses and condos with their turquoise rectangles of pool, the rocky plated tops of the foothills. The plane leaned, wing visible, struts crossing her view, and Lila had the sick sense of falling despite the belts strapping her in.

This is what he had to offer, what he'd always had. The quick thrill: a vision of life seen from above, the world at high remove.

They flew north, following the upsurge of foothills colliding with the sea bottom stretch of plains. They ran the edge between horizontal and vertical, dragging the division behind them, into the spew of smog that enveloped the nearly continuous strip of development running from Colorado Springs up to Fort Collins, with Denver at its stinking core. To the left, past her father's profile, the Rockies swept west in surreal white-capped peaks. They were moving 180 miles an hour and they might have been hovering as the world slid away behind them.

They looped around Denver with its refinery stink, its highrises and still inoperative new International Airport, and the gap of suburbia running to Boulder, then past Boulder. Absurd, this network of veins running the canyons, the big wilderness cut into ski runs and highways, dream houses and alpine golf courses. From this vantage, Lila had a sense of the fragility of the bare-skinned Rockies, condos and cars like ants crawling over some humped dead beast. Maybe from the sky you saw too much. Better to drive those roads and be awed by the spans of Engleman spruce and ponderosa pine. Only from the ground could you imagine you were living inside a Coors ad.

They turned west and gained altitude over the peaks, then were were hit by turbulence, bumps that brought Lila's stomach to her throat, tears to her eyes. She focused on Dad's hands moving, adjusting. Glinting pale hairs, the gold band on his left hand. Wide hands, square fingernails. Lila glanced at her own tapered fingers, long and narrow, their sallow olive tint. His eyes were hidden behind his prescription sunglasses. He glanced over, the plane fell away in a tilt beneath them, and they turned back east until they were running smooth again.

You did things with him during which you weren't with him. If it wasn't headphones it would be yodelly country music blaring, his joke singing voice—the only vestige of his boyhood in Oklahoma—drowning out the silence in which they might know one another. Otherwise he was flying overhead with his squadron, a flock of helmeted ciphers, their planes piercing eardrums, their contrails breaking apart into pale hieroglyphics, the language of vanishing points.

On the ground again, the plane pushed back inside the hangar, Dad was pleased with the results of yesterday's tinkering. He bought them two Cokes from a machine at the office, talked more plane talk with the coveralled man at the control trailer. Then he walked Lila to her dusty, bug-splattered Datsun.

"Car run okay?"

"Seems to."

"You better change the oil before you head back. I'll do it for you."

"Thanks, Dad."

"You are going back, aren't you?"

"Eventually."

It was only when she was seated behind her own steering wheel that she ventured to ask, "Dad, how come you adopted me?"

He pulled on his Coke, kneeled down by her open window so that he was at eye level. "So is this what this is all about, why you came out here all hell-bent for leather?"

"No, I don't know. I mean not consciously, anyway. I wanted to see you guys, but the abortion thing kind of brought it to a head, I guess. It's been on my mind."

"I figured it might. Your birthday coming up and all."

"You haven't answered. Why *did* you adopt me?"

Dad crushed the soda can in his fist, looked around as though to toss it, then changed his mind. He walked in front of the car, opened the passenger door and got in.

"To keep your mother happy, if you want the truth. I didn't care, I was flying. But she was miserable wanting a kid and we just couldn't seem to ace that one."

Lila fingered the keys in her lap. "No, I mean *me*, Dad. Me, not some little Vietnamese boat kid or something."

"Too many bad memories to raise a gook in my house."

Lila grimaced.

"Sorry. Your old Dad ain't PC enough for you. An Oriental. Excuse me. Asian. I couldn't do it. Tell you the truth, I probably would've chosen a boy, but your mother didn't want to wait any longer. I never regretted it, though."

"Thanks a million. I guess you didn't have any bias against Hispanics."

He touched her arm. "Lila, is that what you think you are?"

"Well, I don't know for sure, but what do I have to go on besides the fact I was born in Albuquerque and I look like this?"

"You aren't Mexican, Lila. Your mother was a nice little Jewish teenager who went and got herself knocked up. Nobody knows who your Dad was, since she wasn't telling."

"What?" Lila's heart thrummed in her chest. "You knew all along? How come you didn't tell me?"

"Lila, you know how your mother is about this subject. We agreed we'd just not talk about it."

"But she lied to me outright! She always said you guys didn't know!"

"Take it easy. That's all we knew. We weren't supposed to know that, but your mother's doctor, her gynecologist in Albu-

querque, when we were at Kirtland, he set it up. He knew someone, another OB-GYN, who knew a pregnant girl. Turned out
she was a niece or something. Her family sent her west to get rid
of it."

"It? Dad, you're talking about me."

"Shit, Lila, I'm sorry baby, but you're the one with the way
with words. I'm just a dumb flyboy."

"I can't believe you knew this stuff and never told me. What
right did you guys have not to tell me? So she was Jewish? After
all those churches Mom made me go to. All that Sunday
school."

"Lila, when we took you home you were our kid. Period. We
didn't care how you came into the world or whose genes you
were carrying. And you got to remember it was different times.
They didn't have all this open adoption stuff going on. It was the
terms we agreed to, the rules of the agency."

"Do you remember the name of that doctor? The one who set
it up?"

"Not offhand, but I can find it probably. We had to go off
base for your mother's specialist. Fertility isn't exactly a big concern for Air Force personnel. We had to pay for it ourselves. It
was some Jew name, Rothman, Kaufman, Hoffman. Let me
think."

Jew name. He didn't even get that he was talking about her.
But the idea was as foreign to her as it was to him. Hispanic,
Italian, she'd always figured on some little Catholic girl.

"Look, Lila. You got to do what you got to do. But promise
me, you won't go asking your mother about this. You know
how she gets upset. She's happy here. She gave up an awful lot to
be married to me, and I don't want her thinking she's giving you
up too."

"There's nothing to give up. I'm going to be twenty-one tomorrow, for God's sake. I'm not anyone's child anymore."

"I'm just asking you to keep it to yourself, okay? Whatever
you find out. Your mother loved you better than that girl could

have, Lila. She did what she could under the circumstances." He got out, closed the car door, but left a hand on the half opened window.

Lila put the key in the ignition. "You'll get that name for me?"

"I said I would if I could."

When she was halfway down the drive, Lila looked back at her father. He was striding toward the hangar, head bent, his blue shirt crisp, jeans loose, his running shoes too new and white.

She got lost twice finding her way back. She couldn't keep her mind on the way they'd come in. It was just too weird to take in. Jewish? Or half Jewish. What did she know about Jewish? A girl named Jan Goldberg who lived down the hall freshman year, but they hadn't been friends. The Valedictorian of her high school class, Karen Kessler, who only dated Jewish boys. And before that, in Kansas, Georgia, nothing. Just expressions: Jew him down, Jewish lightning—a fake insurance claim. A Kansas social studies teacher who got in trouble for teaching the conspiracy of the Elders of Zion. The movie *Schindler's List*. For all she knew she had dead relatives in Europe. The Chosen People. Lila the unwanted Chosen Person. Ruth used to say they'd been so lucky because they got to choose her out of all the babies in the world. Ha. And Dad had wanted a boy, which figured. Now he only cared about keeping her from upsetting Mom.

So after all these years of wondering and not wondering, there was information, stuff she could find out. The idea of finding out bloomed like purpose, an antidote to the inertia, the confusion of the last months, as though she'd known, subconsciously, that the time was coming that she could open the files. As if Ruth's inhibitions had blocked her from fully voicing the desire to herself. So what if it was an adoption cliche? At least it gave shape to her restlessness.

The whole process could take months, she knew. And who would she be when she found out? A girl without a job who hadn't graduated from college, with a boyfriend she loved but couldn't stand seeing lately. The same person as before. Or worse, someone with bad news, ugly truths it would be better not to know. No. No matter who her mother turned out to be, just finding out something would offer the clarity that had eluded her these past months.

She went through the rest of the day with Ruth as preoccupied as someone who has fallen in love; she chatted mindlessly, returning to her secret speculations while Ruth compared cuts of beef at the Safeway and sighed over the price of California peaches. She offered to help with supper and admired flowers in Ruth's garden, flowers whose names flew by her as meaninglessly as the names of women who weren't her mother: Columbine, Rose, Violet. Alone in the guest room, she watched afternoon talk shows, Oprah and Montel Williams, hoping for something about adoptees, but all she came up with was women whose husbands were transvestites and the wives of death row inmates.

At supper she watched her father's face closely for a clue that didn't come, and stayed up late watching Letterman on her bedroom TV. Afterward, she lay under the covers, sleepless, alternating between excitement and anxiety. What if he couldn't find the names? But she could find out other ways. There were services. At least now she was committed to looking. That tidbit of information Dad had served up made her birth mother real, somehow. How old was she now? If she'd been fourteen, she'd be thirty-five. If she was seventeen, then thirty-eight. Still young compared with Ruth's fifty-plus years. Almost a different generation. What if she met her and hated her? What if she were dead?

In the morning Lila went for a long walk while Ruth fussed over her birthday cake, insisting on the illusion of surprise. She quickly passed out of the groomed and orderly artifice of Mountain View and headed along the weedy verge of a two-lane country road. A perfect cloudless Colorado morning sky arced overhead. The air hummed with its own clarity. The early sun angled toward the mountains. After years in the East she found the lack of humidity, the sun's high-altitude intensity, eerie and unreal. Her sneakered feet rose and fell on cracked greying asphalt with a regular slapping sound. Crows flapped over a field on her right. Behind her the roar of an engine, and then a cattle truck barrelled down and passed her, whipping the weeds, blaring its airhorn so that she jumped. She could just imagine the driver laughing it up, the jerk. Shivers wracked her even as he disappeared down the road. She felt suddenly weak and frightened. The sleepless drive out and her infection must have taken their toll more than she realized. Lila turned back toward her parents' house.

She let herself in quietly and slipped up the stairs. Through the kitchen door she could see Ruth licking the cage of an electic beater. The rest of the morning she lay dozing, waking, oddly dispirited and uncertain. After lunch she sat in a lounge chair in the back yard, with a *House Beautiful* magazine unread but opened in her lap. Ruth had last minute shopping to do. Lila's "real present" had been mailed a week ago and probably sat waiting for her in Cambridge. But Ruth wanted to get her a "little something."

Kevin called at five, despite their fight wanting to offer a Happy 21st. Lila shaped cheerful words about how they'd celebrate when she got back. When Kevin pressed her for a return date, she hedged. How could she know? She wasn't willing to clue him in on her vague plans for fear he'd try to discourage her. It was only this afternoon that she'd decided she'd head down to Albuquerque no matter what her father came up with.

While they ate their chocolate cake, Ruth presented Lila with a floral sun dress wrapped in shimmery paper. It was demure, sweet, a dress unlike anything Lila wore or would wear—how could Ruth not know? The dress of the daughter she wished she'd had, Lila surmised. That old anxious resentment rose in her but she pushed it away, thanked Ruth profusely.

Dad had taken her car that morning and returned with it washed and Jiffy Lubed. He presented her with cash in an envelope. "It was going to be your graduation present, but this is as good a time as any," he said. Lila opened it and counted out five one-hundred dollar bills. That had to mean something. She was sure he had news. She was grateful, gracious, tried hard to conceal her edginess. When would he tell her?

She suffered through a family drive, a trip up into one of the canyons that ran between foothills. Ruth insisted Lila sit up front for the view. They wound along a creek up into the mountains. How dry it looked at this altitude, the pines widely spaced on the thin, rocky soil. Lila let it pass before her eyes in a blur. Afterward Ruth and Lila drank decaf cappucinos while her father settled for a regular high-test at a downtown cafe that Ruth imagined would remind Lila of Cambridge. Lila could barely keep herself from drumming her nails on the table.

Back home, Ruth came into her room. "It's probably disappointing to have to spend such a big day with your old parents," Ruth apologized. "But you didn't have any friends out here we could invite."

"It was fine, Mom, it was great," Lila insisted. She felt sorry for Ruth, trying so hard, so blind to what Lila was really concerned with. She gave Ruth an awkward hug.

Ruth actually blushed. "That's a rare treat," she said.

Lila pretended to watch TV, but sat on her bed, alert to the sounds of her parents getting ready for sleep. Faucets rushing, toilet flushing. She leaped at Dad's knock on her door. "Come in," she called.

"Here." He took a folded paper from his back pocket. "It's the doctor's name, and the agency." He spoke softly, as though Mom might be eavesdropping from their room down the hall. "It's a start. Don't know if the guy's still in practice or even alive, but I guess the agency can tell you."

"Thanks Dad," Lila said, even though she wasn't sure she should thank him for something he should have given her long ago. "I'm going down there tomorrow. I already decided, even if you didn't get the name."

"I guessed you might. I hope you find what you're looking for. Just tell your mother you're going to see a friend or something, if you don't mind. You don't know what you'll find out, if anything, no use getting her upset for no reason."

"Why do we always have to protect her from reality?" Lila protested.

"Haven't they taught you anything in that college?" Dad snapped. "Don't you know there's more than one reality? Can't you just let her have hers while you go chasing after yours?"

"Okay, okay, okay." Lila gripped the paper. She could be magnanimous now, considering.

"Good luck, honey." He sounded unaccountably defeated. He took off his glasses, peered into them, then set them back on his nose. "On the bottom of that paper I wrote my number at the airport. Call me there to let me know you're safe."

"Promise." She kissed his cheek. "And really. Thanks."

CHAPTER 10

When I can no longer sit in the silence of my Bodhi room, listening too hard to the whisk of broom and suck of vacuum on the other side of the wall, trying to imagine which disciple is assigned to chambermaid duty today, I tie up my hiking boots and emerge, blinking, into the brilliance of early afternoon. There's a conical landmass that I see from the hot pools, and I am determined today to hike to its top. I've heard there's a trail that begins just beyond the Jemez State Monument, a small ruin walking distance from the Bodhi.

I follow the main road, Route 4, as it heads north from the center of town. Men in cowboy hats drive past in pickups, raising an index finger two inches above the steering wheel—the local salute. No one walks here, it seems, except the priests from the Servants of the Paracletes, a retreat for wayward clergy that gained national prominence a few years back with the Pederast Priest scandals. The Mexican-born mother of a college friend used to refer to priests as "boiled eggs," and when I see them jogging slope-shouldered, limp and white-legged, along the highway, the name seems apt.

A silent, crimson-robed nun walks the stations of the cross outside the Handmaids of the Precious Blood convent, which I've learned was once the sister institution to the Paracletes, until the nuns got some version of liberation in the '70s and refused to be the servants of the Servants of the Paracletes any longer.

I visited the town library yesterday (a one-room metal building) and took out a book on Jemez Springs—I needed a break from my own history for a day. This is an odd little mountain town, with three monasteries settled alongside one another on a half mile of road. Perhaps the hot springs beckoned them; Jemez is also the home of a 120-year-old bath house, once the sacred refuge of the Jemez Indians who were forced onto a reservation down the road, now a flourishing business, where locals and tourists soak, take sweat wraps, and breathe in healing scents, before going across the street to load up on "Famous Jemez" green chili burgers at Los Ojos, a bar that offers an impressive array of dead animals on its walls. I went in for a beer and noted a mountain goat with its entire chest and front legs intact. A cougar, a bobcat, and an enormous rattlesnake held their own beside the usual mounted heads of elk and mule deer.

Highway 4 slants up and I'm not acclimatized to the altitude yet. I try to slow my breath. When I was here with you, Lila, waiting for you, or waiting to be rid of you (you might say), I never hiked. I was too pregnant already, too demoralized. I sat day after day in my small room at Philomena's, squinting dazedly through the deep window recess of her adobe house, hiding from the harsh sun and a world to which I didn't want to display my belly.

Philomena was a patient of my mother's sister's husband's brother, if you can follow that. An OB-GYN in Albuquerque. It was all set up through brother Stanley, who had recently hysterectomied a middle-aged woman named Philomena Ruiz from Jemez Springs. I was her boarder. A neat package: my parents didn't want me near home—my father was more afraid of his family knowing than Mom's. As an OB-GYN, Stanley was in touch with infertile couples; he had it all arranged through a colleague, some private adoption agency. You were promised to his colleague's clients before you were born. Stanley might know who got you. All those years I had access to Stanley through my uncle, I never asked. I didn't feel I had the right. And, to be honest, for a long time I didn't want to know. When I finally called, Stanley swore he was kept out of the information loop to protect the adopters, your parents. He has Parkinson's now and said he didn't remember Philomena Ruiz. All he wanted to do was get me off the phone.

Back then, Philomena was alternately solicitous and angry with me. I never knew if it was for my obvious carnal sin or for the future crime of abandoning my unborn child. A few times she hinted that I could stay at her place with my baby after you were born. She had raised her own daughter's child. I don't think she really wanted me though; she was having some crisis of her own prompted by her scraped-gourd innards. More than once I heard her crying in her room.

At another time, I (or some better adjusted Northern teen) might have found spending four months in a home in rural New Mexico fascinating, like participating in a student exchange. But I had no interest in my surroundings. I barely spoke to Philomena except in rude monosyllables. I focussed all my considerable resentment (toward your father, my parents, myself) on her stooped, anxious shoulders. I sneered privately at her crucifixes and Sunday masses and at her bean laden meals. In my own slim defense, I was seventeen, bored, shamed, lonely, and horrified at my lost "potential" and blooming belly.

I drove past Philomena's house a few days ago. Or what used to be her house. The traditional hip-roofed adobe was gone; in its place stood a double-wide mobile home with a swing set and a Rottweiler in the yard. I didn't stop to inquire what had become of her. Dead? In a nursing home? Living with her daughter? Perhaps I was afraid for her to see what the wages of my sins had wrought—I would come to her still childless, without a man, a family, the only things that mattered in her world.

I'm abreast of the Jemez State Monument now. It offers a visitor center, the remains of a church, and standing stone walls the same color as the cliffs that rise behind them. Beyond the ruin, the red canyon walls are topped by beige volcanic tuff, remnants of the Valle Grande eruption that supposedly blew rocks all the way to Indiana.

I cut off the highway shoulder and lurch up a steep weedy embankment above the irrigation ditch, then follow a track until I miss the first switchback and find myself dead-ended above the monument. Huffing, I double back and find the faint trail, then small rock cairns that mark the path as it changes from red dirt to grey, black stone, pumice and grit. The volcanic rock rings hollow when it strikes itself.

I persist dully upward under a blue sky as monochromatic as a child's painting, between clumpy cedar and pinon and scrub. The ponderosa pines stand far above on the higher hillsides, bending to some distant wind. My breath tugs at my lungs like a child at the nipple.

The path cuts under an overhanging ledge. It is the priests' path: little Virgin Mary statuettes stand among the rocks. As I pass under the ledges my neck hairs prickle. I picture mountain lions, cougars, lurking among the crags, waiting to drop on me with their claws and fangs. In the bar I overheard talk of sightings, big cats moving down the hillsides this winter, one shot in someone's back yard. As soon as the image appears in my mind I can't shake it. I can almost smell their acrid cat piss among the stabbing points of century plants, the prickly pear and cholla cactus.

This is one of my little habits, Lila. I'm determined to complete this hike. I know I'm not going to stop until I reach the dunce-cap top of this mountain, and I'm going to torture myself with the fear of wild animal attack the whole way. It's a neat trick I have of ruining solo hikes and climbs. On a travel assignment in Colorado once I vacillated between fear of snakes and bears for ten miles. A way, perhaps, of making myself less alone. Or a distraction, to keep me from what I really fear?

What is that unseen thing that can shape-shift to cougar, snake, bear? In cities it's a threatening man. I used to think it was you, Lila, the guilt and loss that could leap out to grab me whenever I was just going about my life, but now that I'm trying to meet the fact of you head on, what fear still stalks me?

I'm beating myself with amateur psychology and I just want to walk! I try to concentrate on my boots, worn tops and red dust on leather, laces tied in a knot where broken. Above my red wool sock my shin needs a shave. I focus on the miniature puff of dust with each step. The slippery roll of pumice pebbles like ball bearings under my Vibram soles. And still my mind dances back to cougars—their cold-eyed stalking. I've always romanticized wolves, who have never been known to attack humans in North America. Perhaps its their doggy likeness. Cats turn me off. I haven't appreciated them since I was a child and my mother made me hand over my kitty to an animal "shelter" when we moved to our smaller house in Massachusetts. The dog was everybody's, she said, but the cat was only mine. She promised the shelter would find a home for Pixie with some nice old lady, although a black oil drum with a little door, the kitty crematorium, stood right in the driveway.

I suppose it's ridiculous, Lila, to dredge up that old parental crime.

Now the path winds around the back of the upthrust so that I can no longer look behind me and see the town. There's a cooler wind on the east side. I'm still climbing, but I'm close, closer, swinging around to the north. I can see, across the valley, the developments above the Soda Dam, a natural barricade of hot spring residue that erupts, rounded as a huge worm casting, beyond town.

I finally reach the summit and there at the peak stands a huge white cross. More Virgin Mary statues lie about. They are cheaply made, their blue and white ceramic robes sun bleached, shattered. I wonder at this maternity fixation, maternity without sex, that so obsesses not only the "boiled egg" alcoholic, gay, or pederast priests who have been sent here from their parishes, but obsessed, as well, the Spanish colonizers three, four hundred years ago. The mesas hereabouts are named Virgin and Guadelupe.

The truth is, it's not as pretty a view as I'd hoped. Too many new houses, the strip of highway visible. According to the librarian, Californians have discovered Jemez, land cheaper than Santa Fe and not so "spoiled." They're selling their tract houses back in San Jose or their mansions in Laguna Beach to live the "simple" life for a lot less money, pulling in their double wides and log "scabin" kits. A few with taste build adobes or fake adobes and latter-day hippies have created their stucco-covered straw bale octagons, turning this narrow slash of canyon into developments called, unimaginatively, "Area 1" and "Area 2". It's a land boom, a gold rush for anyone who bought here five years ago.

Well, the climb was my achievement for the day. It's so me, Lila, dumbly going forward despite my manufactured fear. I'm a person who needs to be knocked down all the time so I can keep experiencing my own resilience as I struggle back up. Now I'll sit here on a sun-bleached twist of cedar stump, boots kicking in the Catholic shards, and wait for my breath to ease so I can turn around again and head back down.

Lila, I'm losing sight of what I need to tell you. What you may or may not want to know.

Let's see. When I was fourteen I crossed the street if I saw people walking toward me; I was so self-conscious, so sure of my ugliness. And then one day, in tenth grade, my mother sent me in to the Friendly's next to the A&P to buy two ice cream cones—what could I have been doing eating ice cream? It seems incredible. Once I started starving, I never ate sweets, except on a binge. But I do remember the gawky boy with a boat-shaped paper cap scooping cones at the take-out counter. I ordered my mother's coffee ice cream, my mocha almond, and he looked up, ears jutting, Adam's apple poking out like some Norman Rockwell soda jerk, and grinned. "Anything for a pretty girl like you," he said. Like me? I wanted to look around to see who else he might be addressing. I returned to the passenger seat of my mother's station wagon and studied myself in the side view mirror as my tongue licked the melting sweetness. A pretty girl like me?

Overnight, it seemed, I'd been transformed from an ugly duckling into a girl boys mooned over. When I got my first, short-lived job, oddly enough scooping cones at the Brigham's in our town, an older boy waited for me relentlessly, sipping sodas so he could walk me to the lot, to my car (an Oldsmobile 442 my father got free for investing in a car dealership, its high powered engine impressive to boys but wasted on me). Silently he accompanied me outside, angrily kicking gravel, trying to get to the point in which he could ask me out and I could refuse. I was an AP girl who dated no one, too sure of my cerebral superiority to consider boys from lower, even honors, tracks, too frightened and confused by attention to do more than look away, which only seemed to drive them crazier in their pursuits.

I wasn't blind to all the gossip, although I held myself apart— I knew that Aaron Paulson, who sat next to me in English, was rumored to have ground up a litter of baby rabbits in a garbage disposal last year. I observed Maurice La Fontaine's high school romances. Remember Maurice, Lila, from the Karl Marx trial and the Debra Gurwitz fiasco? He was involved with a girl who wore hip-hugger pants and whose bangs fell in her eyes. I knew her from our ski club; her mother drove a Roadrunner and dressed identically to her daughter.

Although AP boys generally knew enough to keep their distance, in Cambridge, townies and Harvard boys followed me, asking, "You want to see a movie? You want to get high?" I wouldn't meet their eyes, gazed instead at my reflection in pastry shop windows, testing my control over temptations.

"Why do you bitches dress like that and then look down your noses?" one guy demanded.

I was shocked. I dressed like that—in minis—because everyone did, even the girls with fat jiggling thighs, even some of our mothers. It never occured to me I was trying to evoke a response.

At school, boys from lower tracks came to sit at my table during enforced library periods, wanting to tell me their dreams of joining the Marines or owning a bar. I sat silent before my stack of research materials. I was a girl of formidable discipline: the only one in my ninth grade history class who didn't have to take the final, the one whose term papers were handed in weeks early. Sure, I was a nerd, but I looked good. My clothes were arranged carefully days ahead, everything ordered and planned so that I would never repeat an outfit in two weeks. My grades were nearly perfect—except for math, my weakness. But I finessed that by lingering after class to beg the red-faced, stuttering young math teacher to help me before exams. He gave me answers, as I knew he would.

In class, while my teachers' voices droned on, I counted and recounted and counted again the day's calories, tried to imagine a life without this strangling obsession—not a life, an hour, a minute in which I wouldn't be observing the density of my own flesh, judging, weighing. I weighed myself fifteen times a day, before peeing in the morning and after, with and without clothes. After eating and after vomiting. Boys could hardly compete with the seductive power of my affliction.

My eleventh grade English teacher, Mr. Teal, plucked me out of my classroom stupor. He was a crippled man with twisted, stunted legs encased in metal braces and a sonorous, beautiful voice. Sometimes Mr. Teal would lift himself by his powerful arms and hover over his chair while intoning verities about *Murder in the Cathedral* or "A Modest Proposal" or Pope's "Rape of the Lock." His gentle voice belied the fact that outside his classroom there was a war grinding on and hippies and Vietnam Veterans Against The War lounged on our historic town common. (When *Life* magazine arrived I studied the war pictures with shame: green and gruesome with bandages. They wore my father's boots.)

Until Mr. Teal, I prided myself on being able to stare at a teacher, simulating absolute attention while computing my caloric consumption. One day he stopped me after class and summoned me to his office. He was head of the English Department, and I had to pass the gauntlet of his middle-aged secretary, who gazed at me with mysterious, open dislike.

"Sit down," he invited, when she'd deigned to nod me in. It was a tiny office, and our two chairs were uncomfortably close. Mr. Teal had an exceptionally large, gentle face. His grey hair parted in the middle and swept symetrically to each side like the pages of a thick, opened book. I carefully looked away from his stunted legs, but his two crutch-like canes with arm braces leaned against the side of his desk. Perversely, it crossed my mind that I could pull them away and leave him trapped and helpless.

"Allie," he said, smiling pleasantly. "You're an A student. You're doing fine, in terms of the rest of the class, but you are capable of a great deal more."

I blinked at him, startled. He'd seen through me.

"I'd like to offer you the chance to go further, to push yourself a little. I'm willing to work with you outside of class, give you additional reading and writing assignments. We could meet here once a week during one of your free periods to discuss your extra work. Would you be interested in that?"

With the self-absorption of any teenager, I had no idea what unnecessary extra work he was creating for himself. Nor was I particularly interested in British literature. I only knew that I'd been selected and couldn't refuse. He sent me on to History with a copy of Orwell's essay about shooting an elephant clutched on my pile of textbooks.

After that, I regularly accompanied him down the halls to his office after class, carrying his books while he painfully leaned into the metal cuffs of his crutches and dragged his twisted legs. I tried to slow my long-legged skittish pace to match his. My stretch of bare, tanned, muscled thigh beside his rocking lurch seemed obscene even to me.

Eventually, Mr. Teal confided that he hadn't been crippled from birth. At Harvard he'd played lacrosse until he came down with polio. He even used to ride with the Myopia Hunt. Our knees nearly touching in that tiny office, mine bare, his above unimaginable withered sticks covered in good, expensive wool, I couldn't picture him young and healthy, taking long strides through Harvard Square.

He lived on Beacon Hill in Boston, which led me to understand that he taught out of love, not because he had to. I drove through once, past his town house, lit by gaslights on the narrow, patrician streets.

That spring he selected me to take tests for a national English award. When I won first place in Massachusetts, my father wouldn't acknowledge the prize, though Mr. Teal beamed so proudly it made me uneasy. I was more accustomed to my father's response: when I showed him a straight A report card, he refused to comment. When I asked, "Aren't you going to say *anything*?" he replied, "I'll have something to say when they aren't A's." The colleges were impressed by my prize though; scores of them sent brochures, inviting me to apply.

One day I was nodded into Mr. Teal's office by the prune-faced department secretary, and found my teacher sitting with his head in his hands. "Mr. Teal, what's the matter?" I asked.

"Oh, Allie, my wife is very ill. Very ill." He looked up at me imploringly. Behind his glasses his eyes looked moist. I was uncomfortable with his distress, Lila. Teachers weren't supposed to display sorrow. Any weakness and they would be torn apart by a pack of teenage jackals. And I was jealous. Jealous that this thick-bodied, stunted man—old enough to be my father's father—even *had* a wife to be worried about. I'd imagined myself to be central to his life in some indeterminate way.

That spring, however, my precious sense of importance was confirmed when the final for our English class consisted of only one poem which we were to explicate: Roethke's "Elegy for Jane, My Student, Thrown by a Horse." I was sure that the assignment, a teacher's words of love over the grave of a student, was aimed at me alone. With thrilling, shameful certainty I read it as a secret love poem. Surely, Roethke described his student with a lover's caress: "... neckcurls limp and damp as tendrils; a sidelong pickerel smile ..." What's a pickerel smile, anyway, that of a darting fish? Perhaps I misunderstood Teal's message. He might have been expressing the emotions of a teacher only ("I, with no rights in this matter, / Neither father nor lover"), one who hoped better for me than I knew how to hope for myself. Did he foresee the fall I'd soon take?

If anything was certain, it was that I looked out, fish-eyed at the world, my face drawn down, my neck strung like a bow. That kind man, so experienced in suffering, must have seen the misery I lived in, a misery that kept me thrashing sleepless in bed and prompted me to steal sleeping pills from my father's dresser. If anyone was alarmed by the fact that I wrote my yearly English/History term paper on the legal and ethical dimensions of suicide, or by my self-imposed hunger, or by the utter aloneness in which I walked the school halls, chin to chest in anguished self-consciousness and self-loathing, it would have been Mr. Teal. Yet, it was just these things, Lila, that made me ripe for the attentions of your father.

You can't (I hope you can't) imagine how inexperienced and isolated I was. I'd only consented to go out with a boy in eleventh grade after my psychiatrist shamed me into it. Let me back up and explain. I was packed off to a shrink in tenth grade after my mother noticed that I never did anything after school but homework and exercise. And I still didn't have periods. I'd spent a week at Pratt, the Tufts Medical School Hospital, being unveiled and prodded by my doctor, always with a horde of male medical students in tow. My psyche was charted by medical students who asked me questions such as "Do you prefer cuddling to intercourse?"

During that week in the hospital, my father refused to let the family visit me. It was his vacation week at the Cape, and I wasn't going to ruin it by drawing my mother away. I lay in bed next to a dying woman whose husband and two preteen daughters were furious with her. They came in and complained about how bad things were at home without her to do the cooking, the laundry. She was on massive doses of steroids and the cartilage in her nose had collapsed in her swollen face—she looked like a sad, punch-drunk fighter.

I told my endocrinologist that there was nothing wrong with me beyond the fact that I was too fat. He scolded me for wanting to look like I'd come from Auschwitz and announced at the end of the week that there was indeed nothing wrong with me beyond the fact that I didn't want to be a woman. So off to the psychiatrist I went.

Dr. Richter, from Harvard Medical School and Children's Hospital, was a narrow-shouldered man who resembled Mr. Rogers—a safe focus for my untapped love. Oh, how resentful I was when he glanced out the window at his children playing in front of his home office, or when he looked at his watch, or when I heard his wife's muffled voice through the ceiling. This gentle man whose office was filled with therapeutic toys once informed me, when I arrived for a session, "You look sexy today." But when I called him up on a weekend to apprise him of a sudden (and most likely minor) insight related to our treasured hour together, he told me that he couldn't be my "Saturday night date." I took it as a slap, a directive to get my own life. I didn't recognize the arrogance of his assumption.

My mother must have been in league with him. When I made a lame excuse to some boy who'd called up to ask me out, she remarked with puzzling coldness, "*I* was never too tired to go out with boys when *I* was a teen."

Of course, we were into a war by then. Prompted by Dr. Richter, I'd begun to question her innocence in the equation I'd always taken for granted: Mom good, Dad bad. I began to notice little instances of provocation and sabotage. I ventured, as she laid out her usual litany of complaints, to point out that maybe if she got Dad's shirts to the cleaners like he'd asked, he wouldn't get so mad. A two-day sulk resulted. (Women's Liberation had not yet put to question her role as shirt-getter in either of our minds.)

When, upon hearing of some favored celebrity's death, she intoned, as she did so often, "The good die young," I replied, my teenage cruelty newly honed, "Then you have nothing to worry about." And, sure of my moral superiority, I scoffed at her lip-service liberalism. She called each live-in worker who passed through our house "her girl." She determined their work-load according to the color of their skin. The Austrian and the English girls were au pairs, but the Honduran and the black woman were maids. I pitied them their lives with us, their warped version of upper middle-class America. The English girl and Austrian got fat on our abundant food; Olivera from Honduras ended up pregnant in the slums of Roxbury. Lillie Mae, from Dixie Moll, Tennessee, however, got revenge, sickening us all one summer when, made to sleep in the bathroom-less basement, she dumped her commode into our well.

I'm getting carried away, Lila. I guess I still suffer from the teenage knack for fault-finding. Back to my first date, then.

John Bailey was an unattractive senior boy from my mixed-grade art class. He had shaggy hair, glasses, a snub nose and bad teeth, and he called me up to say "Molly Hingham and Sara Winchester and Franny Bates can't go to the movies with me this weekend. Do you want to go?" It put me at ease that he was so besotted with senior girls who wouldn't look his way that he didn't realize I was a girl pursued by strangers. Good practice, I figured, so I said yes.

He took me into Harvard Square to see *The Stranger* at an art cinema. We sat in awkward silence punctuated by John's occasional grunt of recognition as he communed with the film. After walking silently, moodily around the streets of Cambridge for an hour, he led me to a Brigham's, and while he shoveled in a hot fudge sundae (I had my Sanka with artificial sweetener) he kept repeating, while mournfully shaking his head, "The Stranger—That's me exactly!" We paid our separate bills and John Bailey drove me home, mercifully without attempting a kiss.

"Home from tramping around again, you little tramp?" my father sneered when I came in the kitchen door.

A few months later I ran into John Bailey in front of Woolworth's; I was suprised when he asked me if I wanted to play poker with him and some other seniors and a teacher that morning. It was a hot day in early June and I wore a pale blue V-necked linen minidress that buttoned down the front and reached only the tops of my thighs. I was tanned from weekends at the Cape. My hair hung straight and black to my waist. I didn't know a thing about poker or boys.

John drove me to school in his VW bug. I'd never been there on a Saturday except to take the PSATs and I was surprised to see how many cars were parked in the students' and teachers' lots. My school had a whole other Saturday existence I knew nothing about—baseball practice on the diamonds, gymnastics in the gym, and in the ground-level lunchroom, a bunch of senior boys sat sprawled around a long formica table playing cards with a young teacher.

I recognized Jim Palmer, whom I knew from our ski club and my art class. He was a big guy who performed daredevil freestyle feats on the slopes wearing lederhosen and a cape, and often lifted a haunch in art class to fart showily. Art class was the only time I could comfortably chat with boys, perhaps because my hands were busy making chicken wire and papier-maché sculptures.

"Hey, Heller!" he called, then switched to mock horror. "Oh, no, you aren't going out with Bailey, are you?"

"No, I just ran into him downtown."

"That's a relief. She's too good for you, Bailey."

Palmer took over the introductions. "These cardsharks here are Walters and Klein." Walters wore John Lennon glasses and a scraggly pony tail, Klein was Jewish-preppy in a button-down shirt, his kinky dark hair cut short in the manner of the lawyer he'd become. "And this is Mustang Mike Patterson," Palmer continued, gesturing at the youngish teacher shuffling the cards. "The only cool teacher in this shithole."

"You can call me Mike," the teacher said, glancing up at me.

Patterson, with his smooth, blunt, even features, bore an uncanny resemblance to Marcello Mastroianni in "The Stranger," except the film was black and white and everything about Patterson was golden: his short, wavy hair; his furry arms, his tan that I would eventually learn came from hours on the golf course. I watched them play a few hands, silently marveling over the oddity of being there with the wall clock jerking out the minutes, the metal kitchen louvers pulled down over the empty lunch counter, students scratching away on test papers, and a teacher leaning back in his chair as though he actually enjoyed the company of these boys. Every once in a while Patterson got up to check on a couple of students planted at the other end of the lunchroom doing make-ups, then returned to the raucous game.

I tried to listen as Palmer explained the rules of poker but I've always had a habit of blocking out instructions; instead I bet wildly and swept up a pile of chips on pure beginner's luck which made them laugh. More cards were passed around. They discussed who was playing at Truc or what was at the movies at the Brattle Street Theatre. They all thought *The African Queen* was tops, as well as *The King of Hearts* with Alan Bates and Geneveive Bujold. I'd seen a poster for *Hearts* in Cambridge and (though I wouldn't admit it) Bates' naked butt had embarrassed me.

When the game was over, the students doing a make-up exam released, I stood and pushed in my lunchroom chair.

"So, you want a ride home?" John Bailey asked. "I mean I got to go that way anyway." Ever the gentleman.

"No thanks," I demurred, computing my 200-calorie walk.

"Come back again Allie," Patterson said as he swept the cards toward his chest. "I like you."

What was to like? I'd barely said three words the whole game.

* * *

I didn't return for poker, but that fall I signed up for Patterson's "Psychology of Violence" course, one of the new untracked electives added for "relevance." In Patterson's class I fashioned a research project at a pre-school, giving four-year-olds puppets and sitting with my notebook before their puppet theatre, comparing the gender differences in the number of incidences of hitting and slamming. Not surprisingly, the boys won hands down. Of course, I couldn't determine how much was innate, how much was cultural. But Patterson was impressed by my "engagement with the question."

He invited me to the Pewter Pot Muffin House for coffee. At the Pewter Pot, Patterson presided over a table of cool kids, including my old junior high nemesis Cara Kaplan, who puffed on Marlboros and talked about all the Valium they pumped her full of at MacLean Hospital, the ritzy nuthouse where James Taylor had stayed. Her parents had committed her for being "oversexed." Stubbing out her butt, Indian bangles clanking on her thick wrist, Cara said the Valium had robbed her of her memory. She looked tired and wasted, and I saw that the girl who'd come to my fifth-grade birthday sleep-over in kitty cat pajamas had stepped through some one-way door of trouble and experience I couldn't yet imagine.

She wasn't the only one who would step through. Donnie Tietz, who carried a briefcase and was a bridge champion in junior high, would go on to drop out of MIT and take a Greyhound across the country before suffering a nervous breakdown. Others would take too much acid or angel dust and just not come back from the ozone; years later I'd see them hanging about our town common with spinning, empty eyes. One boy shot himself a week before the college letters came. And I? I'd live out the cliché that was supposed to fit the poorer kids from neighboring towns like Arlington and Waltham, not upper-middle class Jewish girls with good SAT scores: I got pregnant and gave up my kid. But you know that already.

Patterson invited me, alone, for lunch at Friendly's. We zoomed down there in his red Mustang, its rear window a louvered fastback. The car seemed exotically shallow; my knees jutted up from the floorboards, bare and exposed. I wasn't used to bucket seats or stick shifts. I'd never been in a car with leather lacing on the steering wheel.

Patterson led me into the restaurant, a hand lightly centered on my back, and ushered me to a table. Amidst the suited businessmen hunching over their sandwiches, trying to keep mustard off their ties, and the housewives who'd just filled their carts next door at the A&P, I noticed other teachers from our school lunching in a booth and wondered why Patterson wasn't worried that they might think something was going on. I took his lack of concern as proof of his high-mindedness and admired his refusal to care.

A teacher waved from across the room. She was youngish, blond, cute in a way I considered bland. "Hi, Mike," she called brightly.

He nodded, made a face she couldn't see, and leaned forward to whisper over our table. "Two summers ago when I was getting my masters at the Harvard Ed School, she lived nearby and used to leave mushy notes on my car. It was really annoying."

I glanced at her with contempt and uneasy pity, taking note never to be mushy and annoying.

"That's where I met my wife," Mike continued, sitting back in his seat and studying his menu. "She was a departmental secretary at Harvard."

I was curious, but at the same time didn't want his phantom wife to invade this lunch date. A secretary? How could Patterson love anyone less educated than he was, I wondered with my peculiar mix of AP snobbery and dopey innocence. "What's she like?" I asked from behind my menu.

"My wife? She's a sweet, sheltered girl, Allie. From an Italian family that doesn't think much of girls going to school. I can't talk to her the same way I talk to you, unfortunately." He put his menu down. "And she's pregnant."

Pregnancy was a revolting state *I'd* never enter, one in which even thin people grew disgustingly fat. I tried to imagine him walking beside her, or worse, the two of them in bed.

The waitress appeared with a note pad and we ordered, he a BLT and coffee, me a salad with no dressing and ice tea. When the waitress retreated, Mike said, "Actually, she's my second wife. When I was at Brown, I married my sweetheart from Wellesley. That lasted about two minutes."

"No kids?"

"No, thank God. That would have been a disaster."

"So what happened?" I managed, as though I were accustomed to such grownup conversations. I fiddled with a salt shaker.

"Who knows? We were only twenty-one. We didn't know what we were doing."

"Too immature."

"You got it. I was immature and she was spoiled."

"If I ever get married, which I might not, I won't do it until I'm at least thirty. I think it's important to know who you are before you get tangled up with someone else."

Patterson grinned at me. "How old are you anyway?

"Seventeen."

"You seem so much older sometimes."

I shrugged. "How old is your new wife?" I wanted to hear again about our differences, how he could talk to me in ways he couldn't talk to her. I wanted my specialness reconfirmed like an airline ticket to a foreign land.

"Twenty-four."

Twenty-four seemed plenty old to me. Patterson, I knew, was around thirty-one. I'd figured it out from the sports trophies with his name on them in the case in the main hall at school, from the days when he'd been a student there.

The food arrived. I watched in fascination as mayonnaise dripped from his toasted bread, tomato seeds floated on the plate. I got some peculiar satisfaction out of watching other people eat fattening foods, a vicarious thrill. At home I concocted disgusting combinations of peanut butter and coconut and cocoa powder and made my brother eat them.

"Don't you want anything else?" Patterson urged, watching me stir artificial sweetener into my tea. "I'm treating."

If he only knew how often after our outings I went home and ransacked the freezer, the brownie mix. But to have someone see me eat anything other than undressed vegetables would be as revealing, as humiliating, as someone seeing me on the toilet, or hanging over it with my finger down my throat.

"Did you ever want to do something else besides teach?" I asked. I couldn't understand how anyone, even someone as popular as Mike Patterson, could stand to be a high school teacher. To be so exposed, thirty pairs of critical eyes watching, ready to mock your every misstep, would be horrible. And it wasn't exactly a prestigious job.

"Oh, I thought about it," Mike said. "I could have gone on for my PhD in American history. But I really *like* teaching high school. I'd rather hang around kids than a bunch of stuffy academics." Mike sipped his black coffee. "How about you? What do you see yourself doing, Allie? In college? After?"

"I don't know." I didn't. The goal was always set clearly and simply for me: do well in school. After that I couldn't imagine. I wrinkled my nose. "As long as I don't have to sit in some office every day."

Patterson grinned. "That's the great thing about teaching. Look, I'm getting paid for sitting here with you." He gazed at his watch. "Uh-oh. I've got a one-o'clock American History. We better get back."

He guided me past the lunching teachers whose heads followed our progress, out into the parking lot where his red Mustang sat waiting. He opened the door for me and I climbed in.

"Maybe I'll be a psychologist," I said. "Or a marriage counselor." I looked sideways at him to see if he'd gotten my feeble joke. He was busy fitting the key into the ignition.

"You'd still end up sitting in some office," he said.

"Yeah, but it would be *my* office. Not like working for some corporation out on Route 128."

"With a mind like yours, you'll be able to do whatever you want to," he said breezily. He thrust the car into gear and we careened out of the lot.

It was the early seventies. Who was thinking about what they would be? Maurice La Fontaine was. Debra Gurwitz was. The two of them, acing their advanced placement exams, matching double 800s on the SATs. All winter and spring the halls of our school echoed with the whispered question: What did you get? The other kids looked at me askance: *you* don't have to worry, they said. You'll get in everywhere. We were all waiting for the dread April 15th, the day the letters arrived and, we assumed, the rest of our lives would be determined.

The truth was, as soon as my college applications were filed the wind went out of my high school sails. Except for Mike Patterson, I couldn't think of a reason to attend school. I looked forward to the times Patterson would call me over to his post in the lunchroom to keep him company or beckon me into his office to ask what I'd done that weekend. "Went to a movie alone in Cambridge," I reported one Monday. I was proud of my bravery and independence, even though it hadn't worked out too well. Some old pervert kept trying to sit next to me although I changed rows twice. Still, it was an adventure.

Patterson looked puzzled. "I think going to a movie alone is the saddest thing in the world," he said.

I felt both judged and judgmental; he'd diminished himself by his response, proved himself ordinary. Of course *he'd* never thought of going anywhere alone, never had to.

On April 15th, the letters came. For all the brochures and invitations, no one wanted me, or at least not anyone I wanted. I got wait-listed at a few places. Only Trinity, in Hartford, a school I didn't want to attend but had applied to because my cousin was an admissions counselor there, said yes. I didn't look good on paper and they'd seen through me in the interviews. I had no activities, no sports, no groups. Just my grades and my prize. They'd known who I really was after all: a lonely weirdo.

My father sneered, "Big shot, you should have applied to UMASS." Which was ridiculous, since I had gotten into my "safety school" which was a lot more exclusive than UMASS, although my admissions counselor cousin permitted my father to discount even that as a minor accomplishment. He was angry with me for failing to make a clean sweep he could brag about to his sisters and eager to put me in my place. He didn't need to. It wasn't that I'd wanted to go to any of those schools particularly, merely that I believed myself to be someone who could get in anywhere. Mediocrity was something I had never imagined as my fate. I slunk through the school halls, even more invisible than usual, as everyone exchanged information on their futures. Maurice chose Harvard over MIT. So did Debra Gurwitz.

"You do a year at Trinity, then you transfer," Patterson counseled. "They're idiots. They've made a big mistake and you'll prove it."

"I'm so sorry, Allie," Mr. Teal said.

Two months passed. It was June, school finished in a couple of days. I was trudging the familiar sidewalks home when Patterson pulled up beside me, reached over, and opened his car door. Sun glinted off the shiny metallic finish. I got in. I didn't even stop to consider the calories I wouldn't burn by taking a ride home. He pulled into our driveway. A hedge separated us from the kitchen windows where my mother might have been watching. But she was in her usual tizzy, readying the family for our summer move to the Cape. I'd decided to spend the summer at home in stifling suburban Boston. My father would be there weekday nights, late, after work. We'd be enemy housemates. He was newly angry at me for not having a summer job set up like my industrious brother and sister who would work at the Cape Cod Mall. My only project was to teach myself to type on the electric typewriter I'd been given as a pregraduation present.

Patterson let the car idle in our driveway. He turned to me, hands still spread on the steering wheel. "I'm going to miss you," he said. When he reached over I thought he was opening the door for me but he put a hand behind my neck, pulled me close across the jutting gear shift, and startled me with a hard kiss. Did I stiffen, Lila? Did I pull away? Did I like it? I was stunned. I know it seems hard to believe, but it's true. Not once did I imagine that he was plotting this. Not in all those trips for coffee or lunch did I consider that he might be working out a place or time to make a move. And maybe he wasn't. Maybe it just evolved at that moment, sitting in his silly sports car in front of my parents' house with the semester over and our lives dividing.

I don't want to make him out to be a total jerk, Lila. After all, he is your father, at least genetically, and I've done plenty of things on impulse that could be judged equally poor over the years. Perhaps he was suffering that old cliché, the prebirth jitters, snatching at his last moment of youth before fatherhood grabbed him by the throat. Maybe he honestly liked me, was drawn to me despite—rather than because of—the fact that I was seventeen.

When he released me I opened the door as though nothing had happened, gathered my purse, my books.

"I want to see you," Patterson said, reaching for my arm. "Can I call? Can I come visit?"

"Okay," I replied in what must have been a duck's quack. Then I fled.

He called two days later and asked if he might come over to type his final reports and do his grades at my house. He knew, because I'd told him, that my mother and sister and brother would be at the Cape. My father would be at his job. He wanted to work at my house, Patterson said, because it was too noisy at school and his very pregnant wife was too distracting at home, lately full of demands and complaints.

He arrived carrying an old manual typewriter and a manila envelope of papers. He was wearing Bermuda shorts which disappointed me—Bermuda shorts in the early seventies? I would have preferred cut-offs. But his legs beneath their neat plaid hems were powerful, his calves muscular and tanned.

I set him up at a table in our finished basement because it was cool down there and the only room in the house with an air conditioner was my parents' bedroom. I sat at the dining room table with my typing book propped beside my new machine, practicing finger exercises to the tune of the electric hum. I'd flunked typing class in my junior year, enjoyed flunking a class that wouldn't affect my record. I despised the typing teacher, a skinny old biddy who sported white blouses with ruffled collars over her withered chest, her pipe cleaner legs encased in drooping stockings. She wouldn't let us use erasers or correction fluid and made us retype the entire page for every error. In meager rebellion, I failed. I ran into her in a drugstore a few months later and she grasped my arm with her bony fingers and begged me to retake typing. I leaned back from her intense, imploring gaze, the choking odor of talcum and lilac perfume. "It was the only way I supported my family during the Depression," she divulged. "If you can type, you'll never go hungry."

My dislike evaporated. The poor thing thought she was insuring my future. There, in front of the toothpaste display, I was certain I'd never have to settle for secretarial work like my teacher. I was meant for glories that remained vague and nameless. I would be Somebody. My bright mind and pretty face would carry me there. Or so I'd thought. Now I was teaching myself to type.

From time to time Patterson came upstairs and I refilled his glass of ice coffee. At noon he packed up his stuff and headed for a golf date, giving me a goodbye peck on the cheek.

I was confounded, Lila. I admit I sat at my typing exercises, one ear cocked for the scrape of a chair below, the weight of his feet on the stairs. I wondered if and when he would follow up that kiss in the car. I was willing. My life held nothing but a college I didn't want to go to. Patterson's morning visits had quickly become the focus of my day. I had nothing to do but wait for them, count the calories I consumed and expended, and drift in a heat-dazzled daydream that took on increasingly erotic turns.

When my father came home at night he cursed me for throwing away his moldy foods—his greening bologna and furry cottage cheese that he refused to relinquish. "Money doesn't grow on trees," he harangued, "not that you care. Some of us work for a living around here." When I heard his car in the driveway I hid in my room which was impossibly stuffy and hot. I listened to the thump of cabinets being opened and closed, his feet on the stairs, and then down the hall his air conditioner humming behind his closed door.

One day he came back unexpectedly from a dentist appointment in Boston, in time to see Patterson driving away in his Mustang.

"Who was that man?" my father demanded. "What was he doing here?"

"Just a friend visiting. Aren't I allowed to have friends?" I said, enjoying my father's suspicious glare.

It continued like that for a week or so, and then one day Patterson appeared before me in the dining room.

"I need a break," he said, stretching. "Why don't you show me the rest of the house?"

I gave him the tour. The den where my father presided: we weren't allowed to enter without permission if he was in there. It was the place where he forced us to make his phone calls for him, then challenged "Yeah?" into the receiver when the party answered, as though someone had called *him*. I showed Patterson my sister's old bedroom down the hall, the living room with the smooth avocado carpets and Japanese silk screen. I headed upstairs, aware of my body moving in front of his eyes, my cut-offs, bare legs and denimed bottom.

I showed him my bedroom, embarrassing in its eternal submission to my mother's decorative schemes: the same old mustard and olive and rust colonial wallpaper, the hand-painted furniture and prim twin beds. As neat as ever. Not a poster permitted to mar the walls. My brother's room, its focal point the old black and white TV they gave him when they bought a color set. My parents' room was last. I turned on the air conditioner, stood for a moment in front of its chilly breeze, arms outstretched. It was a dark room, the shades always drawn as my father liked them. My brother and I used to hide in here to study my father's *Playboy* magazines, giggling over "Little Annie Fanny" cartoons and the ones with the old lady whose long scrawny breasts pointed to her toes.

I looked past the dresser, holder of my mother's familiar things: a silver mirror tray, an embroidered miniature pillow quilled with stick pins, a pair of pinching silver earrings for un-pierced ears. Matching fussy lamps with silken shades, two portraits of Grecian maidens hanging in chipped plaster frames beside the mirror—her meager inheritance from her own mother. And in the mirror, my reflection, Patterson behind me, and behind him the stretch of my parents' king size bed.

I watched in the mirror as Patterson lifted the hair from my shoulders and bent to my neck. His lips made me shiver. His hands slid around to my still untouched breasts and in the mirror I saw that even at thirty-one he had creases on his tanned forehead, while my face was round, smooth, unlined.

"You're so pretty," he said, turning me to face him. "God, you're pretty."

I reached my arms up around his neck, searching his eyes for some clue to what this meant. He walked me over to the bed and leaned me slowly back onto the spread, his biceps curving as he supported my weight. His face loomed close to my own. He slid my tank top up over my bare breasts. His tongue lapped my belly and my head arched back. He groaned, "Ahhhhhh. Jesus."

Then he was kissing my face and for the first time I knew the softness of that skin on the inside of lips, the part that's always moist, the part you only feel when someone presses his lips against yours, the luscious intimacy of exploring what you never see. The tickle of his new mustache against my lips, his breath, sweetened by peppermint Lifesavers and a pungent undertone of coffee, his basketball-palming hands pressing my shoulders into the spread on my parents' bed.

His belt buckle cut into my groin as he lowered himself on top of me. So this was how it would be: a married man, a teacher. I felt no remorse, no guilt. I was the student, the teenager, and his wife was his business. It was like winning another contest, although this was an accomplishment my classmates couldn't know about. He pulled back to lift his own shirt and the breadth and heft of him, his golden furred chest with its solid muscling caught me by surprise. There seemed to be so much of him, so little of me, I felt out of my depth.

"What does your wife look like?" I asked abruptly. What I meant was, Why are you here? Was it just her pregnancy that had sent him to me?

He sighed, stroked my bony ribs. "Actually, she looks a lot like you. Long dark hair. Dark skin. Big dark eyes. She has big breasts, for what that's worth."

If he didn't think it was worth much, then why did he mention it? Mine were small, wouldn't even fully develop until I stopped starving, until I moved from underweight to overweight and grew an inch taller in the next year.

"Let's not talk about her right now," he said. He got up, brought a towel from my parents' bathroom, slid it under my hips to protect the spread. He fumbled for a condom in his pocket.

"It's okay," I said, waving the rubber away. I didn't say that I didn't ovulate, I was certain there was no way my hungry body could foster a child.

He unbuckled, unzipped his shorts, pulled down his bright patterned briefs. I saw her, his wife, in a department store, buying them, three to a package, choosing the color thoughtfully, her pregnant belly bulging against her shopping cart.

But then it hurt, it hurt all the way down my thighs and up into my belly. I gasped.

Patterson stopped, suspended above me. "You're a virgin," he said, surprised. "I didn't know."

Why didn't he know? "I never mentioned any boyfriends."

"I don't expect you've told me everything about your life. You always seemed so grown up, so sophisticated, I never guessed. And you said no to a condom."

"I'm on the pill," I lied, "just in case. Are you disappointed? I mean that I'm a virgin?"

He laughed. "God, no. Of course not. You're so cute sometimes. You've got so much ahead of you, sweetie. It'll be better for you next time, I promise." He lowered himself again, concentrated, kept pushing, like banging a log against a door, a battering ram. I bit my tongue, my lip. My mind lifted away from that alien thing, my body, laid out on the bed, and took a tour of the ceiling. Then I heard the air conditioner again as Patterson collapsed on top of me, and the machine cooled our sweat.

When he left I found blood in my panties and was stupid enough to think it meant I'd gotten my period at last.

I wasn't in love with your father, Lila, he was too ordinary, too straight, too content with his Bermuda shorts, his sports trophies, his golf, his adoring students. Maybe I did it for the knowledge I thought it promised, a taste of the world I deserved simply because I was bright, pretty, young—the world that had lately seemed out of reach. Or I did it because I was flattered. I did it because I wanted so badly to be valued by someone and he was my only friend.

No, no, no. I'm lying. Remembering it now, I feel a frustrating surge of desire for the young man he was then: the powerful calves, tanned legs with golden curly hairs beneath shorts. A man so healthy and cheerful and knowing. Or is it desire for the girl I was then: a seventeen-year-old who in wrapping her slender arms around this married man's back, this teacher, this messenger from the world of adulthood, believed I was just beginning to taste all the promises I was entitled to?

God, I'm so fucking jealous of the girl I was then, one who was so fervently, so meaninglessly wanted. The girl whose waist-length hair he wrapped around his palm, that gentle tug as he pulled my head back so my mouth would open, open, my parents' air conditioner whirring as heat transformed itself to ice. The cold condensation the counterpart to the sweat that ran from his chest onto the bikini shaded whiteness of my breasts. His chest, those wiry hairs I gritted between my teeth as he expertly, gently, considerately, forced his way in.

I'd like to kill him for it now, or fuck him, I don't know which, but he isn't that man/boy any longer. I saw his picture on the back of a history text—yes, he did do more than just teach high school, eventually—a thickened face, self-satisfied, the handsome smoothness blurred to bulk.

And I'm not that girl anymore, either.

He said it would be better next time, but there was no next time, not with him. Oh, he came back, not the next day but the day after, with his typewriter, kissing me on the cheek as he had before, going down to the basement to work. I spent the morning upstairs, pretending to type, surrounded by pages of erasable onionskin nonsense: "The quick brown fox. The quick brown fox jumps. Jmppus. Over the lzy dog..." all the while waiting for the moment when he would come upstairs and claim me.

When Patterson was done that day, he put his glass in the kitchen sink. I watched through the doorway that connected kitchen and dining room.

"Look, I've been thinking," he announced, leaning against the sink, studying his big blunt toes in his sandals.

"And?" I turned off my whirring typewriter.

He crossed his arms across his chest, walked to the dining room doorway, filled its space. "What I've been doing is wrong. It isn't fair to you, and it isn't fair to my wife. I've already blown one marriage and I don't want to blow this one. I shouldn't be doing this."

I nodded, agreed silently, numbly. My hands rested on the casing of the typewriter, and I could feel the mechanical warmth emanating through the metal. It was his show, always had been from the beginning. I didn't say, But what about the day before yesterday? Why could you want me then and not today? I wouldn't even think it until later. I pushed my chair back and stood up.

"God, you are pretty." He came over, wrapped his arms around me, smug with his nobility, even though I could feel his erection against my stomach. He must have thought he was strong, giving up a teenager who turned him on. Making the good decision. And I? I was fading, fading, into some darkness that covered all rage.

"I can't come back anymore. It isn't right. You need a boy your own age. Someone without encumbrances."

Of course, I nodded. Of course. You're right. Now he would return to his big-breasted, round-bellied pregnant wife who would soon open her legs to a hard round head and melt back to her own lovely self. While I, for the first time, no, surely not the first time, tasted the powerlessness that came with sex, the piece of you they took away again and again.

I stood out on the brick steps, one hand on the wrought iron railing, while he climbed into his red Mustang. My chest was hollowing, everything draining out of me like water seeping from the delicate underwear my mother left dripping on drying racks, or from the hot water bottle contraption she slung over the shower head. The emptiness was terrifying. He put the car in reverse, backed up, waved.

Idiot that I was, I waved back. When his car had disappeared

I stood in the middle of the kitchen. Now I had nothing; I possessed neither purpose nor definition. I wasn't special, it turned out. I was humiliated. I'd been caught wanting. That phrase can go two ways: caught wanting, as in trapped in desire, or caught wanting, as in lacking. I was both. I'd been tricked into desire and I'd also been found lacking, because if I'd been desirable enough, even his pregnant wife couldn't have drawn him back. This was just one more version of my father taking my horse away again and again or the colleges asking me to apply and then not letting me in. When they found out who I was, they didn't want me. Like Patterson. Fool, fool, fool. I could hear my father's voice: You thought you were a bigshot.

I looked around the kitchen dazed, as though I'd just been whacked in the head by a sailboat's boom and was left treading water as the boat cruised away. The big double-doored refrigerator loomed at me like a beacon, a lighthouse. I opened the left side. Of course there was nothing of interest—my father's horrible salamis and bolognas in the meat drawer, his moldy cottage cheese. I tried the freezer: Bingo. A frozen Sara Lee pound cake. Frozen waffles. And, I knew, there'd be brownie mix in the cupboard. The comforting familiarity made me want to weep. Or something did. But my emptiness roared in my ears, it had to be filled. When my guts ached and I finally leaned over the toilet I couldn't tell my screams from the retching. Only when blood vessels broke in my eyes did I allow myself to stop.

I skipped my high school graduation, drove by to glimpse a sea of blue gowns. I wrote suicide notes on my graduation typewriter and tore them up. Nature abhors a vacuum . . . one day I noticed Maurice La Fontaine sitting on our town green among his friends, with his curly auburn hair and shrewd green eyes, his soccer player's physique, and decided, in an instant's desperate recognition, that what I'd missed was a true high school experience. So what if we'd just graduated? Patterson was right: I needed a boy my own age. It was as though high school hadn't happened and I could go back to the era of that eighth grade dance before I'd begun to disappear.

I pursued him doggedly, ruthlessly, shamelessly. I showed up at his house to his parents' bewilderment. I invited him to take walks. Maurice was willing at first. As I suspected, he'd liked me all those years past. He confessed that he'd beaten up a boy in eighth grade who reported sitting in my backyard in the dark, watching me practice dancing with my reflection in the den window.

Walking the summer nights through the convent grounds where we'd played as children, he said I was the most competitive person he knew, so competitive I refused to compete. He gently chided me when I referred to Carol King's hit album "Tapestry" as being "mellow." Maurice agreed with Woody Allen that soon mellow things got over-ripe and began to rot. Maurice hated sloppy idioms; he preferred the language of mathematics, its elegance and precision.

Oh, we weren't so precise, though, when we grappled on my laundry-room floor—even if *he* did insist on condoms—or when my father came lunging down two flights of stairs to the basement rec room, wild-eyed, screaming that our music was keeping him awake. He threw Maurice out in a fit of jealousy. Years later when I looked him up in Cambridge, Maurice informed me that I had ruined sex for him for years, made it sordid. How could I, insubstantial I, have ruined anything for anyone?

After that, Maurice wouldn't answer my calls. That summer dragged on and yet, looking back, it seems that time speeds up. I lay in my own sweaty sheets and kicked in frustration. I ate. And ate. I couldn't seem to throw up anymore. I felt too sick when I tried. Nor could I starve. Everything that before had been so controlled—my body, my role as rejector of men, my college prospects—was spinning apart and I couldn't maintain one element without the others. I'd starve myself for a day or two and then break down. The weight packed on.

My father was revolted by my sudden gain; he offered me

money to buy "the right foods." I recognized his bribe and refused it. I needed a whole new larger wardrobe for college when I skulked off to Hartford in September. If I hadn't dropped out in October when it became clear even to me that I was pregnant, I would have flunked out anyway, since I couldn't stay awake through class. I knew nothing of progesterone and how it tires you in the first trimester, I only knew that I couldn't seem to get up, talk to my dull roommate, attend anything; I wallowed in a depression that went on and on.

The pregnancy came as an extension of my overall shame. Never again would I wear those little mini dresses. I was a whale, a sea lion, a manatee. The only satisfaction I got out of the whole ordeal was my father's fury. Not only had I humiliated him, but he lost a semester's college tuition when I dropped out. Too late for an abortion, I had to tell them.

This was when my mother offered her tales of being a virgin when *she* got married, about respecting *her* body.

My father was, as always, more direct. "You fucking stupid bitch," he said.

I couldn't help it. I smiled. I'd gotten him good.

But I didn't get you, Lila. I didn't get you.

CHAPTER 11

Lila lay awake long after her father went back to his room. She listened to the indistinct rumble of the nightly news on their TV and then noted the dimness in the hall when their light flicked off. She tried to sleep but couldn't. She needed to tell someone. She crept downstairs and shut herself in the den, turned on the desk lamp and dialed her Cambridge number. Across a dark continent the machine picked up and her own voice announced archly, "You've reached Lila and Marcia. You know what to do. So just do it."

"I'm doing it," Lila whispered into the receiver. "I'm going to look for my birth mother. Call you from Albuquerque."

She replaced the receiver. Having committed herself on tape, she felt queasy with doubt, exposed. Now if she didn't find out anything, or if it went badly, she'd have to talk about it. Lila turned off the desk lamp, sat in the dark, her bare legs chilled against the chair. She wished Marcia were home, tried to picture her out somewhere at, what was it? She flicked the light on, looked at the clock: 10:45. Flicked it off again. So it was close to 1 A.M. in Cambridge. Maybe Marcia was home but had slept through the message. Maybe she was at her boyfriend's. Marcia would approve of her search. She was all for people "coming to terms with their pasts."

Coming to terms. It sounded like a legal process. Something two corporations did through a mediator, or labor and management. Maybe that's what they'd have to do, her birth mother and she, find a mediator, come to terms, if the woman even wanted to know about her.

What if she had given birth to the child she'd aborted a few days ago and handed it over for adoption, what would she want to do twenty years from now? Would she search for it? Or would she rather live as though it had never happened? Maybe she would have followed the current trend, an open adoption, no mysteries beyond the unavoidable, every adopted child's query about what made them not worth keeping.

Lila's eyes adjusted and she deciphered the shapes of the den: the photographs on the wall, the shelves of books on aeronautics and military histories. On her father's otherwise austere desk, a flowery ceramic frame held a snapshot of Ruth and him. Her mother's touch. Lila peered at it, made out her parents leaning close and grinning over a cake. An anniversary? Birthday? She ought to know.

Lila winced. There was a time when she would have seen this picture as evidence that they didn't truly want her, were happier without her. But it wasn't so and never had been. Lately, she'd left them alone with each other far too much, detached herself because she didn't want to belong. And in doing so had punished them for nonexistent crimes. Lila fingered the cool frame. She thought for an instant of stealing it, tucking it into her bag.

Beyond the den window, a streetlight shone on black asphalt and lit the concrete driveway across the street. Lila sighed. Tomorrow she would start her new life, corny as that sounded. She would cast off months of indecision and a lifetime of vague unhappiness. She was ready to face the truth no matter what it offered. Then she could afford to be more generous with her parents. She'd make certain they knew she wasn't rejecting them by seeking out her birth mother. But how could she start a new life when she was still enmeshed in lies? Her father had asked her to deceive Ruth in the name of protecting her. She had lied to Kevin, directly and through omission. That was a Catholic sin, wasn't it, the sin of omission? She wanted to come clean, be freed from these falsehoods. She glanced at the phone on her father's desk. She could tell Kevin everything and really start fresh.

Of course, it was far too late to call him at his parents' house. She'd have to wait until five or six in the morning, when it was seven or eight at the McCarty house.

Lila closed her eyes and imagined punching in the familiar numbers. Waiting for one of Kevin's younger brothers or sisters to rouse him, his groggy "Hi."

"I'm going to Albuquerque," she'd tell him. "I just got some information about my birth mother and I need to check it out."

"Yah really think that's a good ideah?"

"Yeah, I do."

"Yah timing's a little weiyahd, but I guess yah gotta do what yah gotta do."

"That's right." She'd read censure in his tone, respond in kind. "You always accuse me of dwelling on it. You're never supportive. You want me to feel ashamed for wondering who gave birth to me, like it was immature or something to care."

"I just don't want yah to get hurt."

"It can't hurt me. It already hurt me a long time ago." She couldn't see how Albuquerque and whatever she learned there could make things any worse.

Kevin would sigh. "I don't know, Lila, maybe I just wanted yah to be happy with things the way they ah, happy with me. I didn't want any monkey wrenches thrown in. I guess I didn't know how much it meant to yah."

"You don't know me."

"Oh, I think I do, aftah three yeahs, Lila. Not every little tic, maybe, but I know who yah ah."

"No you don't. Kevin. There's a lot of things you don't know about me."

"Like what?"

"Like I had an abortion."

A pause. Then, "Whatevah yah did before we met doesn't mattah to me."

"No, I mean now. A few days ago. I wasn't sick with the flu like I said; I got an infection from an abortion."

"Jesus, Lila. Christ. Yah know how I feel about that. And yah didn't talk to me, didn't let me be a paht of it. That isn't fayuh. It was my child too."

"Maybe it was, maybe it wasn't. I had an affair, Kevin. I cheated on you."

"Lila, are yah just making this shit up fah some crazy reason?"

"I wish I were. But I'm not. He was..."

"Don't tell me. I don't even want to heah it."

"Kevin. I'm sorry."

Silence. And in that silence, terror like an invisible gas would invade her chest, seep into her throat.

"Don't go quiet on me. Goddamn it, Kevin. Yell at me. Tell me what a shit I am."

Then his voice, flattened. "I don't know what yah ah, Lila. I guess yah right. I don't know yah."

Was she crazy? Of course she couldn't tell him. She'd hurt him horribly and the timing couldn't be worse. She'd screw up his final exams. His scholarship depended on his grades. She couldn't be that selfish, risk his future, just to ease her soul.

Yeah, right. Maybe half of it was thinking about Kevin's welfare, and half was fear of burning her bridges, cutting her safety net. She needed him, needed his love beyond all reason. That wasn't the same as loving, though. She didn't know if she were afraid of losing the relationship or just afraid to suffer his desertion. Desertion. A funny way to put it, considering that she was the one who went to the Tara with Richard Warren. Yet that was how it would feel. She knew that much about herself.

But Kevin didn't know her. She couldn't let him.

Albuquerque, she would tell him about Albuquerque. She'd face his disapproval, if that's what he offered, and deal with it. She had a right to find out about her biological mother no matter what Kevin said. But that was all she'd tell him. The affair and the abortion she would tuck away, file in a cabinet under the title "my old life," the life of confusion she was trading for her newfound crusade. She smiled at the thought of herself as some whacked out Joan of Arc, in search of the Holy Mother Grail. She recalled that enormous painting in the Metropolitan. A peasant Joan in a backyard garden, pale eyes cast heavenward in a visionary trance, removed from all doubt.

Not likely. Once again, Lila tried to picture her phantom mother. It was like going on the blindest of dates with someone with whom you hadn't yet had an awkward phone conversation, whose interests you hadn't probed, searching for a common base on which to start a possible relationship. A blind date who might never show, who had already jilted you a lifetime ago. Would she even recognize her if they met?

She used to think she saw her mother everywhere.

Once, when she was riding an escalator, at Kresge's in Kansas City, and was how old, ten? Rudolph the Red Nosed Reindeer blared from speakers. Ruth stood behind her on the moving stairs. Lila idly studied the descending faces, fascinated by the remarkable ugliness of grownups. Then she glimpsed a short dark woman with straight eyebrows, the same brief arched nose as her own, the same thick lips. Nigger lips, the kids had called her on the playground in Georgia. The woman was the right age, not yet thirty. She wore a lavender down coat and carried a Marshall Fields shopping bag in one hand. Lila searched for a wedding ring but her mother's hand was covered by a black wool glove. Lila craned her neck as her mother rode past her.

Without a word to Ruth she headed down the up escalator, squeezing against the crowds.

"Lila," Ruth called. "Where are you going? You'll get lost..."

Lila kept pushing against the shearling front of a man with thick glasses, a woman carrying a toddler on her hip. "Now just a minute," the man complained, but Lila shoved past. The hordes were too thick; they wouldn't part. A roll of wrapping paper poked her in the eye. An elbow slammed her in the cheek. Her mother's dark hair receded, swept away by the crowds. She could see nothing but dark damp wool, parkas quilted into squares. Come back, come back, come back...

Lila searched futilely. She ran to an exit. Out on the sidewalk, shoppers' salt-stained boots churned last night's snow to slush. Her mother's lavender parka was nowhere to be seen. She'd lost her own wool beret and her ears were cold. Bereft, Lila went back inside the overheated store. Ruth found her crying in a ladies' room. "Stomach cramps," Lila lied, curtailing their shopping trip, sending them back to their hotel with a bottle of pink Pepto Bismol. Of course she couldn't tell Ruth she was crying because she'd lost her mother.

The next time it was Senorita Simpson, Lila's seventh grade Spanish teacher. Sophisticated and Bohemian, she'd studied in Madrid and vacationed in Mexico City. She dressed in black and cut her bangs punky; multiple earrings studded her lobes. "She must have worn something else to her job interview," Ruth commented after meeting Senorita Simpson on parents' night. One day she wore a lace mantilla to class, a flamenco costume, and stomped around the room with castanets. The boys snickered but Lila was smitten. She was slim and dark-haired and the right age. Sometimes, in the midst of verb conjugations, Senorita Simpson stopped by the classroom windows, her eyes dark and shadowed and distant, and Lila imagined that she was thinking of the child she'd given up, a child that would be just her age.

In bed, after Ruth came in to kiss her good night, Lila would invent strategies for revealing her birth date to Senorita Simpson. She'd watch for a reaction, know if it were true. She waited after class one day, pretending to need help with an assignment, and offered to carry her teacher's books to the parking lot. Leaning against Senorita Simpson's blue VW bug, Lila asked, abruptly, "Do you have any kids?"

"You know what Senorita means," her teacher said, opening the car door and tossing in her texts and sheaves of student papers. "I'm not a Senora, Lila."

Lila glanced at the messy pile of papers already sliding off the VW's tiny back seat, and it came as revelation that a teacher might not hold student assignments sacred, might in fact have a whole other life besides the one she'd always assumed for them, in which they left school and went straight home to apply themselves to grading papers and forging lesson plans all night.

Senorita Simpson cocked her head. "You're different from these kids," she said. Then she touched Lila's cheek with one slender finger. "Stay that way," she advised. She winked and folded herself in behind the wheel.

Lila felt both honored and dismissed.

Senorita Simpson ended Lila's conjectures by getting herself fired from the Fairlee County School Department for having an affair with a high school junior. A female high school junior. The scandal buzzed through classrooms and was savored at parties on the base for quite some time. Lila had to readjust her explanation for Senorita Simpson's wistful window gazing. Although she missed her spirited teacher, who was replaced by grandmotherly Senora Garcia, she was aghast at the thought that one of her classmates could have witnessed that fleeting parking lot touch. She knew she'd barely escaped the title "lesbo" which they bandied about when talking about Senorita Simpson. She even felt guilty for missing Senorita, for having imagined for a moment that they were allies in their difference. Lila quit seeking her mother in strangers.

Well, at least she finally had something real to go on. Her mother had been a teenage Jewish girl from the East Coast. Lila pictured the stereotypes: a spoiled Princess from Long Island with a personal phone line; a bespectacled oboist from the High School of Performing Arts who'd made it with the bassoon player but didn't want to mess up her future at Julliard. Christ. What did it matter? Whoever that girl had been then, twenty-one years ago, she was someone else now.

Again, Lila felt a bloom of rage that her parents hadn't told her what they'd known. How could she believe they didn't know more? Hypocrite, she chided herself. You're one to talk. She didn't occupy a moral high ground. Only Kevin did, and she'd diminished him by her deception. You could do that to a person, she realized, weaken him in your eyes through your own misdeeds, even though he remained the same good-hearted, upright guy he'd always been. It wasn't fair, yet it was unavoidable. And it sucked.

Lila flicked on the light again, checked the clock. Past eleven now, two hours later back east. She'd call from the road, or once she got to Albuquerque. If she wasn't going to come clean with Kevin, then there was no rush. She needed sleep. She had a long drive tomorrow. Shivering, Lila flicked off the light and climbed the carpeted stairs.

CHAPTER 12

This is how it goes. There's a phone in the kitchen of the Bodhi, but I can't bear to make this call while in the background the students chop onions or clean the oven. I choose, instead, to stand outside the Mercantile, a coffee shop/mini-grocery, in the center of Jemez Springs. It's only a minute walk from the Bodhi. The phone has no booth; it's planted in front of a cement wall that separates the irrigation ditch from the parking spaces. Traffic rolls by slowly. The speed limit is only 25 mph and cops come down heavy here. Across the street is Los Ojos, the bar busy in the middle of this bright mountain day. They are putting a second story deck on it and hammers bang away.

I punch in my credit card number, then the number of the private agency that arranged the adoption. I have had this number for three years, and never once called. I accepted the rules as my uncle explained them, was too confused and scared to fight them. Until your twenty-first birthday, which is today.

Three rings and a voice, female, slightly Spanish inflected answers, "Sandia Family Associates. May I help you?"

My breath ragged now, as though I'm climbing that hill again, as afraid of this voice as I was of phantom cougars.

"Yes, please. Uh. Yes. My name is Allison Heller? Twenty-one years ago I gave birth to a child, a girl, and your agency arranged an adoption." Words coming fast now. Tourists, a middle-aged couple, she in oversized pastel cotton zipper jacket, he in visored cap, unlock the doors to their Saturn. I turn my back to their engine noise, their discussion of heartburn and green chile stew. A finger in one ear.

"I understand that I can leave some written material with you, in the file, I mean, about myself, for my daughter, in case she wants to, uh . . . find me?" Ending weakly, my voice rising as though it is a question.

"Yes, that is permissable."

"So, is there anything there for me? Did she leave something?" I'm pleading with this stranger, making myself desperate, pathetic.

"I'm sorry, we can't give out information over the phone. You can mail in your materials, with the appropriate identification, that would be your birth certificate, social security number, photo ID., and we can mail you a copy of any materials, if there are any, to the appropriate address."

"But I'm here now! I mean, in New Mexico. I could drive in right away and drop them off, and see what's in the file, if there's anything I mean. Could you look in the file, and just let me know?"

"I'm sorry, we can't give out information over the phone. Company policy. There's no way to tell who we're talking to. There's legal consequences."

"Okay, okay, fine. I'm in Jemez Springs. I'll be down in an hour and a half. How do you get there from the interstate?"

I can't drive fast enough, but I know that it's one big speed trap between Jemez Springs and Bernalillo. I saw the local and state cops all along the road driving in. I imagine being pulled over, telling a trooper, "I'm going to find my daughter!" And the cop saying, "Sure, sure, never mind."

But I'm not. I mean, if she's left nothing for me I'll know nothing more than I know now. These private agencies have their own rules. I fantasize about knocking the secretary flat, ransacking files until I find yours, Lila. An address, a phone number.

I pass The Red Rocks, where Indians from Jemez Pueblo sell

fry bread against a gorgeous backdrop of surreal red cliffs. Across the street is the gas station/convenience store they've added. The Pueblo appears unchanged since my last stay, but for the proliferation of single- and double-wide mobile homes. The spine of the Naciemento Mountains rises behind it. This is the southernmost tip of the Rockies, pretty but not particularly lofty; the Rockies peter out here. Even in extremis, I can't help playing the travel writer.

In San Ysidro, gypsum dust soars heavenward off White Mesa; there's a gypsum mine up there. And pumice, gouged out for stone-washing jeans. All in the midst of dinosaur bones. I read in the paper that some little boy dug up a 150 million-year-old dinosaur eggshell in his Albuquerque back yard during a family cook-out. For what that's worth.

I've got the radio tuned to a Santa Fe rock station which loses its static as I turn onto Rte. 44 and head southeast, my fingers numb on the steering wheel. They play Tori Amos' cover of Springsteen's "I'm On Fire," her voice ragged with lust. Is her version meant to be gay? Erotic longing seems so foreign to me right now, an emotion belonging to aliens. But I can relate to the yearning.

There's a woman in my birth mothers' group who confessed that when she finally met her son she immediately fell in love with him, actually wanted to sleep with him. I was shocked. I suspected she'd confused their similarity of appearance and gesture with that frisson of affiliation that accompanies new romantic love.

Yes, Lila, I have loved men. It just didn't last very long.

I whizz around big gypsum trucks, the Texans and Californians toodling along in their oversized sedans. A dead coyote lies belly up on the side of the road. The Sandia Mountains block the eastern sky, a giant blue wall over 10,000 feet high. I pass Zia Pueblo—referred to by the inhabitants of Jemez Pueblo as "The Ants" because their village sits on a hill instead of down in the river valley—then through the Santa Ana reservation and alongside the hideous spread of Rio Rancho development (where you too can own your own home for $49,OOO, according to the billboards) climbing the mesa and sucking up Albuquerque water until it hits Indian lands and can't grow further. To the south, a balloon drifts through smog.

Bernalillo is just an annoying set of stop lights to me. A drive-through liquor store. Pizza Hut, Subway, McDonald's, Taco Bell. Then I-25, where you can go 7O, 75, 8O mph and no one cares. The cottonwoods along the Rio Grande have greened in the week I've been in Jemez, and beyond the Rio Grande, the houses of Corrales and Rio Rancho stretch on and on, beige dust rising from scraped earth. Lila, I know it's improbable, yet I feel that I'm coming to you, closer, close—I can't believe you don't want to find me too.

Sandia Family Associates is located downtown in a shabby building with an inoperative elevator. I rush the two flights of stairs past dingy texturized sheetrock walls, hollow core doors. I knock and turn the handle at the same time. But it's locked. A young woman in narrow black skirt, heels, V-necked red sweater lets me in.

"Allie Heller," I say, breathlessly. "I spoke to you, or somebody, about an hour and fifteen minutes ago."

"Why don't you sit down," she says, gesturing toward a low beige couch, the kind you have to struggle to get out of. I clutch my Lila document, my pages, to my chest. I've included a photo of myself, not that great a picture, but I didn't want to try to glam it up. Just me, staring face front, with a half-smile. Friendly. Welcoming, I hope.

The secretary returns to her desk and buzzes a button on her phone. "Daisy? Mizz Heller is here. Okay." She hangs up, turns to me, no eye contact, just business. "Can you show me your identification now please?"

I leap up like a dog released from the command to sit. I want to wag myself all over her legs, but merely draw out the papers and the card from my wallet. "Fine," she says, and returns to some task at her desk, eyes on a computer screen.

I stand there stupidly, for a moment, then go back to the couch and wait until Daisy, improbably named, appears. She is an extremely heavy woman in a light-blue knit top that doesn't even try to hide the roll of her enormous, shapeless breasts and belly. Matching sweat pants underneath. Short masculine grey hair. The hirsuteness I've noticed on many grossly obese women: furry arms and chin stubble. It must disrupt some hormonal balance.

"Ms. Heller," she says, "why don't you come with me?" She is carrying a manila folder just as I pictured. I try to judge its significance the way we judged those college letters: fat meant acceptance, thin rejection. But that's ridiculous. All I need here is a name, a phone number, an address. Some word that you won't mind my seeking you.

For all my eagerness, terror rises up in equal parts. It's getting too real, suddenly, and I find myself starting to check out a bit, the linoleum floor, black and white squares, locking me into its pattern, until the white rises up and floats above the black.

Breathe, I command myself. Breathe.

Daisy leads me into her tiny office. Photos of pale-haired, heavy children abound, grinning, stuffed into communion dresses and graduation robes.

"This is rather awkward," Daisy says.

Lila, you don't want me to find you. You refuse me, just as I refused you so long ago. I am sinking, sinking.

"We notified your parents immediately. We just assumed . . ." She studies her folder. "Of course, I wasn't employed here at the time. I'm probably about the same age as you are." She smiles, kindly. She knows my age, down to the day.

"Notified them of what?" What business was Lila's decision of theirs?

"I'm sorry, Ms. Heller, but no adoption ever took place. The child died three days after birth. Heart failure, it says here." She lays down the folder. "Your parents were notified immediately." Daisy opens her hands, coming up empty. She has nothing else to offer.

"What?" I shake my head like some sitcom stooge.

"I'm sorry," Daisy repeats.

"Are you sure?" I ask dumbly. My heart is beating in some odd rhythm that isn't mine. I've got that familiar sensation of time slowing down, like when I was a kid and my horse stepped in a hole while galloping through a meadow; I went somersaulting through the air, my head filled with nothing but a swirl of wildflowers.

"Positively. Would you like me to get you some water? A cup of coffee?"

But I am running down the dark staircase and out to the street, squinting in shocking brightness. I cross the street to a jazzily landscaped plaza, brick everywhere and a stupid bronze cowboy sculpture, larger than life: Civic Art.

It isn't possible. Isn't. A filing error. No. I know that you exist, Lila, because I have dreamed you, imagined you, felt you all these years. I've seen your breath in the rise and fall of oceans, heard your cry in babies on the street, felt the tug of milk in my teenage breasts.

This isn't possible. And what does it mean they notified my parents immediately? Twenty-one years and my mother and father never saw fit to tell me? Bastards. No, but it can't be true. I stop at a flat, backless bench. My spurt of energy vanishes and I am suddenly exhausted. I want to stretch out on the bench like some bum; I don't care if muggers and gangs wander the streets.

Shit. Shit. This is big. This is trouble. A genuine therapeutic emergency. I crumple as a mother pushing a stroller passes by, her voice too loud, proud in her Mommyhood, "Tasha, Tasha, don't put that in your mouth, honey. Mommy'll get you a cracker instead."

It isn't until I'm in the car again that I can scream. It's always been my favorite place for screaming. No one can hear you. Who cares if the lowrider passing in his customized Camaro glances over and sees a Munch painting at the wheel of a rental car? But where to go? I've got to go back to the Bodhi to get my things, there's no reason to hang around here anymore. For a moment I consider just heading to the airport, forgetting about whatever I've left in my Bodhi room. I know I'll never be back. But I head for 25 North because I need to stay in motion. An airport waiting lounge is definitely *not* what I need right now. Maybe the cocktail lounge, where I could drink margaritas and make up some alternate life for the Texas businessman who is sure to sit beside me and offer to buy a drink, at least until he sees my red-rimmed eyes.

At a light before the on-ramp to 25, a homeless family has set up camp. A child is sobbing, his ragtag mother pressing him to her chest, patting his back, while holding a "Will Work For Cash" sign. An older boy digs busily in the dirt beside the light post. This world is just too fucking pitiful to stand. "At least you have your kids," I want to shout ridiculously at the homeless mother.

The light turns green and I lurch up the ramp and merge into interstate traffic. I accelerate to speed, my hands and feet automatic and calm, while I scream, "Why didn't you tell me? How dare you not tell me? How could you let me think . . ."

Ahead, to the right and left, the vastness mocks me. The Sandias jut, prickling with great thumbs of rock; to the west the wasteland of development heads toward defunct volcanoes, then there's nothing but scrub mesa to Gallup. Redondo Peak rises to the northwest in the Jemez. Red rock and cactus, ponderosa pine. A sky clear in its enormity, as blank as the ocean. A landscape that won't permit lies.

I think my mother deserves a call right now.

CHAPTER 13

It was under four-hundred miles to Albuquerque from Colorado Springs, less than a day's drive but enough time for Lila to create a hundred different scenarios, from Hallmark reunion to a Kafkaesque immersion in a red tape labyrinth. She kept the music loud. Southern Colorado's east slope undulations gave way to Raton Pass, a rat's ass passway into New Mexico. She'd never been here—wait, of course she had, only she wasn't old enough to remember.

The Land of Enchantment, the road sign touted. Lowriders in Las Vegas, New Mexico, cactus in the overgrazed mesaland. I-25 whipping around Santa Fe, only sixty miles to go. Lila's throat tightened, her chest began to feel weighted and her breath shorter as she closed in. Four in the afternoon. Her little Datsun's engine ticking along. Thunderheads bloomed over the Jemez Mountains on her right, the Sangre de Cristos behind her. The Sandias rose up to the immediate south. Craggy and upright facing west, a long sloping eastern side.

It was peculiar to think of herself driving into town, cruising the motel strips and picking out some base camp. It wasn't as though she'd ever spent any time alone in motels. Stay away from eastern Central Ave. near the Air Force Base, her father had warned. It's a bad part of town.

She could get a paper, look up who was playing at the clubs, take herself to a movie, or failing that kind of energy and courage, huddle in some carpeted room smelling of synthetic bedspreads, synthetic drapes, her back to the motel art, eyes on the TV screen to avoid thinking about what she might find out, if anything, tomorrow, at Sandia Family Associates. She could order in Mexican.

She passed the exits for La Cienega, Cochiti Lake, Algodones, and then, only twenty miles out of town her trusty little Datsun quit humming its steady tune. The heat gauge began to climb precipitously and the oil light came on.

"Shit," Lila exclaimed. "Shit, shit, shit." She veered toward the breakdown lane and hit the brakes. Smoke or steam, some grey cloud, enveloped the hood. Lila snapped off her tape. "Goddammit." She smacked the steering wheel.

Only inches away, tractor trailers roared by, her little Japanese tin box lurching in their wakes. Now what? Lila got out of the car, lifted the hood as though she'd have the faintest idea of what she was looking for, and left it up. Maybe some trooper would stop. She'd have to use up her motel funds, the last of Richard Warren's extortion money, and maybe whatever her parents would send, to get this thing towed somewhere and fixed. Wouldn't you know it would be out in the middle of fucking nowhere?

The thunderheads, which had been gathering force, blocked the afternoon sun. A strong wind bent the sage and wild alfalfa that grew beyond the blacktop verge. Caught tumbleweed struggled to free itself from a barbed wire fence. Lila hugged herself, suddenly chilled. The first big raindrops splatted against the car hood and dented the dust at her feet. Lila got back in the car to wait it out.

Twenty minutes later the rain still beat down. Lila leaned her head back against the seat and closed her eyes. A minute later, she jerked awake. Someone was rapping on her window. She peered up at a guy in a soaking sweatshirt, smiling in at her. No uniform, not a trooper. Rain dripped off the visor of a baseball cap. She unrolled her window half an inch. "Yeah?"

"What's the problem?" he asked. "Maybe I can help."

"I doubt it," she said. "I think it's dead."

"You just going to sit there and wait for some tow truck to wander down I-25?" He was still smiling.

"You got a better suggestion?"

"Let me take a look."

"Be my guest," Lila said. Maybe, though it didn't seem likely, it was something minor, some essential hose or something had just slipped out of place, and could be repaired by a drive-by Samaritan with a screwdriver and electric tape.

He disappeared behind the lifted hood and Lila, although it disgusted her to be so susceptible, snuck a look at herself in the rearview mirror. She stuck her tongue out at her reflection.

He reappeared wiping his greasy hands on his sweatshirt pockets. By this time, Lila had cranked her window down a few more inches.

"Looks terminal," he said. "Blew a rod'd be my guess."

"Great. Shit."

He stuck out a hand. "My name's Steve. Let me give you a ride to a garage. You headed into town?"

Lila rolled the window down the rest of the way and shook hands. "Lila. I'm going to Albuquerque, yeah."

"Come on. I know a decent garage that can send out a wrecker." While she deliberated—it wasn't exactly her preference to get in some stranger's car but there didn't seem to be too many options—an eighteen wheeler roared by, sending up a tsunami wave. Steve got nailed against the back of his legs. He gestured angrily at the truck's wake. "Same to you, buddy."

"I'm really sorry," Lila said. "You better just go on ahead." This was getting embarrassing.

"Forget it, it's just water." He smiled again. "So, you coming?"

"I guess I better." Lila rolled her window up, grabbed her bag out of the back seat, locked the doors, and ran through the downpour to a white, sixties Impala parked behind her Datsun. Steve leaned across his seat and opened the door for her. She settled in, her bag clutched on her lap although he offered to put it in back for her. She studied her rescuer as he peered through the rain-runneled window, trying to negotiate a path back into the traffic. He wasn't bad-looking. She couldn't tell what his hair was like under the hat, but he had nice Sam Shepherd-ish lines in his cheeks. No ring on the wedding hand which rested on the wheel. Dark eyes. She caught the title off a tape on the dash: Waylon Jennings. Oh, well.

"So," he said, easing into the line of cars. "You just drive all the way from Massachusetts or something?"

Where'd that come from, she wondered, then remembered that he as well as anyone else going by could see the plates on her now abandoned car. "Stopped off in Colorado to see my folks."

"Unh-huh. Visting in Albu-turkey?"

So much for wit. "I've got some business to take care of."

"You want me to take you to a garage first, or to wherever you're staying?"

She didn't know where she was staying. Although he seemed harmless enough, she didn't want to ask him to recommend a motel. "A garage, I guess. I can get a cab from there."

"You bet," he said.

"You always go out of your way to help stranded motorists?" Lila asked, feeling duty-bound to make conversation. She really just wanted to get to some motel, soak in a tub, figure out what to do with the car later, but she owed him that much.

"Only when they look like you," he said.

Lila rolled her eyes. Oh, brother. "You couldn't see what I looked like. You were behind me."

"Just 'cause I stopped didn't mean I'd've stayed around," he said. He turned to give her his smile again, then clapped his hand on her jeans-covered knee.

Lila stared at the hand a moment; he wore an oversized class ring. High school, probably. Shit, wouldn't you know it. Some horny bastard who thinks if he stops for you, you owe him something. "I appreciate your help," she said while reaching down to remove his hand. "But I think you've got the wrong idea here."

"No," he said pleasantly, "I don't."

A sign announcing Bernalillo in one mile whizzed by.

"Look," Lila said, "I think I'd just like to get out at the next exit. I can probably find a garage there."

"You don't want to go there," the driver said. "Oh no no no. It's a dump. Too many Mexicans. Back in Texas where I come from, we keep them where they belong. Here they think they own the place."

"Well they do, don't they?" Lila snapped. "I mean, they were here before the Anglos arrived." Racist asshole.

"Whoa now just wait a minute. What's this liberal bullshit you're pulling on me? Are all you East Coast chicks full of this bleeding heart crap?" He turned and squinted at her. "Or are you one of 'em?"

Hispanic, he meant. She considered saying yes, just to see if he'd squirm. Or add the familiar idiocy, "no offense." She could see she'd picked herself a real winner. "Just forget it," Lila muttered. The ramp to the exit loomed ahead. "I'd like to get out here. In Bernalillo."

"I said I'd take you into Albu-turkey and I will."

"Fine." She'd make up some place for him to drop her, any place, the first restaurant or motel she saw. The first garage or gas station. Lila leaned back against the red vinyl seat, gripping her canvas bag. She looked out the window as the Bernalillo exit flew by. The rain had stopped, and the sun blazed again as they whipped past a lumber company, stacks and stacks of greenish pressure-treated lumber, a tiny cemetery cut off by the highway, the graves garish with plastic wreaths and bouquets. A second Bernalillo exit. The Sandia Indian reservation: new government housing up close to the highway, a huge bubble tent casino and a sign advertising "Las Vegas Style Gambling."

"So," Steve said, his voice light again, "after we get your car taken care of, how about you and me going out for some supper? Or a drink? We could have some fun, go dancing . . ."

Christ, what a creep. He thought he could insult her one minute and ask her out the next. But he was obviously a loose cannon, one she'd better humor. "That's nice of you to ask,"

Lila said carefully, "but I've been driving all day and I think I'd really just like to take a shower and get some rest, you know?"

"No," Steve said, "I don't know. I know you're just blowing me off. Where do you get off getting all high and mighty with me? Think you're better'n me, don't you?"

Oh, brother. She should have just said, Sure. Sure I will, then ditched him. Lila stared down at her sneakered feet. A sign announced, "Albuquerque next fifteen exits." Another bragged about the world's longest tramway. Okay. A few minutes and she'd get rid of him.

"Got you pegged, don't I? You don't mind taking a ride with some loser, huh? But you'd never say yes if I came up to you in a bar and asked you for a dance."

How could she have thought Sam Shepherd? He looked more like De Niro in *Cape Fear*.

"I'm just tired," Lila protested. "Really." She had to be diplomatic, avert a scene. "Maybe we can do it another time, Steve. Maybe tomorrow. You give me your number and I'll call you."

"You think you're pretty fucking smart, don't you? Call me, right." He replaced his hand on her knee and gave it a savage squeeze. Lila's breath caught in her chest and her eyes filled. Her mind spun like a revved up engine thrown into neutral.

"Just let me out right here, pull over. Right here. Right now. I mean it."

"I mean it," he mocked in falsetto. He swung into the left lane for the entrance to I-40 east. Santa Rosa, the sign said. East.

"What are you doing?" The world was tilting, going strange on her, the desert light dizzying. "I don't want to go east! I want to get out! Pull off the road!"

"Shut up."

Lila looked around the car wildly. She turned in her seat, wondering if there was something back there heavy enough to whack him with. A few beer cans. A pair of jeans. Running shoes. They were going slowly enough now on the curving ramp that maybe she could just open the door and jump out. She reached for the door handle, but Steve's fist knocked her head against the passenger window. Her vision blurred with the impact, a zigzag of light.

"Now just settle down," Steve instructed. He spoke pleasantly, as though to a child. But beside his thigh, on the car seat, a knife had appeared in his palm.

Lila froze against the door. Her temple and cheekbone ached, but that was a distant pain, one that belonged to someone else. Her heart crashed in her chest, obliterating all sound, and her breath snagged in her throat. She was into something now, way over her head. She had to think. There had to be a way out of this. Without moving from the door, she flicked her eyes toward the lanes of traffic as they merged onto I-40. A steady stream of cars, trucks, semis on both sides, a veering smoking sedan. Oblivious, all of them. Going about their lives, thinking of their dinners, their jobs . . .

"Now you just behave yourself," Steve said. He flicked the knife blade gently with a fingernail. "Enjoy the scenery." It was a narrow knife, with a bone handle.

Kevin, Lila thought. Kevin. Please. Help me. I'm sorry, I'm sorry. I didn't mean to. The landscape blurred past: big egg-shaped boulders tumbling down the slope in Corneuil. An enormous cement factory in Tijeras. A sign for the Sandia Crest Ski Area. And then the east slope of the Sandias flattening away to the high plains of Moriarty, Edgewood. At this higher altitude, wildflowers and clumps of grass grew amidst the sage.

"Listen," Lila said, launching into an absurd babble she was helpless to stop, "I didn't mean to insult you, Steve. Really. We just got off on the wrong foot here, let's start again . . . we could go somewhere tonight, have some drinks . . ."

"You can't insult me, sweetheart. You know why? 'Cause you're nothing. You don't even exist anymore. You're just a story in tomorrow's paper."

Mommy, Lila cried. Mommy. Mommy. Mommy. She

squeezed her eyes shut, and Ruth appeared, pale, freckled, snatching her up from the undertow with her strong, soft arms; piebald wild ponies thrashed through waves, their manes flowing, legs pumping, swimming toward a receding shore.

The Impala screeched off the highway onto a gravel road, rattled over a cattle guard between barbed wire fencing, then bumped over ruts toward a deep ravine which held railroad tracks. He pulled her kicking and crying toward it. Soon the train would come, its big front light blazing through daylight, its force shaking the ground, pushing its klaxon before it, the sound so loud that no one would hear when she screamed.

Stop. Stop here.

Just stop.

This isn't how it happened. I have created your death, Lila, because I had no control over it, because I didn't get to hold you when you died and I don't know, won't ever know who, if anyone, did. I want to think someone unplugged you from the monitors, held you.

I gave you the death I escaped so many times. On highways. Boats. I hooked a ride on freighter leaving a dark dock in Alaska one midnight, fought off the old captain's embrace. I went anywhere with anyone and believed it didn't matter. I threw myself in the path of that train, into the arms of strangers who weren't sick enough or in the mood to do me that particular kind of harm, although they left their marks.

A man who put his fingers to my throat, began to strangle me when he came. Another crashed the little skiff we rode in, but I bobbed to the surface; he was the one who drowned. At eighteen I rolled over twice in a van in Glenwood Canyon, saw the Colorado River swirling green below, and came to rest on a guard rail. Two feet to the left there was none. I crawled out of that battered van to shout curses at the gawkers. And the man who was driving me, he died too. Not there, Lila, but years later, by his own hand, while I survived and survived and survived.

I gave you my death because I can't accept that you had your own without me.

Who held you when you died? Where is the body? My arms pimple up with goosebumps at the horror. I put on the windshield wipers as though a cloudburst has smeared the glass but it is my useless tears making me veer toward the breakdown lane. And then as if I had the power to summon it, one of the big puffy thunderheads that are gliding to the north darkens and rain, then clattering hail, starts battering the windshield. I pull over, my flashers flashing, not caring if I'm about to cause an accident, destroy a family of six on their way to Gramma's who aren't looking and will slam into my bumper at sixty-five.

I picture it: some monitor buzzer going off, a nurse hustling in, maybe some neonatal cardiac team thumping away on your tiny newborn's chest covered with gluey electrodes, or maybe it was different, the buzzer sounds, a lone nurse unhooks you, holds you in her arms until you take your last gasping little breath. God, please let someone have held her. Please please please.

How did they dispose of you? Did they put you into some bin of medical waste like an abortion? A homeless, parentless child, one whose papers I signed. Surely there was no one to pay for a funeral. Or did Mom and Dad take care of that too?

Shit, I just can't stand it. I can't stand it. I'll never be able to stand it. But even as I say it I know it's a lie. Of course I'll stand it. I'm crying over a child who's been dead for more than twenty years. A child I held once, like the baby of some acquaintance, jiggle jiggle then pass it back. The idea of a child.

I'm crying over the loss of the you I thought I might meet. It's a theoretical loss. But I knew you, Lila, down to your moles and shoe size. I knew you because I created you. Twice.

I really can't stand it.

The hail stops as abruptly as it began. A mocking technicolor rainbow appears over the Rio Grande Valley, linking the Sangre de Cristos with the Jemez mountains. Shakily, I pull onto the interstate, blinkers flashing until I reach the Bernallilo exit and head west on Highway 44.

CHAPTER 14

I stop to use the outside phone at the McDonald's on Highway 44, just past the I-25 off-ramp. The phone cubby stands beside the iron fence of an outdoor playland where shrieking children disappear inside huge jointed plastic tube slides and plexiglass bubbles. Their fry-nibbling mothers sit placidly at umbrella tables, assured that any second now their offspring will reappear. In such close proximity to all this unalarmed motherhood I have to turn my back, hunch over the phone as though gutshot.

The phone rings in a disturbingly familiar tone. My hands are shaking, my breath quick.

"Hello?" she says. Her voice sounds uncertain, querulous.

"Mom?"

I can read her silence perfectly.

"Allie." The tone is flattened, stiff. I suppose that underneath it she's glad to hear from me, but she can't show it. It's been three years.

"I'm in Albuquerque, Mom."

"I see."

"Remember Albuquerque, Mom? The place you guys sent me to have my baby."

"Why are you calling, Allie?" She is suspicious now, wary of whatever it is I'm going to lay on her.

"The baby that *died*, Mom. The baby you never told me died." If she hangs up I'll kill her. But instead she expels a tight breath.

"So you found out."

"Yeah, I found out, because I went to the adoption agency to see if I could find her, and they had to be the ones to tell me, no thanks to you, after twenty-one years, that she didn't exist." The rage leaps up like a nasty little pitbull going for my throat. "How the fuck do you think you had the right to keep that from me? What the fuck were you doing?" I'm screaming now, crying, and a mother sitting at the closest table lifts her coffee, her unwrapped burger, and hustles her kids away.

"It was for your own good," my mother asserts. "You were acting so peculiar even before the pregnancy, and I thought you were too fragile to hear anything bad right then."

"So what about the other twenty-one years?" Was I acting peculiar then too? Probably, but that's no excuse. "You made my whole life a lie, Mom. You fucking stole my life."

"Calm down, Allie. Remember when we had to have your cat put to sleep? You were too young to hear that, so we told you she'd been adopted. Sometimes parents just have to make these judgment calls. Believe me, Allie. It was for your own good."

"Jesus fucking Christ, Mom. For my own good? This wasn't a cat, and I wasn't nine-years-old. It was my only child and I had a right to know!"

"I suppose I meant to tell you later, when you were more . . . stable, and then so much time passed it just seemed better to leave it alone. You never asked."

What was to ask? The kid was adopted. Supposedly they didn't know anything else. She wants to make it my fault that she never told me my kid was dead, my fault because I didn't ask. I can't believe it, but of course I can. She'll always have an answer that protects her from blame. She has to cover her flanks from a daughter with sharp teeth and a bitter tongue.

"You've taken everything away from me, everything, both of you. You never wanted me to have anything." It's a child's protest, not even rational, and I'm reduced here, sobbing, hiccupping, afraid that a McDonald's manager will show up in his little uniform with Security to drag me away.

"How can you say that?" my mother says quietly. "I always wanted the best for you kids. Especially you. The move to Massachusetts. That was for you, Allie. I knew you needed a more challenging school. I took a lot of grief from your father for that, and I stuck up for you all the time. I don't have to listen to this now. I've come too far to listen to this. All *you* ever do is tell me what I've done wrong. Don't you think it's time you got over licking your wounds and got on with it? You think it was easy on me in that house? Sure, there are some things I would have done differently. Everyone makes mistakes. Everyone. You're just lucky you don't have a child to point yours out to you all the time. A child who thinks nothing of cutting you off for three years and then calling out of the blue with recriminations."

"Oh, I'm lucky. Real lucky." I sink to the cement walkway, let the phone dangle. Somewhere, thousands of miles away, my mother's tiny voice says, "Allie? Allie?"

I lean my back against the fake brick wall. A balding man in a pale windbreaker and nylon slacks glances away from me as he swings open the door, headed for his chicken McNuggets.

Wasn't that what all of this was leading to, Lila? Meeting you so that you could point out my horrible mistake? This no-win game, either way we'd lose. It would have been a mistake to keep you, a mistake to give you up, and still, it turns out, I would have lost you anyway. And now it's all just one big helix of lies: the lie of denying your existence those early years and then the lie of your imagined, unlived life without me; the lie I constructed and probed like sticking a tongue in an aching tooth, losing you over and over again every birthday, every holiday. The lie of looking for you in faces that could never, it turns out, have been yours.

All that exists of you is this document, a travel writer's record of a journey never taken.

It was a shitty awful trick they played on me. I want to beat my mother with the truth, my only weapon. I dial back.

"Allie?" my mother says before I speak.

"Your father killed himself, you know." The evil words fill my mouth as rich as marzipan, as sickening. "I thought you should know. For your own good."

"I know that," she says quietly.

"You know?" I'm stunned.

"Your father told me a long time ago. I can still see the look on his face. Like a bully on a playground. 'I know something you don't know.' You sound just like him."

Like him? The worst of insults, and one of my greatest fears. The last time I saw him, five, six years ago, I was visiting his house at the Cape. In front of the shingled post office, he sat behind the wheel of his car, reading mail. An acquaintance hailed him, but he continued to pick through envelopes. "Dad," I said, tugging his sleeve to get his attention. Up flew the arm, his face red, neck corded with fury, his instinct to hit me as reflexive as my flinch.

Still, my greatest fear is being like *her*. I try to claw my way back to self-righteousness. "Why didn't you tell me, Mom? You always said it was pneumonia. You lied."

My mother sighs. "He did have pneumonia. I don't know, Maybe I was ashamed. And afraid that it ran in the family. His brother . . . It could happen again. I didn't want you to know. I was afraid for myself, and for you. Ever since that horse accident when you were twelve you've been so . . . troubled."

Horse accident? I'm speechless. What about my life, our life? Wasn't that enough to give a child trouble? In her revisionist universe, my adolescent misery was caused by a concussion. Never mind a normal EEG. She possesses a remarkable defense against reality, my mother. But not a perfect one.

When she begins to cry I feel no satisfaction. I have no weapons left. We've both given up our pitiful secrets. I drop the phone again. I want to vomit. I am sick of myself, sick of us. Inside the McDonald's bathroom I shoulder aside a young mother, slam the stall door and stick a finger down my throat, something I haven't done for years and years. Like riding a bicycle. With ease I bring up the remains of the small breakfast eaten hours ago. Then I retch with dry heaves. Someone enters the bathroom, pauses, retreats. I flush. I am alone here with the mirror; I avert my eyes as I wash my face. No paper towels, just a hand dryer.

I grab a pile of paper napkins at the counter, ignore the stares and swipe my wet face. Squinting against the sunlight, I hang up the still dangling phone and make it to my car. I turn the key and put the snazzy little rental car into reverse. I pull into the traffic heading west on 44. A huge stock trailer stops beside me at the light, one Hereford steer staring at me balefully through the shit-smeared slats. Headed for slaughter. Bon voyage.

On my right there's a tourist shop, Chile Hill. I miss the light at the Santa Ana Star gambling casino, despite the enormous digital display sign, and am nearly sideswiped by a departing gambler in a smoking pickup with kids in the back. Unbelted kids. Did he leave them in the pickup while he gambled? I drift to the shoulder and stop to catch my breath. Adrenaline pumps through my veins; the body does its job no matter what. Like pregnancy hormones, when the baby isn't yours.

We all make mistakes. How profound, Mother. I can mock you, but I can't deny the truth.

Lila, I gave you up willingly. They didn't make me. I could have run off and had you. And aren't I just like *her*? What was I thinking of? I wanted to lay on you all the intimate details of my family horror, describe sex with your father, the same things I curse my mother for laying on me. But I'm *not* like her, I'm not a liar, saying it was for your own good. Even as I protest I see the dented white van I got into that day, in Arlington, twenty-one years ago.

Here on New Mexico 44, a horn blares behind me: I've hit the brakes in the middle of traffic. I press the gas pedal and nearly smash into the stock trailer, which has pulled ahead. But the white van won't leave my brain, and the truth unfurls like some terrible grade school film strip, jerky and inexorable.

Lila, I lied and lied and lied to you. Shit, even talking to you now is a lie, but I've gotten into the habit and can't quit.

Patterson wasn't your father. It could have happened like that but it didn't. Oh, yeah, he kissed me in the car, and he came to my house and worked in the basement and we made out on my parents' bed and he did come back again and tell me he'd made up his mind he didn't want to ruin a second marriage. But we never made love. We never technically had sex. And so I was, in his view, unharmed. But my rage and desolation were just as intense as if we had done it, because he'd made me want something I couldn't have.

This is what really happened: after the gorging, the vomiting that day, the day Patterson dumped me, I washed my face, brushed my teeth. I felt perfectly emptied. I locked the house and started walking down Mass. Ave. thumb out, headed towards Boston. The humidity was choking. Sweat ran down my chest before I could make it to the street. The asphalt shimmered with heat. I wore cut-off shorts, a man's work shirt tied at my waist, sandals, panties, no bra. My legs stuck to the coarse cotton. I would go wherever a ride took me.

I waited by the dry wall embankment that bordered the convent where I used to walk through the woods. It was here, only five years before, that I and Maurice LaFontaine and some other boys had ridden toboggans (I was consigned to sit last so no boy would have to put his arms around me) and thrown snowballs at cars. I was the only one who confessed to my parents when we got caught by cops. "You don't want to be *that* kind of girl," my mother warned. "You'll get a reputation."

The first car that stopped was a grey sedan driven by a man in a suit. A suit in this heat. But the car was air conditioned. My sweat chilled on my skin. He looked about my father's age. Clean shaven, stinking of cologne. Why did some men wear that awful perfume?

"Where you headed?" he asked.

"Harvard Square," I improvised.

He smiled. "You know it's dangerous for a girl like you hitch-hiking?"

I shrugged. Stared ahead. I didn't want any lectures.

"I'm going to Arlington, I'll let you off at the bus station in Arlington Heights if you want. I got a daughter your age."

"Whatever."

"I'd take you further but I got to make a stop. I sell advertising time to radio stations."

I spaced him out, could only think of Patterson. The golfing bastard.

I lingered at the Arlington Heights bus station until the man who sold time disappeared, brake lights blinking, then I crossed the street and put out my thumb.

Arlington: pronounced Ahlington by its denizens. We had no such accents. Ahlington, inhabited by the working class. Across the street, inside an oven-hot pizza parlor, a young man in a white teeshirt tossed a cloud of dough into the air. He blew me a kiss and I turned away. Ahlington. I'd taken the bus into the Square from Arlington often, but never walked the streets. Red lights. Car engines steaming. A thrift store, grungy little glass figurines and dishes in the window. Not hip like the ones in Cambridge. Next to it an H&R Block. A hair salon, the door open, reeking of perms like Mr. Isadore's the day I wouldn't go to school.

The light turned green. I stepped into the street, thumb out, as cars wove past me, until a dented van stopped, backed up, stopped again. I walked toward it. The door opened for me, the guy leaned across the seat. "Wheah yah headed?" he asked.

"Cambridge. Harvard Square." I climbed in.

"Bet yah going to go to Truc, right?"

"Right."

A chunk of car engine and twisted exhaust pipe lay in the back of the van. I breathed in the smell of gasoline, the driver's rank sweat. His hands on the steering wheel, nails rimmed with black grease. Who was he? A cross swung from a chain at his throat. Name: Micky? Mikey? Joey? Not a hippie, not a college guy, a motorhead greaser with a grey front tooth. He was nobody I could want, so it wouldn't matter. He wasn't good looking at all. Hooked nose, big Adam's apple. The only thing attractive about him was the force with which he wanted me.

"Yah in a hurry, yah want to take a side trip with me? Theyuh's a nice little pahk a few streets away. A rezahvwah. We could get high."

I shrugged. He detoured until I figured we were probably in Belmont. I looked out the side window. He lit a joint. I didn't know greasers smoked dope. He handed it to me and I inhaled, held the smoke as I knew I was supposed to, until I thought I'd choke. It was like holding your breath under water, that moment when you think you can't make it, and then you burst through to the light. I'd gone scuba diving in Saint Thomas a few months ago, on spring vacation with my parents. I'd been stunned by the beautiful bubbles rising from my regulator, globes of mercury reflecting the whole undersea world, and then when we had to come up, I was stunned again by the shock of air and wind, the pitch of waves after the silky peace of submersion. A shock like birth. When we got home from vacation, Patterson called me over to tell me I had a great tan.

"You're cute, anyone ever tell you that?" the van driver said. I didn't yet know there'd be a string of men as long as our driveway in my future, men who would ask me that question as if they'd coined it.

Trees hung over residential side streets, their leaves lush with moisture. We used to put maple wings on our noses, split them, wore them. Like sucking pollen from lilacs . . . It didn't matter who he was or where we were going. When Patterson kissed me I was already off track, though I hadn't known it. The van rolled through stone gateposts; he parked behind a thicket of rhododendrons. He rested his hand on the back of my neck. A round pond glittered between weeping willows, trees like a madwoman's dangling hair.

"S'a nice place heah." He handed me the joint again.

Grey tooth, Adam's apple poking his throat, dark greasy hair, a spray of pimples on cheeks pitted with old acne scars.

Where did you get those holes in your face, I asked my father when I was little. Smallpox, he said. The funny man.

We got out of the van and I walked toward the woods, his arm on my neck, my shoulder. As soon as we hit the tree line, he was on me, lips squashed hard against mine, pulling me down, down to the mulch of last year's leaves, grunting, and I was just there, not there, looking at light patterns above me, no breeze, the sticky sweat of him dripping, his breath sour with dental rot. Unh, unh. And even then I was forgetting his name, making this not have happened. Preparing for when I learned I was pregnant, so it couldn't have been him.

The pain, a nail ripped from a board, the screech of plywood sawn. My father used to make me hold the lumber while he slashed with a circular saw; I couldn't block my ears, and I feared he'd cut me. Now I lay sticky with a stranger's sweat, the dirt from the ground on my breasts, grit in my teeth. I never made a sound.

"Jesus fucking Christ," he said when he was done. "Whyn't yah tell me yah was a virgin? I mean what was I to think? Hitching an' ahl. Yah came heah with me." Defensive, blaming.

I didn't answer. Lila, Lila, I can't help addressing you, lost child. I'll say this, your father wasn't without a conscience. Perhaps more conscience than Patterson had.

"You going to go to confession for this?" I asked. "How many Our Fathers will you say?"

"Yah really something," he said, shaking his head. "What the fuck's the mattah with yah?"

"Nothing. What's the matter with you?"

He drove me back to Mass. Ave. where I insisted on being let off. I walked all the way home, four or five miles by that point. I was wet, smudged, semen and blood on my panties, his hand prints on my shirt, over my breasts. My feet aching and blistered in my flat, thin-soled sandals. I couldn't face hitching, but I wasn't as sad as you might think. Because, Mikey, Joey, whatever the hell his name was, had shown me a new-old lesson, the one I'd forgotten since that eighth grade dance: as long as it didn't matter, as long as you didn't care, there wasn't a damn thing they could do to you.

Lila, how could I have been so stupid as to think I could get away with it, giving you a false father, the one I'd rather you had? It's moot now, but you might have looked him up, he'd have denied it, and you could have insisted on blood tests. I would've been caught. It's not that I wanted to trick you, it's that, like my mother, I just "forgot" what I didn't want to remember. I replaced it. I wanted for you a handsome, golden basketball star, a popular teacher, not a slimeball who put his fingers to my throat. Patterson was the one who seduced me, and I got pregnant. Why not put the two together? It happened by accident, and after a while it began to feel true. The memories merged. Honest.

Just as I've believed you to be alive for so long I can't believe you aren't now. I've always had a reality problem.

You know, I kept all those tiny anorexia clothes for so many years, long after they were out of style, as though someday I'd return to that body, slide into those little dresses that barely covered my butt, and resume my perfect true life.

Of course I never did. The only thing that remains with me from high school is a series of dreams I keep having of Maurice LaFontaine, and in every dream he disapproves of me in some new way. As though he, who went on to Harvard and never left, is the arbiter, the judge of my worth.

Yes, Maurice still comes to me as often as once a month in dreams, to tell me in various ways that I'm not who I was supposed to be. Not that AP teacher's pet, Mr. Teal's special one, that studious girl in miniskirts carrying a crippled scholar's books. Always I beg for Maurice's approval, although I want to say, who are you, who have no tolerance for any other choices but your own, whose parents were educated and dignified, who know nothing of my brand of loss? Sometimes I want to say, I'm sorry, forgive me Maurice for using you to fill my gaps. In my dream life, I am always begging for love.

No, I'm not that AP girl. Instead, Lila, I became the one imagining you for twenty years, but that was a mirage, a lake hovering over a highway. My life has never been true. I'm a two-bit travel writer always on the run; I romanticize myself as a "gypsy" instead of facing up to the fact that I'm as disconnected as the tumbleweed I saw blowing across a highway when I was eighteen, had just given birth, was hitchhiking through Arizona high on acid. I saw those hollow balls of spiky brambles buffeted through sagebrush, and thought: that's me. Then, at least, I knew the resemblance.

In all these years there's not been one man I've managed to live with for more than six weeks. Pitiful, huh? Just as it's pitiful that I dragged up that business about my poor gassed kitty for you. Funny, though, that afterward I hated cats. It's easier to dislike what you lose than to mourn it. Like babies. I was never one to coo over them; I felt repulsion at their helplessness, their floppy weak necks and frequent spewings.

Oh, shit. Maybe *she* is the one I'm hating rather than mourning. Isn't that a neat little twist?

Everything I've told you is put to question by the persistent image of an item from my childhood: a yellow eggcup. It was made of glazed ceramic, decorated with a hand-painted green rooster on its bell-like bottom. On top, a smaller half-globe cradled a soft boiled egg in its shell. My mother tapped the egg's crown and lifted fractured shell and membrane with a knife. She sprinkled salt and placed a small scoop of butter into the steaming egg. My spoon dipped, came up coated yellow.

What does this egg cup mean? What about all those breakfasts of Rice Krispies and Sugar Smacks from the box? I taste the golden creaminess of a chicken's unborn offspring gliding over my tongue. There's an entire untold history of egg cups, of soft-boiled eggs, and an egg poacher too, six little metal dishes that floated on a double boiler. They parade around my skull, the way pirates and trunks of jewels swirled around my bedroom when I had a high fever long ago. Mrs. Watson nursed me and nearly died of pneumonia herself. Whoops—there I go, trying to hide behind the memories I've permitted, run from the ones I haven't.

What does it mean that I had a mother who sometimes prepared these egg breakfasts? What shadow does it cast over the history I've chosen: a tale of neglect, disappointment, and cruelty?

Which is true?

They can't both be.

No, Lila, I wasn't going to tell you or myself about my unrequited love for her. Early on I said this is my version, and my version doesn't want to admit to a mother, who, when woken out of her depression, went with me on what I called "Indian walks" to see the little trail I'd found in some yet-to-be-developed bit of brushy woods between house lots, who marveled when I pointed out the beaten down grass where rabbits danced. The mother who read me all of Bambi, not Disney's version, but Felix Salten's original. We loved the chapters about two leaves in autumn discussing what would happen when they fell. Together we pondered the souls of leaves wavering over the abyss. My mother framed my pastels, took me to art class and dancing and riding lessons. I made gifts for her constantly: every drawing or painting or childish sculpture a mommy horse and a foal, a mother holding a baby, honoring my need for her.

When I went to overnight camp I was homesick beyond all reason. I feared that while I was away she might die in a car crash and I wanted to die with her. I knew I couldn't exist without her and didn't want to. But I've always existed without her, haven't I?

Haven't I?

Or is it just that one day I could no longer accept what she had always offered: intermittent love, distorted by her own troubled mind? It was like being given up for adoption, then re-claimed again and again.

It's easier to hate than to mourn, and I've become expert at cursing her failures because to acknowledge them *and* my love for her would be unbearable. These pieces fit about as well as my mother's memories of her perfect father, her recollection of hiding in the toybox to avoid his blows. How did she manage to work those mismatched jigsaw shapes into one puzzled heart?

All these years I hated her because, long ago, I loved her with a passion I've never felt for anyone else. A passion I hoped I'd feel for you.

EPILOGUE

I can't break this habit of telling anymore. It started with Lila, but now I address another daughter, born to me six months ago:

Yours was an unglamorous birth. I was impregnated through donor insemination, your genes chosen from a loose leaf binder, a description of some medical student nearly twenty years my junior—the right height, coloring so that you'd have a chance of looking like me. With only one parent for you, I figured it would be better if there was some resemblance. A nurse practitioner performed the impregnation with a high tech version of the old turkey baster. Some might say I've done it this way so that the child can be all mine; a control freak, I'll never have to discuss child-rearing practices with an unlike mind, never risk a custody battle. But it isn't so. I just knew my time was running out, and with no likely candidate on the horizon, I decided to go for it.

My little daughter, when you were six weeks old I carried you in a pack on my chest through forests. I saw your black eyes mesmerized by the patterns of light in leaves overhead, and I thought, later you will look at light and wind moving through leaves and feel a longing and won't know why.

Who will be there to tell you what your memory has lost? We make up answers or we lie. We reshape memory to make it bearable. And we all live in longing. I was, and was not, a mother for a lifetime before you moved within my womb. Maybe I'll never show this to you, or only after I'm gone, an inheritance to save you from your inheritance. Will you believe me if I say: I've told you nothing but the truth?

I am fascinated by the persistence of deceptions in what we call "family history" and the way these lies move through generations.

When I lived in Brezhnev's Russia, I was intrigued by the parallels between the state version and personal versions of rewriting history.

In my last novel, *The Price of Land in Shelby*, I approached the altered history issue from the point of view of one of the more peripheral characters, "a perpetrator." I was curious about how he managed to live with himself.

In *Lost Daughters*, I'm interested in revealing the lies my characters have constructed in order to manipulate others or coexist with their consciences. But I'm also interested in confronting some of these characters with the consequences of their deceptions. Fortunately for those of us who walk this earth as breathing human beings instead of fictional characters, we rarely have to face such mirrors.